Praise for the Novels of Tom Piccirilli

"Tom Piccirilli's fiction is visceral and unflinching, yet deeply insightful. If you miss Piccirilli you're missing one hell of a treat." —F. Paul Wilson, author of *The Keep* and *Harbingers*

"Tom Piccirilli writes like a crazed banshee. I love his books!" —Ken Bruen, author of *American Skin* and *The Guards*

"Tom Piccirilli may write with the muscle of a 1950s paperback pulp master, but the mood and menace are totally modern. Go ahead and try to stop turning pages. You can't, even though he's got your heart on a hook and he's taken your mind places it never imagined. Piccirilli is the master of that strange, thrilling turf where horror, suspense and crime share shadowy borders. Wherever he's headed, count me in. (As long as I'm allowed to bring a gun.)" —Duane Swierczynski, author of *The Wheelman* and *The Blonde*

THE DEAD LETTERS

"Relentless, mesmerizing, and just damned fine. *The Dead Letters* is the best suspense novel I've read all year, period." —Steve Hamilton, Edgar Award–winning author of *A Stolen Season*

"Tom Piccirilli's voice is dark, disturbing, and truly original. *The Dead Letters* is a riveting story of madness, remorse, and salvation served with a bizarre and brilliant twist." —Jonathan Santlofer, bestselling author of *The Death Artist*

"Piccirilli's latest is part psychological suspense, part thriller, part alternate reality—and boy, can he write! His prose is a joy to read; he has a unique narrative voice, and the dialogue is right on. It's a killer plot with a good mix of fascinatingly flawed characters. The protagonist is full of both wry humor and despair and the villain is psychologically complex. The secondary characters are just as memorable." —*Romantic Times* (Top Pick!, 4½ stars, Gold Medal)

"My God, what a dark treat Piccirilli has created. *The Dead Letters* is absolutely riveting. The writing is gorgeous, the characters wonderfully rich and complex. A truly great cinematic, surreal, sad, and haunting novel." —Patrick Lussier, director of *Dracula 2000* and *White Noise 2*

"Piccirilli has hit full stride with *The Dead Letters,* reaching the ranks of the best writers in suspense and terror.... He just may put out Stephen King's lights or Dean Koontz's eye." —Robert W. Walker, author of *City for Ransom*

"The characters are as real as your neighbors, the setting as close as down the block.... *The Dead Letters* excels as a novel written to blur genre lines.... It's brutal, tragic and at times disturbingly humorous, darkly appealing to just about any audience that loves a good tale well told."
—*Insidious Reflections*

"Tom Piccirilli's new novel is a foray into serial killer territory, but one with his own unique touch. Operating in the same high ground as Thomas Harris' *Red Dragon* and *Silence of the Lambs*...A very intriguing, exciting and thought-provoking ride. Recommended!" —Horror World

"I guarantee you will be mesmerized. Piccirilli's powerful prose and inspiring characterization will have you renouncing the greats and embracing the evolved. This book gets 5 bright, shiny stars! You need to buy this book and I don't care how you get it: borrow, buy or steal. Just do it!" —Horror-Web

HEADSTONE CITY
A 2007 Thriller Award nominee
A 2007 Bram Stoker Award nominee

"A beautiful and perversely funny sort of crime novel... [Piccirilli has] the authentic surrealist's gift of blind trust in his imagination, and that enables him to throw off striking metaphors like sparks from a speeding train. There's a manic insouciance in his prose, along with a persistent, unaccountable melancholy. *Headstone City* gives you the distinctive shiver good horror writing—all good writing—provides: the certainty that the writer's own ghosts are in it." —*New York Times Book Review*

"Alternately funny, sad and thrilling, Piccirilli's stellar supernatural crime novel plays haunting riffs on old mob standards.... Stoker-winner Piccirilli plays cleverly with his hero's paranormal ability, keeping the reader guessing—and jumping—by blurring distinctions between the living and the dead." —*Publishers Weekly* (starred review)

"The author's picture of Italian family life in Brooklyn is stunningly vivid.... I hope Piccirilli has room on his mantle because it won't be surprising if *Headstone City* brings home another Bram Stoker Award. Grade: A." —*Rocky Mountain News*

"A tense and sometimes sorrowful yarn with just enough supernatural elements to lift it above more typical crime fiction fare. Subtle and masterful." —*Rue Morgue*

NOVEMBER MOURNS

"Piccirilli successfully blends character and incidents to conjure a spirit of the strange that plays a key role in the tale's surprising but fitting finale. In lieu of a tidy conclusion, this loose and episodic horror novel tantalizes with hints of awesome mysteries that defy complete understanding." —*Publishers Weekly*

"Dark, ambiguous, strange, and sometimes surprisingly sweet...The taint in the land brings William Faulkner to mind, while the taint in the people is pure Flannery O'Connor. Piccirilli has taken Southern Gothic imagery and woven it with his own poetry to create something uniquely his own, a book of terrible beauty and beautiful terrors." —*Locus*

"Tom Piccirilli is the master of the Southern gothic, quietly building horror where the chills grow with increasing strangeness....When he is done, the uneasy horrors of Moon Run Hollow are in your bones." —*Denver Post*

"Beautifully written, *November Mourns* mesmerizes from the start and never lets up." —*Talebones*

"If Victor Frankenstein had stitched together pieces of Flannery O'Connor, Stewart O'Nan and James Lee Burke, his creature might have risen from the slab to write Tom Piccirilli's haunting new novel, *November Mourns*. . . . Piccirilli manages, like the best magic realists, to create landscapes pulsing with otherworldliness, places out of time that seem wonderfully disconnected from our own world. . . . This is a place you find yourself wanting to experience for yourself." —*Colorado Daily Camera*

"*November Mourns* is a literary arrow—roughly handcrafted here, finely carved there; splintered and ornate—fired with a deft hand and a keen eye. And its path is true—there are no diversions, no meandering tangents: this one goes straight, and it doesn't miss its mark." —*Cemetery Dance*

"Tom Piccirilli breaks genre form with a potent brew of poetry and atmosphere to concoct his unique brand of shudder-inducing, highly literate horror." —*Rue Morgue*

"If you go down to the woods with Tom Piccirilli, make sure you have eyes in the back of your head. Scary, engaging, this story gives a totally new meaning to the phrase 'cliff-hanger.'" —Graham Masterton

"No one else *writes* like Tom Piccirilli. He has the lyrical soul of a poet and the narrative talents of a man channeling Poe, William Faulkner, and Shirley Jackson. . . . After you begin reading *November Mourns,* you will not be able to put it down: and when you have finished it, and have returned it to your bookcase, you will not be able to forget it. Ever." —T. M. Wright, author of *A Manhattan Ghost Story*

"A novel of supreme and mesmerizing power that reads like a head-on collision between Flannery O'Connor and M. R. James." —Gary A. Braunbeck, author of *In Silent Graves* and *Graveyard People*

"Brilliant and deeply unsettling." —Poppy Z. Brite, author of *Liquor* and *Prime*

A CHOIR OF ILL CHILDREN

"A wonderfully wacked, disorienting, fully creepy book from which I never once reeled in revulsion even though as a reader I am admittedly a bit squeamish. I didn't reel because the poetic nature of the prose and seriousness of intent carried the day in every scene." —Dean Koontz

"Riotous, surprising, and marvelously gruesome." —Stewart O'Nan

"In this compelling Southern Gothic, Piccirilli . . . presents a searing portrait of twisted souls trapped in a wasteland. . . . The novel will appeal both to genre fans and to readers of Flannery O'Connor and even of William Faulkner. James Lee Burke and Harry Crews devotees should also take note." —*Publishers Weekly*

"Lyrical, ghastly, first-class horror." —*Kirkus Reviews*

"A marvelous fable about family, responsibility, and owning up to your nightmares." —SF Site

"Tom Piccirilli's work is full of wit and inventiveness—sharp as a sword, tart as apple vinegar. I look forward to all his work." —Joe R. Lansdale, author of *The Bottoms*

Also by Tom Piccirilli

The Dead Letters
Headstone City
November Mourns
A Choir of Ill Children

And coming in 2008:
The Cold Spot

THE MIDNIGHT ROAD

TOM PICCIRILLI

BANTAM BOOKS

THE MIDNIGHT ROAD
A Bantam Book / July 2007

Published by Bantam Dell
A Division of Random House, Inc.
New York, New York

This is a work of fiction. Names, characters, places, and incidents either
are the product of the author's imagination or are used fictitiously.
Any resemblance to actual persons, living or dead, events, or locales
is entirely coincidental.

Bantam Books and the rooster colophon are registered trademarks of
Random House, Inc.

ISBN 978-0-553-38408-6

Printed in the United States of America
Published simultaneously in Canada

www.bantamdell.com

OPM   10 9 8 7 6 5 4 3 2 1

For my wife
Michelle

And to Dean Koontz

ACKNOWLEDGMENTS

Special thanks need to go out to the following for their friendship, support, encouragement, and inspiration during the writing of this novel: Norman Partridge, Ed Gorman, Jonathan Santlofer, Robert W. Walker, Steve Hamilton, James Langolf, Gerard Houarner, Matt Schwartz, Stephen Romano, T. M. Wright, Brian Keene, Patrick Lussier, and David Morrell.

And for kicking ass and taking names (mine & mine): editor extraordinaire and amateur bowling-pin juggler Caitlin Alexander.

THE
MIDNIGHT
ROAD

ONE

Flynn remembered the night of his death more clearly than any other in his life. The black details of it forced him from the wild slopes of his dreams back to the beginning of his pitch through the ice, down into the dark waters below and the midnight road beyond.

There'd been a moment's premonition as he drove up the long narrow curve of the Shepards' driveway to their minimansion. A faint whisper of what was to come. The storm had ended a half hour earlier, but a heavy burst of wind had rattled loose a cluster of icicles high in the canopy trees. They slammed down against his hood so hard and unexpectedly that he overreacted and jammed the brake, his dead brother's '66 Charger going into a lissome power slide. He eased off the pedal and turned the wheel directly into the spin. They were the relaxed, familiar motions of someone who'd done a lot of street racing in his youth. The positraction got the car straightened almost immediately. The tires hit a dry patch of brick and let out a squeal like an animal cry of fear.

His stomach tightened. It was the kind of bad vibe he

usually made an effort to ignore. Before his death he'd been an even bigger idiot.

There were no streetlights here in this chic area of the North Shore, close to the Long Island Sound. Maybe it was a sign of wealth, having to wind your way through the night all on your own.

He looked out the frosted driver's side window, seeing the world like watching a film noir. Black and white, intensely sharp around the edges.

From the moment he saw the two pale figures wafting like white lace on the snow-filled front lawn, meeting and parting and joining again in the moonlight, he had fifty minutes left to live.

Flynn's headlights flashed across the terrain and immediately the grim nerve worked through his chest again, twitching under his heart. Late November, locked in the worst winter in a decade, night having dropped like your grandmother's velvet drapery, and there in the frozen yard were the girl and a dog prancing about, no parents in sight.

It wasn't a good sign but he didn't want to jump to conclusions. Most anonymous tips to Child Protective Services could be traced back to the neighbor across the street or on either side of the home in question. Except the Shepards had no neighbors within view. Dense lots of brush rose up around the huge house.

It was a three-tiered home built in the late seventies when art deco was losing ground and the holdout architects were really blowing their cool. You had a nice little family residence hidden within a bunch of mortar and rock face, metal and large, well-lit empty windows like wide, blind eyes. It looked schizo as hell and Flynn couldn't imagine living in such a place, even if it did sell on the open market for a mill and a quarter, maybe a mill and a half.

The tipster had said a child was in danger at this address. No other comment. There didn't need to be one. It was all CPS needed. If somebody said a kid's welfare was at risk, you had to move. You catch the call, you take the ride, even in a snowstorm.

The girl stopped traipsing and stood at attention in her white ski suit and snow boots, watching him. The dog was a French bulldog, all white except for a black ring around one eye, wearing a white knitted sweater and little plastic booties. It sat at her heel with its chin up, head cocked, staring intently at Flynn as he stepped from his car. The only color in the world seemed to knife out from the huge windows and the twin bronzed lanterns bordering the two-car garage.

In the glow he saw the girl was about seven. A swathe of snow clung to her chin. Her breath blew white streamers that burst against his belly as he approached. The dog's breath broke across his legs.

He had to play it carefully. This was always a little tricky. If he approached the kid and she got spooked, screamed and ran into Daddy's arms, then the potential for big trouble went off the chart. You had to try to keep things easy and friendly. Just introducing himself as an investigator for Suffolk County CPS put everybody on the defensive. All kinds of hell could break loose. Fisticuffs, maybe worse. Nobody wanted to be called a child molester, not even the ones who were guilty of it.

That's one of the reasons why most investigators were women. A woman could appeal to the wife, seem less threatening to the husband. Flynn still wasn't quite sure how he wound up on the job, but one of the big perks for him was when some bitter, middle-aged ex–high-school jock who liked working over his old lady and kids decided to throw down and Flynn could cut loose. It was childish, he had to admit. But you took your action wherever you could.

Men weren't really wanted in the ranks. They had to take evaluations and psych tests semiannually to make sure they were trying to save kids for the right reasons. The shrinks had to weed out the CPS dudes who jumped out of broken marriages just hoping to find some beautiful young teen in trouble. Wanting to nurture her with poetry and bubble baths, maybe woo the mother just to make it look right on the books. The peds hunting fresh meat. Flynn came into work every day and faced cagey, cautious attitudes tossed at him all day long from nearly every corner. It pissed him off, but he tried to understand. You never knew where the next big breakdown or blowup might come from.

It was late. He should've been here over an hour ago, but the storm had hit while he was stuck in traffic on the Expressway. Nobody could get anywhere as the freezing rain came down and the slush on the road turned to ice within minutes. Even cars that weren't moving started to slip sideways into the median. Within a half hour there were a hundred fender-benders as drivers tried to roll off to the shoulder, park and wait it out. The storm didn't last long, but the freeze was so bad that everybody had to get out of their cars and start hammering away at the layers of ice on their windshields.

He didn't want to frighten the girl. She didn't really seem spookable, standing there looking at him, but he wanted to go extra easy. She took two steps through the snow, her blond hair squeezing out from around her white plastic hood, framing her cute face.

"Who are you?" she asked.

"I'm Flynn."

"I'm Kelly." Then, pointing to the dog, "This is Zero. What are you doing here?"

"I'd like to speak with your parents."

"Okay."

"Aren't you cold out here this late, Kelly?"

"Yeah," she told him. "I wanted to see the storm, but my mother wouldn't let me until it had stopped. We're about to go inside. I'd invite you in, but I'm not supposed to do that. How about if you stay right where you are until I get to the door, then you can follow, all right?"

"Sure," Flynn said.

Smart kid. Practical, even. He always got thrown by smart kids. He'd be getting ready to talk baby talk and they'd suddenly start speaking like college grads.

More icicles clattered in the trees overhead. Flynn walked back and leaned against the Charger, watching the girl make her way to the house, the small dog fighting his way through the drifts.

There were strict codes on how investigations were supposed to proceed, and he adhered to them pretty well, despite the occasional self-defensive brawls. He'd been with CPS for five years and neither his boss nor the

District Attorney's Office ever gave him any static. He was proud to know in his heart he'd saved lives. He'd put child molesters behind bars. He'd gotten good people with anger issues and drug problems the help they needed.

He was the best caseworker CPS had because he didn't have much of a social life to interfere, which sort of put the whole thing into a spartan perspective, if he stopped to think about it. He rarely did.

Flynn slipped twice just stepping up to the front door.

Mrs. Shepard answered before he got a chance to stomp the snow from his shoes. Kelly stood behind her, and the dog sat behind Kelly. Flynn got the feeling he was entering a very orderly household. One of those intensely domestic homes that ran with military precision and generally creeped other people out.

Mrs. Shepard kept a flaccid smile soldered in place. She stared at him through the storm door and said, "Yes? How can I help you? What's this about?"

There were rules. Too many of them, but he did what he could to make them work to his advantage. You had to be up front. You couldn't rope anybody into anything. Couldn't sneak in and snap pictures, no matter what you saw. You had to ask to be allowed to look around the house. They could deny you. They could claim you were an intruder. They could shriek about lawyers. You tried not to shake them up too much for fear they'd take it out on the kid. The child's welfare always came first.

He told Mrs. Shepard his name and showed his identification. He explained he was with CPS and that an anonymous complaint had been registered. She nodded as if she knew all about it and let him inside. He clarified his position and asked that he be allowed to check the house. While he spoke, he casually surveyed Kelly Shepard. No bruises on her face or arms that he could see. She seemed like a regular, happy kid.

Flynn waited to register Mrs. Shepard's response. There wasn't any. The lady just kept smiling and said nothing. The bulldog sat there looking sort of humiliated to still be wearing the booties.

"Mrs. Shepard?" Flynn asked.

Finally the woman said, "Yes? What is it you want? What do you think goes on here?"

"Mrs. Shepard, as I said—"

"I'm Christina."

"Mrs. Shepard, I—"

"I just told you. I'm Christina."

She was all riptide intensity. Flynn could sense the conflicting tensions inside the woman but had no idea what they were or how they would affect him. Her smile looked scraped into her face by a fishing knife. This lady's teeth were drying out, the high gloss fading. The faint aroma of scotch trailed from her. She was maybe thirty, quite attractive, with burnished copper hair that fell in two wide, sweeping currents. The glaze in her eyes kept him from getting any kind of a real bead on her.

Now might come the questions, the defensiveness. She might grab Kelly and hold the kid out in front of her like an offering. Some of them did that. Some parents stripped their children in front of Flynn to prove there were no bruises. Some broke down and dropped to the floor. Some went for a kitchen knife. You never knew what might be coming next.

He'd given the spiel he was supposed to give. He'd amended it a bit to make it sound like he had a little more authority than he actually did. If he snapped the sentences out fast enough, he came off like a cop with a court order. It was good to lay it down on the line as hard as he could. It set the parameters and usually let him know which way things would go. Whether they'd confess or go for the shotgun in the closet.

He waited, feeling the current riding up his back. He knew she'd be different, that she was going to pull something new here.

"Would you like some tea?" she asked.

There it was. That was a first. No one had ever offered him tea before. "No thank you," he said.

"How do we proceed?"

"Do you have any other children?"

"No, Kelly is our only one."

"I'd appreciate a tour of your home."

"And what will that prove? If I'm beating my child to the point that a neighbor—the nearest of whom lives several hundred yards away—can hear her screams, wouldn't she be battered? Are you looking for pools of blood?" The smile had downshifted into an almost amiable grin, except it was way too wide.

"I'm just doing an on-site evaluation. It's very standard."

"Not for me it isn't."

"I realize that. I'm very sorry, Christina, but once a complaint has been lodged we have to follow up."

"This late? It's almost Kelly's bedtime."

"The storm kept me. Again, I apologize for the intrusion."

Christina Shepard was given to dramatic movements. Swinging herself around and gesturing with her hands like she was scrawling signatures in the air. Kelly and the dog intuited her motions and stepped along with her, keeping just behind her. It was a weird kind of ballet he was watching, the three of them so gracefully maneuvering around in the front hallway.

"All right," she said, giving him the thousand-watt leer again. "Let's take a tour of my home."

She walked him through it, all three floors. She offered to open drawers even though he said it wasn't necessary. She opened them anyway. Her hostility came off her in waves, the way he expected. But there was something more there. Flynn couldn't figure out what it might be, and his curiosity was really starting to bang around inside him. He stared at the side of her face as she led him from room to room, propping open armoires and dressers.

She put her hands on him only once, gripping him by the upper arm and steering him toward the master bedroom's private bathroom. This lady had some serious muscle. He felt her coiled strength and the furnace of her agitation. She opened the medicine cabinet, grabbed a handful of pill bottles and started reading off labels. "Zyrtec, this is for allergies. Flexeril is a muscle relaxant for my husband, Mark, who has a bad back. Zoloft is medication for depression. I suffer from it. Surely that's not a crime."

"No, it's not," he said.

"Thank God for that. Would you like to speak to my

daughter? Ask her questions?" The mask slipped another notch as she called for Kelly. The girl and the dog paraded into the bedroom like Marines landing on a foreign beach. "Foul questions, no doubt. What kind of a man wheedles his way into working with children every day, Mr. Flynn? What thoughts go through your piggy mind?"

He let it slide. She had a head full of serpents herself, he decided. He'd heard a lot worse on the job and Christina Shepard didn't seem angry with him so much as she appeared flush with clashing forces.

Flynn turned to the girl and said, "Kelly, I work for people who look after children in case someone is hurting them. Maybe even a friend or someone in the family. It happens sometimes. Do you have anything you want to say to me?"

She peered at him like he was a puzzle missing a few pieces. "Are you asking if my mother and father hit me, Mr. Flynn?"

"Yes."

She let out a titter and covered her mouth, and the bulldog did a little dance in his booties and barked happily. "Of course not! Why would you ask me something like that?"

"There, are you satisfied now?" Christina said.

Her lips were doing something between the freaky leering smile and the too-wide grin. It was an expression of satisfaction, but he saw a lot more in there, a hint of panic. Like she was trying to hold herself together just until he was out the door, and then she would let herself go.

"I'd like you to leave me and my family in peace now," she told him.

Flynn said, "Thank you for your cooperation, Mrs. Shepard."

"Fine. Just go."

She didn't follow him as he left the upstairs bedroom, but Zero the bulldog did. It got in front of him and dropped a chew toy at his feet. A plastic hamburger. Flynn tossed it down the stairs and Zero shot off after it. The dog waited at the bottom of the stairway until Flynn got there, then dropped the burger at his feet again.

Flynn bent to grab it one last time before he left, and the black nerve twitched inside him again.

He didn't know why at first. It took a second to figure out. He looked left and right. He glanced back up the stairs. He was leaning over with his face near a heating vent.

He heard humming coming from somewhere deep in the house. A man murmuring a childish tune.

You didn't expect to hear a man sound like that. It wasn't a guy singing lullabies to his kids. There was more to it. The man *was* the kid. Flynn's stomach tightened and his scalp prickled.

He looked back over his shoulder. Christina and Kelly Shepard were still upstairs in the master bedroom. Zero was still waiting for Flynn to toss him the burger. Flynn did so and the dog went scampering. Flynn looked along the length of the walls and tried to track the vents in the direction he thought the sound might be traveling. He walked past the living room to the large kitchen. There were three doors there. One led to the garage. Another was a huge closet that was like a storeroom, full of massive boxes and gigantic cans and enormous jugs, the kind of oversized packages you get at a cost-cutting warehouse. Even though the places were presumably set up for the middle class, only the rich could ever shop there. Only they had the room to store all this shit.

The last door led to a cellar.

Flynn had twenty-seven minutes to live.

He didn't like the look of it. There were two sets of locks, both open. His bad juju detector was already blaring. He pulled out his pocketknife, worked the hinge pins free and put them in his coat pocket. The way the door hung, it looked exactly the same, but nobody would be able to lock him down there.

He was playing it all wrong but something kept telling him this was the only way to play it.

His dead brother's presence felt so strong around him now that he could imagine spinning fast enough to catch sight of Danny.

Flynn didn't have any evidence for the cops or his boss, Sierra, who was already going to read him the riot act for the way he was botching this case. He'd be lucky to stay out of the pokey himself.

But some things couldn't be helped. You decided on your course, and you saw it through.

Flynn hit one of several light switches and descended the stairs.

The outlandish house had thrown him once more. It wasn't a cellar, but a damn nice basement that had been turned into a guy pad. It was the kind of room that men without sons spent a lot of money on while awaiting the arrival of their first boy.

A flatscreen high-definition television sat high against one wall. Shelves were packed with DVDs. An ample L-shaped leather sofa made Flynn think this was the place where all Shepard's friends watched the Super Bowl and the World Series every year. There were sports collectibles in glass cases all around. Signed photos, footballs, catchers' mitts, boxing gloves. Mark Shepard had invested a good chunk of change and really liked to show off his collection.

It would've been a hell of a nice place if not for the guy in the cage in the middle of the room.

Flynn just stared for a second.

Sometimes you needed an extra breath to help you decide where it was you wanted to go next.

The cage was pretty small, the size of a boarding kennel for a German shepherd. Bars were half-inch steel, and the frame had been welded together with precision. The door was padlocked.

Inside sat a naked man with a misshapen head, as if someone had flung him against a cement wall as an infant. His slack lower jaw bent too far to one side and threads of drool slid down his chin. Thick, knotted scars and brandings cross-thatched his entire body, even his inner thighs. His left arm had been broken, poorly set, and now tilted slightly backwards at the elbow. He was still humming, and his gentle brown eyes, which were about an inch too far apart, just kept on watching Flynn.

"Hey, hello there," Flynn said, trying to make his voice

sound as natural as possible. "I'm your friend. I'm Flynn. Can you talk to me? Can you understand me?"

The man grinned, his gaze full of bewilderment and delight. Something started to crack in Flynn's chest. After all he'd been through, the guy was still glad to see another person, still singing. The nerve throbbed so painfully through Flynn he had to put his hand against the bars of the cage to steady himself.

Zero appeared at Flynn's ankle with the plastic hamburger in his teeth. The booties did a good job of soundproofing his paws. The cellar door creaked and slipped off one of the hinges. Up there, the girl let out a small cry of surprise. Zero circled the room and Kelly appeared on the stairway. She held a handful of cookies wrapped in a napkin.

She walked down the steps, saw Flynn, but showed no surprise, just a smidgen of irritation. "Did you break the door?"

"Sorry about that," he said.

"You found Nuddin. He's my uncle."

Bending to the cage she handed the cookies through the bars. Nuddin accepted them and chewed them down with joyous noises. He only ate half of each one, then offered each remaining half to Zero, who ate from his hand.

Nuddin?

Nothing?

"How long's he been here?" Flynn asked calmly.

"Since before my last birthday."

"Okay. When's your birthday, Kelly?"

"June. June 15. I was seven. I'm seven and a half now."

More than six months the man had been down here.

Flynn had seen it twice before. Mentally challenged children locked up in back rooms, imprisoned in chains, but that had been in the south Bronx. In areas that looked like they'd been invaded, blitzed, nuked, where the rules dried up and things got savage, and superstitions burned out of control. Roosters ran wild in the streets, kept on hand for Santeria rituals. Maybe it *was* Santeria. New religions were being born every day in the slums. Flynn had seen a lot in his time, but you just didn't expect a retarded man to be caged in the basement of a million-dollar house out on the North Shore.

"Kelly, where's the key?"

"My mother has it."

"We need to get him out of here."

"Why?"

"Because it's wrong to keep people locked up like this."

"Well, yes, I know that. It's *often* bad, that's *usually* the case, but this is different. I bring him cookies ... and fudge ... and cake sometimes. I gave him a big piece of my birthday cake, it even had a rose on it."

"You're very nice."

"My mother says he can't leave, he might hurt himself. I wouldn't want that. He's not only my uncle, he's my friend."

Zero dropped the burger at Flynn's foot and started pawing at his shoe, trying to get him to play some more. Flynn started back for the stairs, hoping he could get the drop on Christina Shepard, but she was already there, perched halfway down, holding a Smith & Wesson .38 trained on him.

He was beginning to think that the rules he was supposed to handle his business with were really very fucking stupid.

"He's my brother," she said.

"Jesus Christ, lady."

"I love him. I love him too much to let him go to one of those homes. You know what they do to them there?"

"They don't lock them in three-by-four cages."

"My father has been ill the last few years. He couldn't care for Nuddin any longer. My brother became my responsibility. It came down to me to shoulder the burden. We take such things seriously in my family. Our name is important. Our history."

"You're living in the Middle Ages. Where's the key, Mrs. Shepard?"

"We don't abuse him! We let him out sometimes. He plays. We let him play. You don't understand. We're protecting him."

"From what?"

"From the world. From temptation."

She didn't look like a religious nut, but then again, what did a religious nut look like? He'd seen them in all shapes. "What the hell is that supposed to mean?"

"You can't understand."

"You're right." Always keep someone with a gun pointed at you talking if you could. "What about all his scars?"

"That's from—" She clamped her mouth shut, then took a step closer, the revolver aimed at Flynn's belly. "We let him play. My daughter gives him cookies."

"I told him," Kelly said. The kid was taking it in stride. Her mother holding a gun on a stranger couldn't rate all that high on the Holy Shit Barometer if your own mentally handicapped uncle lived in a cage in your basement. Was that just another sign of practicality?

"He has a good life," Christina Shepard went on. "Believe me, considering the choices, he has nothing to complain about. He plays a lot."

This was always the worst part. Listening to their admissions and rationalizations, their explanations about why they do the terrible things they do. No accountability. Blind denial of their ugliest behavior and intentions.

Flynn said, "I want the key. Now."

"It's not here. I don't know where it is."

"He likes it in there," Kelly said. "He doesn't want to leave."

"You see!" Christina said. The barrel of the gun wavered. "You see? He likes it in there. We don't abuse him."

Flynn had met crazy once or twice before, but nobody had ever poured on the bad juju like this lady. There were rules, and he tried to stick to them, but when it got ugly he tossed them to the curb. It was pretty ugly right now. He stepped up, grabbed the woman, shook her hard. It was like putting your hands in the ocean. The immense power could rise up and crush you at any second.

She raised the pistol and shoved it under his chin.

He thought maybe he had a death wish like his brother Danny.

"Where's the key to this damn cage?" he said. It was tough talking with a pistol barrel jabbed into your jaw.

"Don't take him away! You don't understand—my father, he'll—"

Footsteps pounded upstairs and Flynn knew things were about to get even more funky. He squared his shoulders and moved to the side of the stairwell so he could try to prepare for whatever was coming now.

Christina switched gears, reverted back to sweetness, her voice full of honey. But she kept the pistol pointed at his head. She called, "Mark, there's someone here."

Mark Shepard flipped the rest of the light switches on his way down and the basement practically glowed with reflections in all the glass. He stared at Flynn and Flynn stared back.

Shepard had the eyes of a man who'd been living with a guy caged in his basement for the last six months. He was frayed, his gaze faraway and at the same time way up close, like he couldn't get anything into focus. He was a couple years younger than Flynn, maybe thirty-five, but he had the look of someone who'd been battling a terrible illness and losing fast. His thin face had grown long with shadows. He stood very still but seemed to somehow be trembling. Flynn knew immediately that Shepard had made the anonymous call himself.

"You're late," Shepard said. "Why were you so late?"

"The storm," Flynn said.

"I was waiting. I should've stayed away but I couldn't." For a guy who wanted to keep the call anonymous, Shepard was too fried to play the game in his own house. He snapped and gave up the truth without anybody even pushing him for it. He looked at his wife. "Christina, I'm sorry."

She gave him a murderous glare. All the dizzy attitude had fled her now, leaving behind only that tension. The gun was still loosely pointed at Flynn, but he could tell she was thinking of shifting it over a little and aiming it at her husband.

Flynn wondered if she was going to make all three of them get in the cage. It would be cramped. There'd be a death struggle for the cookies.

She moved in on Shepard. "You did this? But I thought you understood. You told me you understood. You agreed!"

"I did, Christina, but—"

"Liar!" she shouted. Flynn had a tough time watching her, those pretty features squeezed together, as if stuck in a vise, deformed by rage. "My father was right about you!"

"Your father's never been right about anything in his life, that crazy son of a bitch." Shepard managed to raise his maladjusted gaze high enough to find Flynn's eyes. "I don't know what to do."

"You made the right choice," Flynn said. "But she does still have the gun and all."

"You're a fool. You don't know what's happening. You have no idea."

"Maybe not. So enlighten me."

"Nuddin will do that for you. It's not over. It's just beginning. I'm not doing anybody a favor, I'm just passing trouble out of my hands."

"You should've done it sooner."

"I know." Shepard reached into his pocket, and tossed Flynn a key. "Take him and go."

Nuddin went, Oh oh oh.

Christina lunged at Flynn with a nasty intent. He realized he didn't have that strong a death wish after all. In fact, he was getting a little worried here as the lady got closer and started to cock the revolver. Her husband dodged in front of her. He was fast. They were both very fast. She said, "Get out of my way, Mark."

"I can't do that."

"Get out of my way now. You can't let him take my brother."

"That's exactly what he's going to do."

Shepard moved as if to embrace his wife, like he was asking her to dance. His hand closed on her right wrist and he spun her around and gripped her in a loving hug, pulling her hands tight against her chest, the gun useless in her fist. She let out a sharp grunt of disgust and anger. Knotted black veins stood out in her neck. Her arms were all corded muscle.

Flynn had a rough call to make. He still wasn't certain about Kelly's safety. This was a buggy house and he didn't like the idea of leaving the kid behind. But if he tried to take her, Shepard might lose his head and Flynn would have to deal with both these nutjobs. He'd never run from a fight in his life, and he could handle himself pretty well, but the look in Christina's eyes definitely made him think that if everything went to hell, he'd be leading the train.

It was a good thought to have. He had fourteen minutes to live.

He unlocked Nuddin's cage, reached in and grabbed the guy. He was so light he might've been made of balsa wood. Nuddin laughed and pressed a papery hand to Flynn's face, patted him there. Flynn wrapped his coat around Nuddin, carried him up the stairs, through the house and out to the Charger. They slipped and hit the ice twice. Nuddin got up and sort of loped through the snow, running on the balls of his feet. The blind eyes of the house burned behind them.

A silver Cadillac Escalade SUV was parked on an angle next to the Charger, as if Shepard hadn't known what to do with himself—drive into the garage or back out again and take off. He'd been torn in half about even stepping into his own home.

Flynn wrangled open the Charger's door and strapped Nuddin inside. He had the driver's door open when he saw that Zero had followed him outside, and the girl had followed the dog. Zero hopped into the driver's seat and sat there as if waiting to whip out onto Route 25a. Flynn just shook his head.

"Get in," he told Kelly.

A gunshot punctuated his words. He grabbed the girl by the arm and flipped her into the backseat.

"Buckle up," he ordered and climbed in himself, shoving aside the dog. A moment later Christina Shepard broke from the twisted house and ran onto the lawn through the heavy snowdrifts, holding the .38. She moved extremely well, with her arm extended, firing with great precision.

She got off three rounds. The first hit the front quarter panel, the next ripped a furrow across the hood and the last tore off one of the wiper blades and cracked the windshield directly in front of Flynn's face.

She'd snuffed her own husband. And what kind of a

woman shoots at a car when her seven-year-old daughter and retarded brother are inside?

Maybe Flynn had never really met crazy before. Maybe this was his first time.

He wheeled out of the driveway, onto the dark road, and gunned it. In the rearview he watched her jump into the Caddy SUV and saw it fishtail after him, the headlights coming up fast.

"Why is my mother shooting at us?" Kelly asked.

"Because she's shithouse crazy, kid. But don't ever tell anybody I said that."

"Okay." She laughed. She was having a good time. He knew the feeling. The speed and bluster and action could be appealing to a kid. Even the gunshots. It brought on a powerful sense of wonder and awe. Flynn remembered his brother in the driver's seat, four cop cars blaring sirens behind with the old-fashioned cherry tops on them, Flynn just a little boy in the passenger seat, strapped in, smiling just like Nuddin.

The Caddy had all-wheel drive, all-speed traction. It cost a bundle but was worth it in the winter. Christina was chewing up the distance between them. Flynn turned his head, looked at Kelly in the backseat and felt a vast onrush of pity for the girl. What would've happened to her in that house over the next few years?

The next bullet creased the driver's door. Just a couple of inches over and it would've gone into his spine.

"She's a perfect shot," Kelly said. "Normally."

"She is?"

"She's on the range three times a week. She likes skeet

too. I go with her if we don't have choir or violin practice. We went the day after New Year's."

"It's good for a family to spend holiday time together," he said.

"I think she's missing on purpose."

"It would be nice to believe so."

Nuddin started singing, La la la la.

Flynn wasn't very familiar with the area but knew they were about ten minutes from Port Jackson. He swung out in that direction thinking maybe he could lose Christina Shepard on the town roads, assuming they'd been cleared enough to travel on and he didn't wipe out along the way.

He had to admit, there was more to it than saving the girl and her uncle. Even more to it than running for his own life. Behind the wheel his ego went off the chart. He didn't like anybody trying to outdrive him, even on streets as bad as these.

He gritted his teeth. Christina Shepard came up hard and smashed into his bumper. The Charger rocked and bounced, and the wheel bucked wildly in his hands. He tightened his grip until the steering column started to groan.

Flynn had imagined his brother's death in this seat ten thousand times during the last thirty years, and now it surfaced again. He checked the rearview and saw an old man's eyes peering back at him. He'd lived to be twice his brother's age, but still he thought of Danny as the older one, the sharp one, the hip one, the guy with the moves, slick, tough, cool. What did it say about you when you looked up to a ghost already three decades gone?

Christina laid on the horn and slammed into them

again and the hideous noise of tearing metal ripped through the black-and-white night.

It was ridiculous. He couldn't get over the feeling that they were all part of a very stupid joke that was going to end with a duck on somebody's head. Flynn kept flipping it around in his mind, thinking the answer had to be here someplace, but he simply couldn't see it, just couldn't find it.

They made a series of lefts and rights and eventually came out of the snowy retreat of suburban side roads and into the quaint township of Port Jackson. They were doing sixty on icy streets that would've been unsafe at forty on a June day. He kept hoping to find a cop or a sander or a snowplow driver or somebody who might call it in, but no one else was on the road.

A traffic circle opened up in the middle of the Port Jack pier, a flagpole dead center, some kind of snow-covered statue pointing a cutlass. Flynn knew this was going to be bad. They were too close to the water. If Christina rocked them from behind again—

But she didn't. She was nuttier than that, this lady. She swung out to the other side of the traffic circle and came up hard on his left. It was suicide. He saw her face closing in from the shadows, an expression of pained purpose distorting her features. The SUV looked like the beautiful fury of heaven. The cars smashed into each other hard and the ice took them and they slid over the jetty together.

Nuddin going, Wah wah wah.

"Hold on!" Flynn shouted.

And here came the punchline. *So this mook spins out of*

control, hits the mooring where the ferry takes off from in the summer, blasts through the retaining wall and crashes into the ice upside down! He was going to die pretty much like his own brother did, and get this—in the same car!

Flynn just didn't get the joke.

He came to with Danny's voice loud in his mind but the words were unrecognizable. He'd been out for no more than half a minute. He saw stars because the bulldog had bounced off the back of his skull.

The Charger was on its roof down on the frozen surface of the Long Island Sound. The ice had been thick but four tons of Detroit production line had cracked it wide, and the noise was like a splitting glacier. Sixty feet of water lay beneath them.

The tires were still turning and creaking. Freezing water had started to seep into the car. Flynn tried the door but it had buckled. The window was busted but he realized now they were lying at a forty-five-degree angle, the driver's side facing down. There was nothing but ice here. He couldn't get free this way.

Through the windshield he could just make out the tail end of the Caddy about ten yards in front. It was rightside up. Christina Shepard had the driver's door open but she was hung up in the seat belt. She was still holding the gun. He'd never seen anyone look so damn resolute. A wet thunderclap rumbled and the SUV started sluicing down, dragging Christina Shepard along as she frantically tried to get free of the belt. She wasn't going to have enough time. She was already halfway underwater. She let out a whimper. Flynn made a similar sound. He hoped to Christ the little girl wasn't watching.

The broken ice flailed open like a trapdoor and swallowed the woman and the SUV whole. They dropped into oblivion and there was another crashing roar as the great lid of ice resettled almost perfectly back into place.

And then there wasn't a goddamn thing, there was absolutely nothing more.

Christina Shepard had actually done it. The crazy bitch had killed herself and probably murdered the rest of them as well. Flynn stared at the empty ice for another second as his heart chopped at his ribs.

"Kelly!" he called, craning his neck to look behind. "Kelly, are you all right?"

"I think so," she said. He could hear the trembling sob about to break in her voice.

Flynn tried to get his seat belt open, but the damn thing was jammed. The belt should've been part of the punch line too. You survive the crash, you're alive on the ice, you've been an ace driver since you were fifteen but this little busted button is what's going to do you in.

He smelled Danny's cigarettes. The French bulldog, sitting on the ceiling, stared at Flynn.

"My door's no good," Flynn told her. "Can you climb up here and get out the other side?"

"No."

"You've got to try."

Kelly clambered forward from the backseat, stepped on the dome light and stretched across Nuddin. "The door is stuck!"

"Can you roll the window down?"

"Where's the button?"

"This is an old car. You've got to roll it down. See the handle?"

Nuddin reached out from behind the passenger seat and cranked the handle. The window slid halfway down and shattered. The car shifted with an enormous moan.

"Climb out!" Flynn shouted. Kelly got her hands on Nuddin's seat belt and popped it in an instant. Of course. Nuddin swung out the busted window and slid from view. "Both of you! Go!"

"Where's Zero?"

"He's right under me, he'll follow in a second."

Nuddin going, Woowoo woowoo.

"There's water!" Kelly screamed. "I'm slipping! The ice is breaking!"

"Don't stand up. Lie flat. Can you crawl?"

"It's cold, Flynn! It's too cold!"

"Crawl for the pier!"

"Come on, Zero!" she shouted.

The dog was just sitting there and wouldn't leave. Flynn didn't know what that meant, but it felt like there was a great weight to it, a huge significance.

He twisted his neck as far as he could to see what was going on, watching in the rearview as Nuddin and Kelly crept over the splitting ice back toward the pier. He saw lights there now. Figures silhouetted.

He kept yanking at the belt. The Charger shifted again. The front bumper dipped underwater and just kept going.

"Christ," he whispered. The fear he'd been holding back so desperately catapulted through him as the ice continued to break. It sounded like an avalanche. The car lurched forward and dropped, the front end looping around as it sliced into the water. Flynn felt like he was somersaulting in midair as the car jerked loose and started to descend. The dog flopped backwards into his face. Ninety-five seconds left.

The freezing water raged in, and with it came the intolerable cold and the crushing pressure of a darkness he had always known but had never had to endure before. Every nerve burned and schizzed out at once, and then there was only an insane numbness. The overwhelming terror soon swelled into something like comfort. He had only an instant to take a last breath and wondered why he should bother. Zero looked him in the eye as the water rose and covered its face, bubbles bursting from its nose. The dog let out a noise that was more growl than whine, as if to say, *Ah fuck all, we're gonna snuff it. We're dead.*

Flynn watched the midnight road open beneath him and he cut loose with a screwy giggle under the water, burning up the last of his oxygen, seeing his brother Danny far below smiling at him with a cigarette hanging off his bottom lip. Flynn was thinking, Christ, I am. I really am. I'm about to—

Time.

TWO

The potential for breath.

An option to flow.

A crack in the black.

A warm light pulsing, way out of reach.

Awakening was pure hell without thought or reason, without identity or even definition. All that remained was human emotion spread out like an oil slick across the width of the midnight road.

Maybe it was fear. Maybe hate or remorse or guilt. It was so pure it couldn't be distinguished.

Slowly it took on value and made itself known. Flynn didn't exist anymore, but his futile and wretched hope remained. It straddled spheres. It was everything left after his heart had stopped.

He began to drive back up the road to his former self. His foot was hammered down on the gas as he broke from the depths of his own death and took his first breath in nearly half an hour.

Twenty-eight minutes pretty much on the nose before his body came back up through the hole in the ice—a one-in-a-million shot right there—and they got him out

of the water and jabbed him with adrenaline directly into
his busted heart and got him wired up and burned him
back to life.

Somebody's eyes searching.

They were his own. They didn't remember yet how to
blink. He couldn't shut the world out. The noise of it
made him scream. A rush of memory encompassed him,
and he knew his name but not his purpose.

He saw a round, eager face that he took for God. Thinking God looked a lot like a puffy-faced bald guy who
smelled like Hamburger Helper and Tabasco sauce.

God stared at him with a gap-toothed smile and said,
"You're the luckiest son of a bitch I've ever heard about.
You got angels watching over you they never taught us
about in St. Vincent's, let me tell you."

It surprised Flynn that God didn't have a more civil
tongue, but maybe it was a holdover from the whole
Philistine thing, slaughtering heathens and smashing the
Egyptians. Flynn turned his head and saw that he was
in the back of an ambulance. He had an IV in his arm.
Flashing red and blue lights flared behind him, stoic cops
standing around staring in his direction.

God turned out to be a paramedic. He was still grinning as he toyed with a plastic tube snaking into Flynn's
nose.

That first minute back—what some people would call
his miraculous resurrection but which Flynn called his
Holy Fuck I Ain't Dead revelation—he felt like he used to after he'd been on a weeklong bender. It hot-wired his
memories and dragged them back from great distances.
He saw Danny with his forehead propped against the

steering wheel, lifelike but utterly lifeless. Next to him, Patricia Waltz's head had gone through the passenger window, her right ear cut off and a squirt of blood dripping down the outside of the door.

He spotted Marianne's face, saw her at the beginning and the end of their marriage. The night he proposed to her, holding out the ring to her at Rockefeller Center a couple hours after they'd lit the big tree. The two of them skating together—ice, more ice—as she slid around into his right arm and he held the ring box in his left palm, sneaking it up to surprise her. Her eyes went wide and then she was leaping at him like a forward end and they both went down on their keesters. The ring flopped out of his hand and she went diving for it, fat kids eating pretzels circling them, Japanese tourists doing figure eights and snapping their pictures. She fell onto his chest and put the ring on and he reached up and held her tight, thinking you live for these moments. She planted a kiss on him that felt like it would never end. It went on and on and on, the back of his head getting frosty but her keeping his lips and his heart so damn hot. The best kiss of his life.

Then flashing forward as he watched her climb naked from the loins of a cat named Alvin. Marianne even introducing them, saying, This here, this is Alvin. Then Alvin scurrying for his pants folded precisely over Flynn's desk chair. Alvin dug sharp creases. Alvin going, Oh Jesus, man, I didn't know, she didn't, she didn't tell me. Of course, she wouldn't have. Marianne had to end a relationship with the broadest stroke possible. She'd shouted and blamed it all on Flynn while Flynn stared at Alvin, frickin' Alvin, feeling sorry for this guy with his crank hanging out.

Like life wasn't tough enough, you had to catch some cat in bed with your old lady and waste your remaining sympathy on the dude. Flynn could taste rum. His past pitched and rumbled. He saw abused and dead children who had been stowed away in carefully sealed compartments at the back of his mind. His own death had blown all the locks.

Flynn whispered, "...the kid?"

"Don't talk."

Jesus Christ, the Tabasco stink was like a blast furnace. Flynn hoped like hell he was stabilized because if this guy had to give him mouth-to-mouth, it might flatline him again. "...tell me."

"I said shut up. You guys, you come back from the dead, and you always want to talk an ear off. She's fine. Not even a scratch. I checked them both out. She and the retard are drinking cocoa. They're going to be staying at Stonybrook for a couple of days of observation. I'm driving them there in a minute, as soon as I finish with you."

"The cops—"

"They got a lot of questions for you, that's for sure. There were witnesses who caught some of the scene—your spinout, the SUV chasing you."

"She was trying to kill us..."

"Save it for the cops, all right? They'll be on your case at the hospital after you get checked out." The smile faded as the paramedic leaned in, the heat of the sauce like an open flame. "Now, why don't you lie back now, Miracle Man, huh? It's not every day I drag a corpse up out of hell. I'm feeling good about it, so don't ruin my high. I really don't want to think that you were stealing that kid from her mother and the lady died for it, right? So shut the fuck up and let me do my job, and the police can sort it out."

The EMT loaded Flynn into the ambulance, where another EMT hauled him forward and started asking him questions. What was his name? His date of birth? Flynn craned his neck and saw the pudgy guy with the Tabasco breath climbing into the back of a second ambulance, where Kelly and Nuddin were huddled under blankets drinking hot chocolate.

Flynn said his name and his birthday. The doors slammed shut, the EMT called over his shoulder to the driver and told him to get going. The engine growled and knocked hard. It needed an oil change, was down at least a quart. The siren started up and began its looping whine. They hooked a hard right and supplies on the shelves hit the floor and scattered.

He was alive.

The next morning, after a pair of hard-edged cops finished shaking him, Flynn heard his boss Sierra's three-inch heels stomping out there in the halls. He imagined coma patients waking up after fifteen years, rattled out of their sleep by those shoes.

Sierra stormed in, carrying a cactus. Like that's what you give somebody just back from the dead, a cactus. Well, all right. She threw it down on the windowsill and stared at Flynn lying there in a foofy hospital gown, a catheter in his crank and a bag of blood-threaded urine hanging from the bed rail. You'd think they could hide the damn disgusting things better, but no, they put it right out there to sink everybody's stomach.

Sierra leaned close and peered into his eyes. "They say you might be brain-damaged. Is it true?"

"It must be," Flynn said, "for a second there you looked good."

"God in heaven, you really are screwed then. Maybe I've been setting my sights too high. Instead of looking for a surgeon, I need to prowl around the patients."

"The brain-dead ones. It would probably be in your best interest."

Sierra Humbold was fifty and looked sixty because some of the plastic work hadn't completely taken. Due to a crushed cheek, her left eye was significantly lower than the right. The corner of her bottom lip pulled obscenely aside so you always got a look at a couple of her dry, nubby teeth. She wore a different wig every couple of weeks because she'd had some blunt trauma to the head. There must've been suture scars, maybe plates. Defensive scars and mottled bite wounds gouged the backs of both hands, forming a flotilla of evil smiles. She had lines dug in by time and more than a few by knives. They diagrammed the blueprints of her past.

She went two hundred pounds of hard muscle and could kick the ass of a jacked-up rhino, so Flynn had a hard time picturing the mooks who had worked her over. All she ever said was that she was a screwed-up kid who liked bad guys like her father. Her old man got shanked to death at Rikers when she was a child. He was doing an eighteen-year stretch for serial rape. Her last lover put a

.22 bullet in her lung. It took her years to find her own hate. Before that, she had swapped it out for love.

Now Sierra had the difference down cold.

"You know what happened to you?" she asked.

"Doctors and nurses come and go, but they haven't told me anything. Neither did the cops. The paramedic said I snuffed it."

"You know another euphemism?"

It almost made him grin. "Yeah. *Iced.*"

"Flash frozen underwater for about twenty-eight minutes, according to eyewitnesses," she told him. "If the water had been a degree or two warmer, things might've turned out different. By the way, half an hour? It's nowhere near a record."

He opened his mouth to snap out a retort, but he felt the icy water pour down his throat again. He steeled himself and tried to pull away from the memory.

"You talk to God?" Sierra asked. "See a white light or anything?"

Flynn yanked his thoughts back from the midnight road. "The kid," he said. "Kelly Shepard, and her uncle, they called him Nuddin, where are they? The cops wouldn't say anything."

"The cops aren't going to tell you shit and I'm not going to either until you explain to me exactly what the hell happened." She drew the only chair in the room over to the bed and sat waiting, her face hard but expectant. She wasn't cutting him any slack because he worked under her. Probably less because of it. There were enough internal investigations always going on, everybody suspicious of the guys who worked kid cases. They were right to be.

He gave her the report down to the smallest detail. The house. Nuddin in the cage. The plunge onto the ice, the dog refusing to leave, awakening to a puffy god. Even the way his thoughts seemed to be skittering a little too loosely. He had Marianne on his mind again, for the first time in a couple of years.

"Now tell me where the girl and her uncle are," he said.

"With me."

That wasn't the way it was done. Sierra already had five foster kids, but none of them came from cases she worked. Not even ones she was peripherally involved with. "What? Why?"

"No other family members have been tracked down yet. The police are taking their time on that house. They found the cage in the basement. Your story is checking out, but they're still worried you may have instigated the whole situation. I figured I'd watch over them to make sure nobody separated Kelly and Nuddin. They could easily get split up in the system."

"How are they doing?"

Sierra plucked at her wig the way any woman might toy with her hair when she was keyed up. She didn't show it but Flynn almost dying had left another lasting mark. The case had her knotted up. "The girl's acting all right, for the time being, but Dale says she's still in shock. It'll be a few days before the upheaval begins to display itself. He expects her to go into fits, the way any normal kid would. Right now she's on vacation. She's having fun, playing with the other kids. I taught her to make pasta last night. When she realizes she has no home left to go back to, that her mother's gone forever, she'll either shut down or act out. He thinks she's in for some bouts of rage."

"Who the hell isn't?"

Dale Mooney was the head CPS shrink. Flynn and Mooney didn't like each other, which didn't matter much except during the semiannual psych review. Mooney loved to project. He'd take Flynn to task for handling cases wrong because, Mooney said, fifteen years down the line the kids might evidence severe emotional scars because of something Flynn had done poorly or hadn't done at all. Flynn thought Mooney was mostly full of shit.

"Nuddin?"

"He's low-functioning autistic," Sierra told him. "So separated from the world that it hardly affects him. I wonder if he even felt any of the torture he was going through. He walks on the balls of his feet because there's more pressure exerted on the nerves that way. He likes to be hugged hard. He can stare into a mirror for hours, unable to fully realize he's looking at himself. There are certain treatments that can help but he's too old for most of them. Jackets lined with weights so they can feel the form of their own torso. Heavy boots so they can feel the ground under them."

"He sings, though. And in the car he understood when I said he had to roll down the window. Can he talk at all?"

"No. I'm not sure how much he understands, but it's not much. Maybe at a four- or five-year-old level."

Flynn shut his eyes and a dark wrapping of cool exhaustion tried to take him under again. His eyes snapped open. He had a lot more questions.

"And the husband? I heard the shot. Did he buy it?"

"No," Sierra said, "he's at Stonybrook. The bullet wedged under his heart, but it's one of those things where he's able to move all right until they open up his chest and go after it."

"He was the tipster. Has he been talking?"

"He won't shut up. He talks about the wife, their happy, beautiful home, his job on Wall Street. But when it gets to the dicey stuff, he winds it down and says he wants to talk to you. And he won't say why. But he seems scared."

Flynn thought he already knew the answer. He'd learned a lot on the job. Spouses witnessed occasional horrors beneath their roofs. They allowed the secrets to grow and taint them, until they were just as guilty. Sometimes it went on for months or years, until they took a stand. Wives got out the meat cleaver. Older siblings performed ritual patricide. Husbands dropped a call to CPS and drove around the block waiting for their family crimes to be solved by other men.

"He wants to explain why he called in the tip," Flynn said.

"You sound sure of it."

"I am. Shepard was a regular mook caught up in something beyond himself. But the wife? She's the one who ran that show."

"You don't have to go."

"Of course I do, and you want me to anyway."

"I want to know everything about that guy. If it has to do with Kelly and Nuddin, I want to know about it." She tugged at a nylon curl and the wig shifted forward. "The newspapers are pretty much split down the middle about you."

"What do you mean?"

"Half are making you look like a hero. The rest are saying she was only trying to save her kid and died for it. They're trying to juice the situation up as much as they can."

Flynn thought about a retarded man in a cage, a crazed woman with a gun, a car chase through the slick back roads, a flip onto the ice, the yawning mouth of an icy hell sucking down a Cadillac SUV, and wondered why the hell anybody out there needed more fuckin' juice.

"All someone has to do is look at the scars on Nuddin's body."

"You make it sound like reporters care about facts and evidence and little stuff like that."

"I live in hope."

"You need to forget that now," Sierra told him.

She was right. The media could massacre him. The cops might scapegoat him. A dead woman's word held a lot more weight than his own did. She'd been rich and pretty. She'd had a beautiful home, a loving husband, an intelligent and sweet daughter. He was an outsider who trucked in during a storm and blew the American dream off its foundation. Shepard would have high-power lawyers. They could play all kinds of cards. Say that Nuddin was being cared for personally, by family, instead of being sent off to a filthy *asylum* run by uncaring, corrupt attendants and fat, cruel nurses. Before it was over, Flynn could be looking at jail time for manslaughter.

"Do a background check on Christina Shepard," he said. "She had a thing about her name. She forced me to say it."

"We'll run the usual and I'll go deeper if I have to."

"You will. She mentioned her father, acted afraid of him. She said he'd become too sick to care for Nuddin. Shepard called him a crazy son of a bitch. I'd guess the father was the one who tortured Nuddin."

"Okay, I'll look into it. This is going to be the big ugly story for a while. A crowd of reporters has been waiting for you to wake up so they can tear you to pieces."

"It's nice to be loved."

"You'll contend with it. Just stay the course. Don't dodge. You know you were right in what you did, don't let them deflect you."

Flynn thought about Sierra's household. The layout of the place. Big yard, short hedges. You could see the kids playing in back from the street. He wondered how safe it was. "I'm going to drop by now and again."

"You can't for the time being. If the cops see you near Kelly, you'll stir them up even more."

"I can handle that."

"But she can't. Don't come by until I say it's all right, you hear me?" She waited for him to answer. When he said nothing, she kicked the bed frame hard enough to make his catheter rattle. "You hear?"

"Jesus Christ, yeah, I hear."

"Good."

An oppressive weariness dropped over him. It was the timed pain meds feeding into his system through the IVs, except he wasn't in any pain. "What about the dog?" he asked.

"The bulldog? Kelly keeps crying about it. They found it in your car when they got the Charger up off the bottom. You're special. Usually they leave shit like that in the Sound because of the cost, but everybody's been raving. It was only fifty feet down. They had guys in these super scuba suits going after it with winch lines. Poor bastards nearly froze too."

"Did they get the Caddy?"

"They got photos of it and brought her body up. She was still holding the gun." Sierra stood and started for the door. "Are you going to take care of this cactus?"

"You don't water them, so what's to care for?"

"I thought that would be your attitude." She retrieved it from the windowsill, held it close, but not close enough to scratch her. Flynn realized there was a metaphor there, but he was too tired to fully examine it. She gave it another minute's worth of love and warmth before abandoning it back on the sill.

Sierra put her hand on the door knob and checked the hall before stepping into it. She turned back and said, "Well, it's good you're not too brain-damaged anyway. Hey, they're showing *Out of the Past* at the Paradigm if you want to take it in."

Iced. For nearly a half hour. And still it wasn't a record.

But Flynn wasn't so sure of the brain-damage part.

Because a moment after Sierra shut the door, the dead dog Zero crawled out from beneath the bed where he'd been hiding, still wearing the white sweater and little booties, looked up at Flynn and said, "The Paradigm, huh? I love Robert Mitchum."

THREE

A different pair of cops came around before he was released. They warned him not to discuss an open investigation with the media. As soon as Flynn was wheeled out the front door of the hospital he covered his ass and talked to every reporter who wanted to listen. He suspected the cops were building a case against him and he wanted his side of the story out there building momentum if they came after him.

The media was hopped up and merciless. Flynn did his best and told the truth, but it wasn't nearly enough. Nobody wanted to believe him. Rude as the story was, it was even nastier to point the finger at him. It was too difficult for them to come to terms with a beautiful, high-class woman keeping her retarded brother locked in a cage. It was easier to call Flynn a pedo on the prowl working for CPS.

None of the stations came right out and said it. They edited his footage to make him sound thick and a little high. He couldn't handle the spotlight well and they took advantage of it. Every time they showed his face on television he looked sweaty and guilty as hell. Sierra gave him pointers on how to do it right, but when the lights were in his face and the journalists were sticking their mikes under his nose, he just tried to explain himself and give the facts. He appeared dazed. It was his own fault. All the pretty reporters sounded so sincere that he was easily duped.

The papers did better by him, but nobody read the papers. He started receiving death threats in the mail and over the phone. He recognized at least one voice, a woman whose husband used to beat her and their eleven-year-old daughter. Flynn had investigated the case and got the husband put away for a nickel. The woman spit venom and used some foul language he'd never come across before. It was spooky. Her vitriol downshifted into broken sobbing when she admitted her name and told him how betrayed she felt, that he was doing the same things her husband used to do. He talked to her for more than an hour before she hung up, furious and calling him a liar. He hadn't taken a drink in eighteen months but could only fall off to sleep that night after killing a half bottle of Jack.

Despite all he'd seen and survived, Marianne used to call him terribly naive. He was starting to understand what she meant.

He went back to work. He ran two investigations, following up complaints that turned out to be from angry in-laws who didn't like their grandkids watching too much television. He ran another case and found a father with his belt in his hand beating the shit out of his ten-year-old son for missing a few blades of grass while cutting the lawn. Flynn kept his cool for about eight seconds.

He got into it with the guy and broke his jaw. The police kept him for three hours of questioning. They sensed he was going savage.

It took more than a week before he felt ready to face Mark Shepard. It was bad timing. He was too slow off the line. By the time he got to the hospital, Shepard had been under the knife for four hours while surgeons extracted the bullet near his heart. Flynn decided to wait it out.

He wandered the hospital and sat down in the emergency room. He watched the battered and the ill come in by the truckload. Every time a child cried he hiked up a notch in his seat. He tried hard not to think that Christina Shepard had been right and he had piggy thoughts squirming away in some corner of his skull.

Zero hopped around and followed tight-faced paramedics racing through the corridors. The ghost dog had a nose for blood. He discussed Mitchum movies and kept up a running commentary on who might live through the night and who was definitely dead. Zero's eyes fixed on a coughing kid and he said, "This one, he's been bitten by a spider and he's severely allergic. His throat's closing up fast. By the time they get him on the table, he'll be going into anaphylactic shock. He's almost there."

It wasn't so bad, really, knowing you were either crazy or haunted. Flynn had felt that way most of his life anyway. Now things had just been kicked up a notch. His mother, on her deathbed, had roused from a coma long enough to lock her eyes onto him. Her hand gripped his shirtfront and proceeded to crawl up his chest until she snagged his collar. Her flesh was bloated and yellow as mustard. Her kidneys had stopped functioning days earlier. A quarter million in machinery did nothing but stare and keep time with its flashes and jazz-riff wails.

His mother's gaze was distant but clear. She'd had nothing but ice chips for a week, and not even that the last forty-eight hours. Her voice sounded full of dust and silverfish. She said, "Wings like shiny gold coins" and died clutching his shirt.

Danny went out of the game with a beautiful teen girl riding next to him. Flynn didn't know why he was stuck with a French bulldog, but everyone had to play the hand they were dealt.

He didn't so much mind that the ghost of a dog spoke to him as he did the fact that Zero spoke with Flynn's own voice. It was embarrassing.

The coughing kid was getting worse. Maybe Zero had something down right. Flynn watched, getting to his feet for a slow approach. It scared the boy's mother while she stood at the desk filling out the insurance paperwork. She pulled the clipboard closer to her so he couldn't see her name or address. He asked her, "Is your son allergic to anything? To insect bites?"

"What?"

"Your son—"

The emergency room had a security guard. Like if you got pushy while you were having a stroke, the guard might arrest you, put you in hospital jail until you learned your manners. Pick a number, get in line. Yo Stroke-boy, settle your ass down.

The security guard braced Flynn. Big guy, no weapons Flynn could see, but the dude was acting like he might yank a taser. "Sir, do you have a medical emergency?"

"This boy, I just wanted to know if—"

"Sir, if you don't have a medical emergency I'm going to have to ask you to leave the ER."

A wave of worry passed over the boy's face as he stared at Flynn, his cheeks growing ashen, tears spurting onto the floor. The mother's hand reached out and touched her son's shoulder, turning him away. The guard started getting in close, invading space. Flynn wondered if anybody here would cut him some slack for coming back to life after twenty-eight minutes on the bottom. He was a Miracle Man, after all. Not everybody could do it.

The kid was turning a soft shade of blue. His breathing made it sound like he was whispering backwards.

The room seemed to be getting brighter. Flynn felt his lips drawing back. His teeth dried in the air. He began to grow short of breath. He weakened and nearly went to one knee in front of the guard.

The guard kept repeating, "Sir? Sir?" but wouldn't lend a hand.

You'd think with a word like emergency right there in the name of the room, they'd take things a little more seriously.

Zero said, "What would Mitchum do, huh?"

Ole Bobby wouldn't have allowed himself to get into this position in the first place. Neither would Danny. Neither would Sierra. Someone braces you, you slap him down. Flynn was trapped someplace between being too hard and being too soft. He also didn't trust the dog. He hoped the dog was wrong about the whole situation.

The mother turned in the paperwork to the woman at the desk. She didn't look like a nurse. Just someone else who worked there not acting official or grim or caring enough. She took the forms and bopped away, ponytail swinging. The boy continued whispering. Flynn was fifteen feet away but he thought he felt a drop of water land on the back of his neck. The kid's tears were covering ground.

Flynn knew he should fight to win back his cool, but he'd dealt with enough dying children who couldn't catch a break and he didn't want to add another one to the list. Not even if he might have to go to hospital jail for a time-out.

He tried once more. "Get a doctor here now!"

"Sir—"

"Get out of my way."

"Do you need a doctor? Is this a medical . . . ?"

"Get out of my way!"

Flynn backhanded the security chump and watched him drop onto his ass and sit there gaping in fright. Mitchum would've been ashamed of Flynn. When you were a hero, you took on the roughnecks and the bootleggers and the mob. When you were on Cape Fear, you took on hotshot attorneys who owed you a debt of years wasted in the joint. You didn't put the bite on some loser with a cap and no gun, whose bottom lip was trembling.

The boy settled it for all of them. The kid pitched over backwards and, for the first time, Flynn could see that the boy's throat was so swollen that his coat zipper was gouging into his skin. The mother turned like she was seeing him for the first time, and said, "Jeff? Jeffie?"

Flynn yanked the kid into his arms and broke the zipper apart. It seemed to give Jeffie some relief, let him suck in some air. Flynn held the boy close and kicked through a pair of sage green doors at one end of the waiting room. The hall beyond was lined with beds and patients. Doctors congregated in groups with nurses, chatting. One guy turned to Flynn and actually smiled. It was a leftover leer from some joke one of the other doctors had just finished telling.

Behind him, the mother was screaming, "My baby! My baby!" They really did that, it wasn't just in the movies.

Flynn put the kid on an empty table and said, "Anaphylactic shock from a spider bite!"

"Who are you? You can't just come in—"

Flynn thought, Good, he was finally going to get a chance to crack somebody in the head, but one of the other docs, maybe the one who'd been telling the joke, began shouting orders. He questioned the mother and she told him, "I don't know who that man is or what he's talking about. My son has asthma! He's on *Azmacort* but ran out of his inhaler spray!"

Three doctors, two nurses, all of them pointing at Flynn, several voices calmly speaking as one, said, "Get him out of here."

From behind, someone drew him gently out of the hall. Flynn was surprised at how easily he allowed it to happen, his body responding without his will. He spun and saw a young woman beside him, her hand on his wrist pulling him along. From this angle he could only glimpse the barest hint of her face. She wore her blond hair long and straight, the way women had in the midseventies. He used to watch his friends' older sisters actually iron their hair on ironing boards to get it that straight. Some of Danny's girlfriends had done it too. Patricia Waltz. Hers had been the same.

The woman knew the hospital and skirted the emergency room, leading Flynn down halls back toward Shepard's room. Her purse had weight to it and swung with real momentum. He was scared it might clock him in the crotch. She walked with an angry authority, never turning her chin. He kept waiting to see her face but she never showed it to him.

As they turned another corner he stopped abruptly, hoping to break her hold on him, but she had good reflexes and stopped with him, still gripping his wrist. He started up again and so did she, drawing him on. They entered an alcove waiting area with a view of the parking lot. It was snowing again.

She turned and he recognized her. She was a reporter for *Newsday* and she'd quoted him accurately. Her name was Jessie Gray.

"Was there a reason for all that ruckus?" she asked, sitting on a small love seat, leaving just enough room for him to squeeze in beside her. He remained on his feet.

"Probably," he said.

She was dressed in jeans, heavy boots and a well-fitted insulated ski jacket. He got the feeling that she was never unprepared, that she always wore exactly what was necessary and was never caught without chains on her tires or sunscreen at the beach. She stared at him with an air of control and influence.

"I was trying to save a kid's life," he told her.

"Why did you think he was going into shock from a spider bite? It's winter, there are no spiders around. Why were you arguing with the doctors?"

"You following me?" he asked.

"I was hoping to interview Mark Shepard again before his surgery but they rescheduled him from the afternoon to the morning. He went in before I arrived." She gave him a good eyeing, her pert mouth like plastic rose petals, deep twin lines edging out from the corners cleaving her cheeks. She looked young enough to be doing a story for a high-school paper. "Please answer my questions."

She was pretty, and guys always got pumped up to talk bullshit in front of a cute girl. Jessie Gray had the appealing features of the girl next door even if there'd never been a girl next door like this. His mother would have called her *bonny*. His weaknesses were hot-wired into his head by his brother's girlfriends. She looked more than a little similar to Marianne, and Flynn felt himself wanting to impress her with his quick wit, even though he didn't have one.

She stared at him with dark eyes that revealed a glint of indulgent humor. He thought she was probably deciding on the best way to draw out all the hidden facts of his life. He thought she might be carrying a concealed tape recorder that was catching his every stutter and fuck-up.

"I've seen the signs before," he told her. "Nobody was taking the situation seriously enough. The boy was turning blue."

"I only came in at the tail end of that scene," she said. "You were scaring hell out of everybody, you know."

He liked the way she talked. With an in-your-face,

whip-snap quality. He liked how she handled herself but Flynn still wasn't certain he should level with her or any reporter anymore.

"Did you speak to Shepard before he went in?" she asked.

"No."

"You were finally willing to talk with him?"

"Finally?"

"He's been asking for you for over a week."

"I've been busy dealing with reporters."

"And working your caseload. And scuffling."

"I can promise you," Flynn said, "I don't scuffle."

"Fight, then. *Brawl*. Are those macho terms more to your liking?"

"More accurate anyway."

The snow was wet and collected on the window in varying patterns that reminded him of hitting the ice. He wondered if the snow wanted in just to finish the job. Marianne would say he was just being paranoid. He'd always had a touch of it. It was a way to salve the ego, thinking you were important enough to be on other angry people's minds. He noticed that in the past two weeks his thoughts had been firing pretty randomly. He didn't mind the dead French bulldog nearly as much as the fact that he was actually listening to it, doing what it told him. That he had believed in Zero.

"I'd like to do a follow-up interview with you," Jessie Gray said.

"It's only been, what, six or seven days? There's nothing to follow up on."

"How you're getting on. What life is like for you after your near-death experience."

He couldn't quite make out if she was being facetious or not. Being flash frozen for a half hour wasn't quite the same thing as missing out on a heartbeat or two. He realized it all came down to ego again. Like someone was taking something from him if they weren't in awe that he'd driven back from the midnight road. Now he had to be called Mr. Miracle Man or what, he'd go pout?

"Life is very much the same," he told her. He wasn't sure if he was lying.

"No grand revelation or epiphany on the nature of our existence? How precious each waking moment has become?" She moved out of the seat and weaved about him, lissome, somehow ephemeral, as if she was vanishing and reappearing moment to moment. She was used to putting old men off-balance. She was turning on her appeal and dispensing pheromones. She was poking fun, probing for a deeper truth. "Have you put past regrets and bad blood behind you?"

He thought about it for a minute and said, honestly, "I don't have much of either."

"No?"

"No."

"How about telling me why you conceded to speak to Mark Shepard?"

"It was time."

"What's that mean?"

Flynn said, "It means it was time."

"The press has been treating you like hell, hasn't it?"

"Yes," he admitted.

"What did you think of my article?"

"It was exact. And well written."

That loosened her lips a little, brought out a real smile. "Thank you. So don't you think you could trust me to tell your story?"

"I don't have a story to tell," he said.

"Everyone does."

"Yeah? So what's yours?" he asked.

"Mine's boring. Twice married, twice divorced, both marriages ending within a year. My fault, mostly. They didn't want to be married, but I did, and I chased them until they cracked. I know I don't look old enough to have two ex-husbands, but there it is. I didn't deserve my position on the paper. My father is a journalism professor at Hofstra University. He's got a lot of friends and pulled some strings for me. I earned my station pretty fast, though. I'm compulsive. When I see a chance to tell a unique story, I go after it. I chase the truth like my men, no matter where it leads, even if it hurts, and sometimes it does. I'm obsessive. It's an ineradicable flaw in my character."

He got the sense she'd been asked the question before and had this all down as a prepared statement. Probably hit on all the proper psychological lures and decoys to get an interviewee to open right up, start spilling his own guts. Flynn had no idea why it wasn't working on him.

"At least you're self-aware," he said.

"Very. Now, what do you think Mark Shepard wants to tell you?"

"I don't know."

"What are you hoping he'll say?"

"I have no idea."

"Is there anything you want to say to him?"

"Miss Gray, one of us isn't taking the hint here."

She nodded and stood, waited for him to move off first and when he didn't, she gave a quick flip of that long lovely hair and started down the hall. She was a woman who would always need the final word, and most men wouldn't mind allowing it.

"I wonder, though, if it's you or me, Mr. Flynn?"

He decided, Screw Shepard. Maybe it wasn't time after all. Maybe it would never be time.

Flynn got lost in the hospital. He peeked into rooms and startled the hell out of old people and candy stripers. Memories and associations started peeling up from the back of his head like cheap plastic tiling. Shards struck him and dug in. He turned a corner and looked through an open doorway and saw a woman very much like his mother, hooked up to the same types of machines, and just as dead. Her mind gone, her lungs forced to work on and on, serving no purpose.

He nabbed the elevator and saw a guy in there holding flowers, hunting for the maternity ward. Flynn had been holding candy and a stuffed teddy bear, late for the arrival of his own son. He'd been stuck in traffic, in the snow— *always* stuck in traffic in the snow, forever, forever like Sisyphus and his rock—and had gotten off on the ward to be met by the anemic faces of Marianne's parents.

Both of them crying. Both of them with their arms open. Both of them trying to hug him. The bear gazing on. The baby in the morgue. Marianne in her room, alone, with the Weather Channel blaring. She held her arms out to him too. She'd named the kid Noel because of all the snow. Frickin' Alvin out there somewhere in the world waiting to make his way into Flynn's bed.

Flynn hit the automatic doors and the cold burst against his warm face and he let out a breath that had been pent up for days. He looked for his rental car, a blue Taurus, but the snow was heavy enough that it had blanketed the lot. He started wiping off hoods trying to find the car. He felt embarrassed without reason, and a subtle flush of anger continued to well inside him.

From the street side of the lot a vague shadow of a woman approached, black parting veils of white.

Orchid tattoos twined up her neck and reached out across her jaw, the first thing anyone would notice about her. Knotted ropes of hair hung across her face, these deep dark eyes peering out from the shroud. She had piercings going all around her ears, four or five in each lobe. Her face hung slack, burdened with hard mileage. Fishnets even in winter, a leather jacket a few sizes too large, lots of chains and studs.

Junkie was an outdated term no one used anymore, but nothing more PC had replaced the term. *Drug dependent* didn't cut it. *Crack whore* was too glib, but it might prove accurate. Flynn rarely got approached by hustlers on the street anymore because he had enough cred behind him for the girls to smell law. Maybe he was losing the musk now that he was on the wrong side of the cops.

She was too attractive to be one of the under the 59th Street Bridge gals. She looked more Greenwich Village or East Side action. He couldn't figure what the hell a Manhattan pro might be doing out here in the Stonybrook Hospital parking lot in a snowstorm.

He could see she was stoned. "Aren't you cold?" he asked.

She drew a slip of paper from her pocket and held it out to him. "I have to give this to you."

"To me?"

"Yeah."

He was reluctant to take it. He scanned the lot to see if anybody else was around, if this was a setup of some kind. Shepard's lawyers at work, trying to tap him with kiddie porn. The girl took another step closer. Snow was piling in her hair, the white blotting out her tats. He let out a small groan of frustration, hoping he wasn't being a sucker. He took the note.

On it were the neatly typed words:

THIS IS ALL YOUR FAULT

Flynn glanced up at her and said, "What gag is this?"

"It's no gag. I mean, I don't think it's a gag."

"Who gave this to you?"

"I'm not supposed to tell."

"Tell me anyway."

"I can't."

"What's it mean?"

"Don't you understand?"

He stared at her knowing this was some kind of new game he'd never played before. He frowned in puzzlement and she smiled sadly back at him, and he watched as her black hair billowed as if from a great wind, and the snowflakes dusting her flew off at once, turning pink and then red, and her eyes widened in perfect clarity without reason. Her forehead seemed to jut forward from the center before splitting apart, first in half and then into quarters and many pieces afterward, the orchids coming closer, proffered, as she rose up onto her tiptoes to meet him, lifting further and vaulting into his arms, and then he could see nothing because her brains were in his eyes.

FOUR

The Suffolk County homicide dick looked like a stiletto blade with eyes. The black nerve inside Flynn started throbbing away as he picked up a serious threat vibe. He'd expected to see one of the cops he'd talked to before. Now he'd been turned over to a hard-ass, someone who'd make something stick. Even before the detective introduced himself, he squinted like he thought every word that would ever come out of Flynn's mouth was bound to be a velvet lie.

Flynn had met a lot of cops. The front line of the donut brigade. The hard-core men of justice who put solving crimes before spending time with their families. The scuzzballs with badges who busted teenage girls so they could spook them into backseat favors. The ones who were a hair away from being career criminals, who liked to pal around with the goombahs and hustlers on their off-hours.

So far, he didn't know what to make of this one.

They were in the emergency room. The storm had worsened. All the sick folks were pressed together in one half of the waiting area while cops and forensic photographers kept swinging in and out of the hospital nabbing hot chocolate and stomping snow off their shoes.

The sick people kept staring at Flynn. He didn't blame them. He'd bolted in grabbing at his face and immediately vomited on the floor. The security guy kept calling, "Sir! Sir!" behind him. Flynn had found the bathroom on a blind run and practically drowned himself in the sink washing himself off. His forehead stung with two parallel scratches from flying skull splinters. The dead girl was in his mouth.

Flynn's clothes were still covered with her blood. A janitor had cleaned up his puke but the stink of it remained heavy in the room.

The security guard was bitching to the police, gesturing to Flynn with his chin and keeping his arms crossed over his chest.

The stiletto stood about five-seven, went maybe one-fifty. He looked light enough to pick up and sail across the room like a paper plane. He was padded in a black raincoat with heavy lining, black gloves, the top third of his black three-piece suit on display. The tie he wore was double-knotted. Hair black, eyes a hazy gray, skin the off-white of a dirty motel sheet.

"I'm Raidin," the detective said. He had a priest's soft voice. The name lingered there in the draft. Flynn knew he was supposed to respond but had no idea what to say. He just nodded and hoped it would be enough. The cop continued with a polished politeness. "Could you please go over what happened in detail one more time?"

Flynn did. He told it exactly as it happened, starting with waiting to speak to Shepard and the circumstances with the kid choking in the ER. He wasn't going to be able to make himself look good. He was going to appear unhinged, which maybe he was. He wasn't discounting anything. Raidin made heavy, sustained eye contact as Flynn laid it out. Flynn didn't let it shake him. He realized that as soon as he was done telling his story Raidin would try to knock it down.

"Did you know her?"

"No," Flynn said. "Who was she?"

"You never met her?"

"No."

"You never slept with her?"

Flynn gave it a five count, trying to shrug back into his cool. Raidin was going to be one of those cops who wore away at you like Chinese water torture, one drip at a time. "Wouldn't that constitute knowing her, in its broadest definition?"

"Yes, I suppose it would." Raidin offered a grin that looked sharp enough to slice paper. "Her name was Angela Soto. Twenty-one. She grew up out here on the Island but she'd been working Manhattan the last couple of years. A known prostitute, both in the city and in Suffolk. In and out of rehab. She'd tried cleaning up her act but kept creeping back into the life."

"She have any kids?" Flynn asked.

"Why?"

"Maybe the CPS has something on her."

"We don't know yet if she had any children."

"Who'd she work for?"

"Strictly freelance so far as we know at the moment. Every now and again she'd come out here and visit her mother for a few months, wind up working a few side jobs in Centereach. She's got a detailed rap sheet."

"She was pretty, and young. I bet a lot of people felt a need to help her."

Watching the tip of his own finger, Raidin tapped Flynn's chest gently, prodding the stains. "And nobody could. That's the way it is."

"Maybe he was one of her johns."

"Who?"

"The hitter."

It made Raidin's face tighten. "The hitter?"

All the film noir euphemisms slid through Flynn's head. *Torpedo. Shooter. Button man.* "The guy who shot her. He chose her for a reason. He probably knew her."

"We'll check."

Flynn's eyes darted around the emergency room. More kids in assorted states of illness and injury stared blank-eyed. Elderly people who wouldn't last out the winter appeared to know their fates and accept them with a common but assertive dignity.

The smell of the place, and himself, and Angela Soto's blood and excavated interiors began to swarm up against his face again. He had to put the back of his hand over his nose and wait for the stinging in his nostrils to pass.

"Any idea where the shooter was standing?" he asked.

Raidin let his lips slide into the smile again, but his eyes were heating with controlled resentment. He didn't like answering questions from someone like Flynn, but he wanted to engage in dialogue, get a feel for who he was talking to. "East end of the lot, close to the building, probably back where they park the ambulances. With a rifle. Damn difficult shot from nearly a hundred yards off. In a storm. This perp's had some experience. Or he's lucky as hell."

"He had plenty of time to ice me," Flynn said. "He waited for her to approach from the other direction."

"And you didn't see anyone?"

"No."

"You're absolutely certain about that?"

"It was snowing. I have a rental Taurus and couldn't find it. I didn't notice anybody else out there. Maybe folks were coming and going, but I didn't pick up on it."

"And so he waits until she delivers the message," Raidin said.

"She was the message."

Raidin nodded, already on the same track. It made talking out loud so much simpler. He thumped Flynn's chest again, same spot, a little harder. The way an excited friend might do it. "Sent as a warning. From whom? And what for?"

"I don't know."

"I see." Raidin drew out a little plastic bag containing the note. "And why would someone do this do you think? Go to all this trouble to send you a message? What is all your fault?"

"I don't know."

Raidin turned the bag over and over, holding it out as if he wanted Flynn to take it, like this was some kind of card trick. "You receive the note and she immediately dies."

Flynn didn't know what the hell else to say. He nodded and waited.

"Have you tussled with anyone recently? Do you have any enemies that you know of?"

"Who would kill somebody else *instead* of me? That I don't know."

"How about in general? In conventional terms. In the broadest definition, as it were."

They were definitely going to hunt down and interview Marianne and Frickin' Alvin. Flynn talked about the death threats but didn't mention the woman whose husband had been tossed into prison. He knew she was just acting out because she felt betrayed, unwilling to give him the benefit of the doubt. "In general, you'd have to devote a lot of man-hours. The list is long and varied."

"And if you had to abbreviate it?"

"Christina Shepard's father might be at the top," Flynn said.

Raidin's features emptied of all human expression. He might've been alabaster, his face something you put on for a masquerade. "You believe this connects with the Shepard situation?"

"I don't know," Flynn said. "But maybe, in some way." He was saying a lot of things Raidin already knew, but the cop was making him say them anyway. An understandable power play. His questions seemed dumb but the man definitely wasn't. If Flynn wasn't so sick to his stomach, he might be feeling anxious, even juked up. But Raidin wasn't going to get very far under his skin today, and the man appeared to know it.

"The father's been dead six months," Raidin said.

That made Flynn lift his chin. He wanted to know

more but didn't want to question Raidin and get even farther on his bad side. Sierra would find out the facts. "Christina Shepard said he was ill but talked about him as if he were alive. So did the husband. She was afraid of what her father might do if she let her brother free."

"Some families, they still lock up the mentally handicapped in their attics, chain children to the radiator for months at a time. They think they're possessed by Satan. Diseased. Wicked."

"I know," Flynn said. "I've seen it."

"He's out of surgery, by the way. Shepard. Critical but stable. He won't be responsive for a couple of days. Heard you wanted to talk to him."

"He wanted to talk to me."

"About what?"

"I don't know."

"Do you believe he tipped you about the brother?"

"Yes."

"Maybe he feels guilty about his wife."

"Maybe he's got a reason. Did you get anything out of him?"

It was a pushy question but Raidin didn't mind. "No. His attorneys won't allow him to talk, and we can't exactly pressure a guy who has a bullet in his heart."

"I guess I can see that."

"Now, explain this scene with the boy in the emergency room."

That was trickier. Flynn tried to be deliberately vague. He said he'd seen anaphylactic shock before and thought the boy was dying from it. Whatever the cause, the kid had been about a minute away from suffocating. Doing a good deed for an unknown reason made his actions dubious. Nobody was going to pin any medals on him. The mother would never say thank you. The docs would always give him the stink eye. Raidin kept watching.

"How's the boy?" Flynn asked.

"Fine. He just had a bad asthma attack."

They stood there like that for a while.

Then, again with the poking. The thin index finger, rapidly tapping, determining the thickness of Flynn's sternum. "Half hour with your heart stopped, that's a pretty long run."

"I've been informed it's nowhere near a record."

"So what was it like?"

Flynn thought about it. There'd been no euphoria but no despair. No guiding divine presence but no abominable evil either. He'd seen his brother but he always saw his brother. Danny was forever prevalent in his mind. He'd seen an endless dark road, but every road seemed immeasurable when you were stuck on it.

"Pretty much just more of the same," Flynn said.

FIVE

In the city, at the Paradigm, the dead dog wouldn't shut up during the afternoon showing of *I Wake Up Screaming*.

Zero commented on how hot Betty Grable was, what a shame a first-rate actor like Laird Cregar couldn't break wider in his career because he was so overweight and how sad it was that Carole Landis bumped herself off when she had such a nice rack. Zero kept pawing at Flynn's arm wanting Milk Duds. Flynn was starting to get a little annoyed.

He didn't mind the dog talking all the time so much, saying a lot of the same things Flynn felt about the movie, in his own voice. But he damn sure wasn't going to sit here feeding his Duds to the talking ghost of a French bulldog in booties.

You had to draw a line with the dead.

It made a kind of sense that the dog showed up. Flynn was open to hauntings. He'd been chasing his dead brother for most of his life. His ex-wife was still very much on his mind. He relived old cases with eerie repetition. Kids he hadn't seen for years would show up in his dreams. He thought of his lost son Noel, who he'd never even seen. He fell in love with film noir actresses fifty years dead.

Zero was right, Betty Grable still had it. Flynn inserted himself onto the screen and elbowed Victor Mature out of the way. He knew how the movie ended, he could save Betty and clear up the mystery in half the time. He could get on with things. The past pulled him backwards.

"You're really not going to share the candy?" Zero asked.

"Really."

"Selfish prick."

It was okay to talk. The projectionist was some college kid working part-time who spent his hours in the booth studying calculus and advanced physics. He probably never even looked at any of the films he ran, and in six months he'd graduate and start building satellites for the military or cell phone services.

The real movie buffs, the obsessives and disability cases who couldn't work a job because they lived inside film stock and nitrate, wouldn't turn up until the next showing. It was too early for most of them. They were just waking up now, readying themselves. They'd flood in carrying buckets of chicken and burgers and bottles of wine, and move from theater to theater all night long.

"You're just mad because they make you wear sweaters and little booties in the afterlife too," Flynn said.

"They don't let you have anything," Zero said. "You have nothing because you are nothing."

"That's not what Sister Murteen told us in Catholic School."

"I don't think you should put much faith in what that woman told you. Sister Murteen is a drill sergeant in hell."

Every time Flynn shifted in his seat the .38 he'd started carrying on his hip would thunk against the metal arm and an ugly note would chime. Victor and Betty were about to go swimming in a crowded public indoor pool at 2 A.M. The forties were definitely different. Vic showed off his physique, smoking a cigarette. Betty put her hair up in a plastic cap. She showed off the legs that kept a couple million servicemen brimming with hope while they knocked back the Nazis and jungle-wrangled the Japanese.

Funny, he saw Betty up there taking a dip but he was thinking about Marianne and Alvin, frickin' Alvin, Marianne on top of him, hearing Flynn at the front door and shifting into high gear. How his wife must've hated him, and hated Alvin too to put the guy in that position. Maybe she wanted them to throttle each other. It would allow her to walk out free and clear, tiptoeing across the bodies.

Instead, she'd clamped onto ole Al and turned her chin to look over her shoulder at Flynn stepping into the room. She smiled up at him. Sierra called it a cry for attention. Sierra figured Marianne had been sending up all kinds of flares for years, but Flynn was too stupid to see any of them. It must be true. He'd never noticed she was unhappy with him, not until the day he met Alvin.

"They're lying, you know," Zero said. "It wasn't asthma. The cops know it. The mother was wrong. As soon as the doctors examined the boy they realized it was a spider bite. The kid and his mother live in an apartment complex that's being renovated. They're digging up the foundation. The spiders are migrating all over the building. That's how the kid got stung. You think there are no spiders in winter? You think they're all dead or something?"

"I don't know."

"You don't *know*, is that what you just said?"

"That's what I said."

"Betty would never go for you."

Flynn had to swallow down a Dud before he could answer. "Why not?"

"You lack style. She dated George Raft. She liked bad boys, guys who were mobbed up."

"She was searching for someone who'd have a deeper understanding of her pain."

"You're too soft," Zero told him.

"But she'd go for you, I suppose."

"It's a well-documented fact that Betty liked dogs."

Maybe so, Flynn couldn't remember.

He wondered if Christina Shepard might be floating about, just out of eyeshot. Maybe seated in the row behind him, also coveting his Duds. Every now and again Zero would perk his head up and look off in some direction as if he were being called. His nubby tail would wag for an instant and he'd shiver with excitement, and it seemed he only remained with Flynn through a great act of will.

The movie finished and Flynn rubbed his eyes as the lights came up. Zero followed him out past the poster for next week's showing of the 1932 classic *I Am a Fugitive from a Chain Gang,* starring Paul Muni. Zero started running around in happy circles, saying it was one of his favorites, and why didn't Flynn just buy the DVDs?

"I like the big screen," Flynn said.

"But the seats are murder."

Flynn hit the street and had to search the area twice before he spotted the undercover police car parked on the corner. He used a calling card at a pay phone to check in with Sierra.

She said, "Why is it that you don't have a goddamn cell phone?"

"The idea of instant communication bothers me."

"I'd think after the past couple of weeks you'd want to have the police, the fire department and your local priest all on speed dial."

"Maybe after my next swim in a frozen harbor," he said. "Anything on Christina Shepard's father?"

She paused, and he could hear her flipping papers. "Tell me again. What exactly did she say to you?"

"Jesus Christ, you and your 'tell me agains,' you're as bad as the cops." Flynn shut his eyes and ran through the night of his death. "She said, 'My father has been ill the last few years. He couldn't care for Nuddin any longer. My brother became my responsibility. It came down to me to shoulder the burden. We take such things seriously in my family. Our name is important. Our history.'"

"That word for word?"

"Pretty close."

"I'm surprised you can remember, after what you went through."

"I remember that night very clearly. Shepard told his

wife, 'Your father's never been right about anything in his life, that crazy son of a bitch.'"

Flynn realized Sierra was looking out for him, the way a mother decides what's good and proper to share with her children.

She hesitated and cleared her throat. Flynn knew it wasn't going to be good. She was trying to keep the fear out of her voice but he'd picked up on it anyway. The vibe was strong. He wondered what in the hell could manage to frighten Sierra enough for her to tap-dance around like this.

"Okay," Flynn said. "So tell me."

"Christina Shepard was born Crissy Bragg. The 'Crissy' is official, it's on her birth certificate. Her father, Martin Bragg, was hard-core military, a lifer. She grew up an Army brat, mostly down South."

"I knew I heard the accent."

"Mother died of cancer when she was nine. She went out of this world in a bad way, in pieces. Had to have her vocal cords removed, then a lung, both legs. Et cetera."

"Jesus Christ."

"Ole Marty Bragg retired a colonel three years ago after he was diagnosed with brain cancer. Tumors. They wanted to open his skull, but he refused any kind of treatment."

Flynn figured he'd do the same when his time came. After seeing his own mother die slowly, surgery by surgery, he'd never go in for radiation or chemo or wait his turn to go under the knife. He didn't have that kind of strength.

"And six months ago he croaked?"

"Two years back he started acting unpredictable in public. The cancer was eating into his brain's center of rational thought. Wild shifts in personality. He started carrying his guns in public, thought the Russians and the Koreans and whoever the hell else were flying overhead. It became worse over time. He got off a few rounds at a school playground one afternoon. The kids were in class and no one was hurt, but he started yelling about throwing babies in a well and it made the local authorities come down on him. He was arrested but the Army doctors stepped in, got him released. They were going to have him committed, I suppose, but instead he jumped in the Chatalaha River, which branches into the deep cypress swamps. As you might guess, the body was never found. Which is why Crissy Shepard may have spoken about him in the present tense."

"Or maybe his corpse showed up at her house one day with Nuddin in tow."

"There is that," she said. "And he might blame you for her death. And he might want revenge. And he is going insane."

Flynn said, "There is that."

He tried to work out the angles but kept hitting walls. He thought he just wasn't crazy enough to see his way clear, or at least not crazy enough in the way he needed to be. It was a pretty rude awakening, knowing that his brain damage just wasn't the right kind. "But if he wanted me dead for killing his daughter, why wouldn't he just zap me? Why have a pro deliver a note and then whack her instead?"

"Listen, I dug a little further into their family history.

Even though they're proud of their heritage, the Bragg dynasty is not known for its mental and physical well-being. A lot of it's just hearsay and rumors, but it's the kind of thing that winds up in reports and on file. People write down their suspicions, and they're believed down through the years. Bragg's forefather slave owners would do naughty things with the field hands out in the tobacco patches, then throw the mixed-race newborns down a well."

"Ah-ha."

"Ah-ha is right. Who knows what he had in his head at the end."

"If it was the end. What'd you dig up on Nuddin?"

"Nothing. No record of him at all."

"How can that be?"

"You've seen it here in New York, for Christ's sake. People ashamed of their kids, locking them up in cellars, crack babies born in apartments in the Bronx."

"But most of them still had birth records and documentation."

"Most isn't all. They were down in swamp country, they do things differently there. Midwives."

"Maybe."

It was a reach. An Army bigwig wasn't a burnt-out prostitute living in squalor off the social radar. But who knew what kind of thoughts Bragg had in his head even before the tumors. Flynn hoped Shepard didn't die in his sleep. He had to talk to him.

Flynn leaned against the phone and watched the foot traffic through Greenwich Village. There was a Ray's Pizza stand nearby and he caught a whiff of mozzarella and his stomach rumbled.

He could hear Sierra shrug in her chair. "I suppose a colonel could have certain documentation destroyed if he wanted. Out of shame. Fear of stigma, maybe. But why go to the trouble of caging him up? Why not just put him away? If Bragg had so much pull and could cover his tracks, then he could've put Nuddin away in a facility with no publicity. Nuddin could've been helped."

"Or Bragg could've just killed him," Flynn said.

"Yeah, there's that too. Shepard's not awake yet?"

"No, and there've been complications. His blood pressure took an almost fatal dip. They're calling him 'unresponsive.'"

"Nicer than saying he's in a coma."

"They say he's going to wake up, they just don't know when."

"Speaking of unresponsive, you haven't been in to the office."

"Very sweet segue," Flynn said.

"Don't try to divert me. You've got cases."

"Turn them over to someone else. I've got to stay off the map for a while until I figure this thing out. See if Angela Soto was targeted because of me. If it really has to do with Shepard or not. Find out how involved I am. If it really is my fault."

"You doing this for us? To make sure nobody hands us little notes to give to you?"

"Well, let me ask you, do you want a bullet in the face?"

Sierra let out the laugh that he always dreaded. "As a matter of fact, I've already had two," she told him, which put him back on his heels. You never could get over on Sierra by talking that kind of shit.

He let it go by and asked, "How are Kelly and Nuddin doing with you?"

"Kelly was fine until we told her about her mother. It was such a shock that hearing about her father being shot hardly made a ripple. I haven't mentioned he's in a coma yet, and she hasn't asked. I dropped Bragg's name to her but she showed no recognition. Either he's just Grandpa to her or she never met him or she doesn't remember him. She's withdrawn and a little sullen, but she never broke down and still hasn't cried."

"When it hits, it'll hit hard."

"You got that right. Hopefully it'll happen soon, and she won't keep it pent up until she's thirty. As for Nuddin, he's playful and loves being with the other kids. He's good for Kelly, watches over her. He likes television even though he doesn't know what's going on. If there's a laugh track, he laughs along. Whenever the kids play ball, he sits on the sidelines and cheers."

"No moodiness? Anger or resentment?"

"None. He doesn't sleep well and sometimes I find him sitting alone in the dark or walking around in the kitchen. That's normal enough. Despite having the mentality of a child, he is a grown man and probably doesn't much like going to bed at nine o'clock. He sits a lot with my oldest kid, Trevor, and watches him play video games. Trevor, he's sixteen, a juvie with both parents in prison for selling cocaine. He's very responsible, helps out with the younger ones a lot. There's abuse in his history and I think he's picking up on Nuddin's damage as well. He's a little more taciturn than I expected, but not everyone takes to the mentally challenged, you know? Nuddin looks a little weird, it's bound to strike a chord in some people, especially teens who think they look and feel a little peculiar themselves."

"Is it going to be a problem?"

"Nothing I can't handle."

"Who watches him during the day, when the kids are at school?"

"Trevor dropped out. He got his GED and wants to go to college, but for the time being I pay him to watch over the others, and he takes online courses. It works to everyone's benefit. Anyway, don't you have enough troubles of your own without worrying about my house?"

"You'd think so, wouldn't you? Can I see Kelly yet?"

"No," Sierra told him, hitting him with that fed-up tone the way his mother used to do. "After she vents she'll begin to heal. Sometime after that you can come around, although I don't know why you would want to."

"Yes, you do."

She let out a raw sigh. "Yeah, I suppose I do. How are you holding up?"

"Fair," he said.

He almost told her about Zero but couldn't quite commit to doing so. She was already giving him enough attitude, he didn't need more.

She said, "If I found out all this, about Bragg, then so did the cops. That Raidin is playing a loaded hand with you. Keeping you out on the street as bait. He should have you in protective custody."

"It's only a theory so far, and I'm still too iffy at this

point. Raidin thinks I'm directly involved somehow and not telling him the whole truth." The police car tailing him had moved around the corner and was parked on the opposite side of the street now. He could see the cops talking in a bored fashion. He imagined they were discussing whether they should run out and nab a slice of Ray's pizza. "So they're gonna keep watching me."

"Your phone might be tapped then."

"What do I care?"

Flynn scanned the surrounding rooftops and fire escapes, trying to catch a glimpse of Bragg up there with a high-powered rifle, maybe with a telescopic sight centered on Flynn's right eye. What would be going through the mind of a man like that? Cancer destroying his mind black inch by black inch, hoping there was time enough for one final act of personal justice. A guy who imprisoned and tortured his own son for being imperfect. A husband who'd lost someone he loved to the doctors and machines, bone by bone. A man driven by some of the same horror that Flynn had endured. A soldier who learned to murder without any hate in his heart. A father with a drowned daughter who had taken her frenzy to the cold depths. A maniac whose great-great-grandfather had drunk water from a well filled with dead babies.

SIX

The Charger sat in the parking lot behind his apartment complex, near his front door, frozen cement solid. After examining it for evidence, the cops had towed it to his parking lot and plunked it down in the exact spot he'd always parked in, practically outside his patio. What the police expected to find in a car washed to the bottom of the Long Island Sound, he didn't know, but they seemed to run in small circles with very little knowledge of why they were doing the things they did.

Flynn kept hearing Danny's voice in his head, telling him not to give up on the car. He would start to answer aloud and stop himself in time. Of course he planned on repairing the Charger. It would take as much money as time, but he had no choice. Both he and his brother had died in it. He'd blow his savings to get it back up and running. The car had some kind of mystical resonance now. It connected him to himself more than ever. The car was packed full of ghosts, including his own.

He awoke in the middle of the night to find his mother standing over his bed, staring down with a brittle expression. It happened three nights in a row. They didn't feel like dreams.

He was waiting for the next message.

The following morning he drove over to Sierra's and parked down the block, watching her place hoping for a glimpse of Kelly and Nuddin. It was important to see the girl, to quell some of the fear about her welfare. He had to put it to rest and know she was all right. He kept his hands on the wheel of his rental, squeezing tightly and feeling none of the muscle or cool he would've gotten from the Charger.

Some of the older foster kids rushed out the front door, heading down the block toward the bus stop. He waited impatiently, feeling more and more awkward just sitting there parked with the engine running, wondering if anybody was going to call the cops and try to get him rapped as a pedo. His heart hammered, the anger rising because Sierra refused to let him see the girl when he needed to. She didn't fully understand. She hadn't been down in the basement or out there on the ice.

He watched Sierra step out the front door and walk the smaller kids to the bus stop, the way that Flynn's mother used to take him by the hand every day and lead him up the sidewalk. Children hung on Sierra and she swung them along while they laughed, refusing to put their feet down. His mother had called him a little monkey and these kids were doing the same kind of thing. Sierra moved along, careful of the ice on the cement. The older children were firing snowballs all over the place.

A moment ago Flynn had been getting pissed but now he felt a sudden warmth for her, knowing how strong and loving she was, how hip and on the ball, especially given the life she'd had to lead.

Kelly trailed at the back of the line of children, walking easily, chin up, smiling even though no one was speaking to her. It made Flynn grin. She looked a little unhappy, but not gloomy or heavily pensive the way he had thought. Just seeing her shifted his whole mood. He felt the muscles in his back loosen. She was doing all right.

The bus swung past him, grinding down into second, then first, as it passed him and pulled over to the curb, blocking his view. He only had another moment to watch Kelly, an aching loss already building, and then he could only see the side of the bus and the blurred movements of children moving down the aisle. He waited for her face to appear in one of the windows closest to him, but she must've sat on the opposite side. The bus pulled off and he watched Sierra trundle back to her car, climb in and drive off to work.

He waited a little while longer and saw the teenager, Trevor, and Nuddin in the kitchen window, standing by the sink. They were washing dishes together. Trevor rinsing, Nuddin standing with a dishrag but unable to quite get the circular motion of drying down. He hoped Nuddin would lift his gaze and make eye contact, but he never did. Flynn put the rental car in gear and drove back to his apartment.

A pair of cops came around while Flynn was working on the Dodge. He'd started replacing parts and he liked working out in the cold. It reminded him of when Danny used to show him around an engine. Flynn, maybe ten years old, would climb up on the front grille and peer down into the machinery and try to make himself one with it. The thrum of the Charger would work into his chest until he felt like his heart might stop the moment the engine quit. Sometimes he'd get in the driver's seat and his brother would shout for him to turn the wheel, or step on the gas, and he'd sit with a great sense of himself, as if he could will himself larger until he took his position on the road. Flynn would feel like a best friend as well as a baby brother, justified by trust. He still felt that way.

The cops didn't bother introducing themselves. They were terse but polite. They wouldn't explain anything except to say that Detective Raidin wanted to speak with him. Flynn went inside and washed his hands and hid the .38 in his closet while the cops waited in the living room.

He piled in back of the cruiser behind the cage and his stomach started to tighten as they headed in the opposite direction from the precinct. At least a dozen noir scenarios ran through his head, all of them ending with dirty cops laughing with blood on their fists and him lying in a ditch. Sometimes he regretted having so many movies so far inside his head.

The cops took him down to the south shore toward Bluepoint. They started arguing over directions and got turned around a couple of times. Flynn knew the area pretty well and wanted to ask if he could help, but figured he'd wait it out and see what happened.

Because they got so lost, Flynn didn't start to recognize the neighborhood until they were almost to Grace Brooks's house. The tightness grew worse and climbed up his chest.

Out in the street were three cruisers, forensic vans and the M.E. The cops parked, let him out and walked him shoulder to shoulder inside.

On the living room floor, wearing a black mourning dress, covered in dried vomit, was Grace's body. She hadn't been dead long. He got a very strong sense that somebody had been just a little too late to save her.

The forensics guys were taking photos and bagging carpet and fibers and bits of her puke. Her stepfather, Harry Arnold, was dressed in a black suit, sobbing violently at the dining room table. They were asking him questions and he was answering in a voice full of blubber. Flynn didn't even have to turn around to know Raidin was behind him, gauging his reaction.

Flynn got as close to Grace as he could, looking for blood. He didn't see any. He didn't spot a note anywhere. He stared at her face and thought she looked even prettier than the last time he'd seen her.

Her clothing was a mess. Her hair disheveled in a sexy, postcoital disarray. She wore no makeup. She did not appear to be at peace. Her brow was ridged. She seemed to be frowning. She looked angry with herself. The vomit blotted her chin and neck in a powdered, delicate pattern.

Flynn spun. Raidin said nothing, merely watched him. Flynn was tired of the tap dancing and said, "Grace Brooks. She was a case of mine."

"When?"

Another question he already knew the answer to. "Four years ago."

"Seen her since?"

Flynn did the math. "Twenty months ago. She was

eighteen, and planned on heading out to L.A., she said. We had lunch and she talked about her plans."

"What were they?"

"What else? She wanted into the movies. But she was smart, didn't go on about trying to be a major star. She just cared about acting and wanted to be on a soap opera. She said it was a good training ground. She had the dream and the drive. I thought she had a chance."

"Any letters or phone calls since then?"

"No. And don't ask me if I'm sure."

Flynn was piecing some of it together, but the sight of Grace on the floor, mobbed by so many men, kept distracting him. He had to fight the urge to pull a crocheted blanket from the corner of the sofa and drape it over her.

"Was there any note?" Flynn asked.

"No."

"Was she shot?"

"No. Pills."

"What kind of pills?"

"Percocet, Vicodin and Valium. Appears to be a suicide."

"What's she doing on the floor?"

"There's traces of vomit on her bed. She threw up but not enough. Looks like she got to her feet and made her way downstairs, passed out in the center of the room. There's a cell phone on the coffee table. It's possible she changed her mind, tried to call for help, but couldn't get to the phone."

"Jesus Christ." Flynn felt a rushing wave of grief rising up trying to swamp him. He wanted to go with it but had to keep clear a little while longer. "So it's not connected to—"

"To you? To Angela Soto? What do you think?"

Raidin looked at him. The homicide dick was still feeling him out. This whole show was for his benefit to see how Flynn behaved. How he replied, rebutted, responded. To find out what might shake loose. Flynn didn't blame him.

"Tell me about her," Raidin said.

Flynn did. He explained how Grace's mother was pathologically jealous of her daughter. She was physically and mentally abusive of her, started doing little things like shredding all of Grace's clothes, slapping her around, calling neighborhood teen boys and telling them to stay away from her slut of a daughter. Did other funky stuff like chasing her up the street with a butcher knife. Took a girl with no self-esteem and burned her to the ground.

Grace OD'ed at school once and a gym teacher saved her. Flynn stepped in four years ago and had the mother put away at Pilgrim State for a period of observation. She went in to avoid charges. The shrinks confirmed she was a paranoid schiz and held on to her. Harry Arnold said he couldn't handle the stress of caring for Grace and a sick wife. So Grace was shipped out to an aunt.

The mother was away six months, came back and her bad triggers were pulled again almost immediately. She went back into Pilgrim. Flynn had checked in on Grace until she'd turned eighteen. She was starting to get some work in magazine ads and even a couple of commercials. She planned on trying her hand at soap operas. She said the soaps were the best training an actor could have. Flynn knew she had the looks but thought she was still too fragile for cities like L.A. or New York. He tried to talk her out of it over lunch, but she seemed so intent he didn't want to slap her down like her mother always did.

Now she was on the floor, wearing black. Harry, in black. The mother nowhere in sight. Flynn figured she was dead and today had been her funeral. He wondered if Grace had carried so much misplaced guilt that she'd come around to see the world through her mother's eyes and found it too sick and too sad. He had a tough time buying it, but he hadn't seen her for almost two years. L.A. could've followed suit and caved her in.

"The mother?" Flynn asked.

"She died three days ago. Committed suicide."

"In Pilgrim?"

"No, she was here in the house. Pills in the bedroom. The same ones the daughter used. The viewing was this morning. There's another one due for tonight. They came home, the father went out to get a pack of cigarettes, drove to the store, had a crying jag in the parking lot for a half hour. By the time he got himself together and came back, she was dead."

Flynn looked over at Harry Arnold and snapped the pieces together as fast as he could. "Check her for rape."

"It sounds like you're giving me orders."

"Yeah, it does sound like that," Flynn said. "Have the M.E. check her for recent sexual activity." He looked over at Grace, without makeup on, recently showered. "There might not be much to find. I think she cleaned herself up afterward."

Raidin let the sharpness back into his attitude, got the knifelike edge back. "Simply because she had intercourse in the past forty-eight hours doesn't mean rape. The M.E. does know his job."

"Make sure he doesn't slip up. Harry Arnold over there, he's not her father. He's the stepfather, married in eight or nine years ago. Always a lot of friction in the family. The mother was psychotically jealous of her daughter, but I don't think it was Grace who set her off. It was Harry sniffing around Grace."

"Did the girl tell you that?"

"No," Flynn said. "She may not have recognized it. She was just a kid."

"Then you have no real evidence. She was sixteen, you say?"

"Yeah."

"That's not much of a kid. You're just obsessing on bad daddies."

Flynn shook his head. "He sent her away after the mother was committed. I think he was fighting the urge. But it finally got ahold of him." Flynn stared over at Harry, sitting there with his face screwed up, still sobbing, but no tears on his cheeks. "He caused it. Shake him up, he'll spit it out in a minute. He wants to."

"You're not given to much doubt or reservation, are you? You have the dubious quality of making things sound true simply because you say them."

"He drove Grace to it. She was a beautiful girl. He watched her grow from a gangly preteen into an attractive young woman. The mother was a battle-ax who just got worse as time went by. After she was dead, he couldn't control himself anymore. They came back here after the viewing. He's alone in the world, Grace's back from L.A.

It's in his head, how it's not illegal anymore, she's not his daughter, he's free. He put the moves on her, probably raped her."

"There are no signs of that. No struggle, no ripped clothing."

"She was probably showering. He couldn't take the idea of her naked behind the door. Raped her at her mother's own funeral. Probably blamed her for it, saying she drove him to it. That she'd ruined the family. That she'd caused her mother's death. It was her weak point."

"You know all of that after being here only ten minutes."

"It's what I do for a living. He said he went for cigarettes. Did he actually buy any? Get a receipt? Anybody see him in the store?"

"We're checking."

"You're always checking on some goddamn thing or other. You know he did it. Brace him and he'll crack. He wants to crack."

"How do you know that?"

Flynn scowled and said, "Can't you smell it?"

He was surprised Raidin wasn't already rousting Harry, hammering at him. It was a misstep on his part, Flynn figured. Or maybe not. Maybe it was just a chance to kill two birds with one stone. Setting Flynn up to set up Harry Arnold. He searched Raidin's eyes and got back nothing. No, it wasn't a mistake. This guy was slick. This guy was using the whole scene as leverage on Flynn. Raidin wanted him to pull something funky, act up, cause a scene. The more he saw, the better he could gauge Flynn.

Flynn wanted to move and he didn't want to move. He

wanted to talk to Harry Arnold. He wanted to get Raidin off his back. He shot a glance at Grace on the floor and he thought of how happy she'd looked in the diner the last time he saw her, telling him about L.A.

"Okay, if you won't shake him, I will." Flynn started across the room.

Raidin reached out to grab Flynn's wrist. His grip was surprisingly strong, backed with wiry muscle and stolid intent. He latched on tight. It wasn't a cop thing. This was short-guy syndrome. It had to do with being the toughest kid in the room. Raidin didn't like Flynn's attitude, but he especially didn't dig the fact that he had so little effect on him. That he couldn't intimidate Flynn or force him back a step. It was about as schoolyard as it got. Flynn was taller but suffered the same. The longer he stood in this house, the more conscious he was of the feeling that he belonged here and everyone else didn't.

Flynn snapped free and walked over to Harry Arnold. He'd always suspected the guy was a borderline pedo. The man had lost a wife and a stepdaughter in the last three days. Death clung to him heavily, and so did his guilt. Harry would break down and admit he'd raped Grace a couple of weeks down the line. Flynn didn't feel like waiting.

He sat down across from Arnold at the dining room table and said, "Hello, Harry. Condolences."

Harry Arnold raised his chin. His bottom lip hung slack and his eyes were hooded. Flynn got the feeling that Harry couldn't quite see him, so he leaned over the table and flicked Harry on the forehead.

One of the cops made a move to grab Flynn. But Raidin

was making heavy eye contact with his men. He wanted
to see how this played out. The atmosphere shifted from
crime scene to potential action. This was as much a test of
Flynn as it was of Harry. It was rope. One of them was
bound to swing soon. Maybe both of them. Flynn never
questioned for an instant that he was right. He didn't
know much, but he knew predators.

Harry Arnold's eyes were opening wider.

"There we go," Flynn said. "How you doing?"

Harry recognized him. He glanced around to see what
was happening, wondering why Flynn was there, why the
cops let him get away with flicking a bereaved father's
head. Something uncoiled in Flynn's chest, warming him.
He smiled. Depending on the situation, his smile could
be charming or disarming or he could look a touch de-
ranged. It came in handy. Harry quit making sobby noises.
His eyes cleared and filled with suspicion and fear. He
sniffed one last time and said, "You. Why are you here?"

"I'd like to ask you a question."

"Go away."

"I wish I could, Harry, I really wish I could." Flynn's
breath came in short sharp intakes. The edges of his vision began to blacken. He wondered if he was hyperven-
tilating. He had a particularly crazy idea that, having
survived underwater for so long, he didn't really need to
breathe anymore.

"I don't want you to ask me any questions."

"No, I don't suppose you do. But that's why I'm here."

Harry's gaze wandered over to the cops, moving from
face to face, pleading. None of them responded. They
were going to let Flynn run with it.

"Why'd she do it, Harry? Why'd Grace kill herself?"

"Her heart was broken," he whined. "Because of her mother—"

Flynn's hand flashed out. He slapped Harry hard across the nose. Bad dog. A man had a lot of armor and shielding. Quickest way through was to treat him with complete disdain. It's what Grace's mother had done to her, breaking her apart from the inside out. Pedos and rapists were all about imposing their own will on others, abusing power. Show them they had none and they'd implode.

Flynn was aware of Grace on the floor. He knew her death was due in part to his own failure. If he'd smacked Harry around four years ago she would've had a better chance to put her pain behind her. Flynn hadn't been careful enough. His arm stretched out again and he caught Harry's nose and twisted it. Harry let out a tiny, girlish squeal. He didn't get up from his chair, though, and didn't fight back.

"Tell me about it, Harry. Tell me what you did."

"I didn't do anything. I went out for a pack of—"

"No, you didn't."

"You're not a cop, what are you doing here?" he whined. This was it, all it would take was a small push in the right place.

You had to connect to them. You had to say what they'd never voice themselves. You pulled the words out of their brains and shoved them one after the other into your own. Your voice became theirs. You began their confession for them, hoping they'd pick it up and run with it.

"Let me tell you how it was," Flynn said. His eyes unfocused and he began to speak of watching a beautiful girl growing from a flat-chested pubescent into a sexpot beauty no man could keep his eyes off of. The anger and resentment that built up. The hatred of libido. The failure of will. The parceling of guilt and anger. The passing of lustful grudges and envy onto a bitter wife. Flynn's voice took on a silky tone that he despised. The black nerve pulsed.

Harry Arnold squirmed in his seat with his hands doing infantile things in the air. Small sounds began to emerge from the back of his throat. They made no sense. They weren't words yet. It would take time.

Soon Harry said the name with a hallowed and almost loving tone. "Grace." He repeated it under his breath in a hymn of pain and deliverance. It rang through the house in a dull chord of confession. He was asking her forgiveness.

It was easy to find the weakness. It was one that many men had in the depths they never ventured. Some ignored it. Some fought it. Many denied it. Subjugated, imprisoned, but never fully managed to kill the urge. Occasionally the weakness reached up into their minds and consumed them. It released a man's evil into the act of love.

"What'd you do to her, Harry? Tell me."

As if a series of locks inside him were opening one after the other, Harry Arnold slowly filled with enough real emotion to darken his face. His eyes widened, seeing something beyond himself. Flynn knew the look. Harry was meeting his own memories. He started crying. Real tears this time. He couldn't stop saying her name. It took on a bitter timbre as Harry's mouth filled with salt. "I couldn't help it. I couldn't help myself."

Flynn had to jump-start him again. He spoke Grace's name himself, putting an edge of finality to it. Harry Arnold admitted he sometimes acted poorly.

"You drove her to it."

"I couldn't stop myself."

"Say it out loud, Harry."

"I did some things to her when she was younger. I did them again. I made love to her. It was love. It was all the love I had."

"You lousy motherfucking piece of shit."

Flynn stood and thought that one solid punch to Harry's nose—hearing the cartilage snap, seeing the burst of blood—would make him feel much better. But Grace was still dead on the floor, and this wasn't about Flynn's rage. He'd failed her. He hadn't done enough. There was still so much to do, for so many others. He had to try harder.

This wasn't connected to Angela Soto. Flynn stood and glanced over at where Grace's body had been lying, but it and the M.E. were gone. He backed away and headed for the door.

"You enjoy using your fists," Raidin said.

"I didn't use my fists. I just flicked him."

"And slapped him. And tweaked his nose."

"Still not fists."

"What would you have done if I hadn't been here?"

"The same thing," Flynn told him. "He'll admit what he did to her now, in detail."

"It's still a suicide."

"He raped her. He's sick, he ought to be put away."

Raidin grunted at that. It wasn't a cop's providence to worry about what ought to be done, just what could be done within the boundaries of the law. "There's nothing for us to charge him with."

Getting up close, nose to nose, only three inches separating them. "You people aren't worth a good goddamn, you know that?"

"You play a risky game."

"Everybody does."

Raidin wasn't about to give points. He pulled a face and said, "Are you certain you didn't know Angela Soto?"

SEVEN

The reporter from *Newsday*, Jessie Gray, phoned and said, "You're becoming quite the story."

"Through no fault of my own."

"I was hoping we could have that follow-up interview soon."

"Man, you weren't kidding. You really are compulsive. Still checking up on me to see if I've had any epiphanies or revelations? Or regrets?" Flynn felt a thick tether of anger tightening inside him and yanking through his gut, pulling him forward. He leaned farther into the phone.

"That, and if you have any thoughts on who murdered that prostitute. After all, the hitter wrote you a note."

She had good sources. And she respected them. The note was a piece of information left clear of the police reports as a way to weed out the admission addicts who'd be calling the hotlines falsely confessing to the crime. She'd left it out of her latest article too. But she knew about it.

He could just see her grinning there on the other side of the line, thinking up more things to hit him with. Her voice, with a lilt of humor because she was doing what she did best. "The police think you know more than you're telling them."

"They're just trying to comb through a major mess," he told her. "It makes sense they'd latch on to me."

"It doesn't make you upset?" she asked. "That you're a suspect?"

"I'm not a real suspect. I'm just a character of questionable repute."

"Does that salve you in any fashion?"

"More accurate anyway."

A subtle scratching drifted over the line. He heard her writing, pen on paper. It sounded like doodling, the pen point circling and circling, digging through the sheets. If it was a sign of frustration, he couldn't hear any in her voice. "You use that word quite a bit. Accurate."

"Do I? I hadn't noticed." Actually, he had.

"Yes. As if you fear distortions and bias."

"I have respect for precision."

"Let's discuss it more. Say tonight? Dinner on me?"

The noir conventions drew him in. He imagined her wafting through a high-class nightclub toward his table. The poise and confidence and clean, moderate good looks catching some attention but not enough to give her date a jealous twinge. Him sitting there in a tux, friends with the owner. Cops at the door, he and Jessie escaping out the back past a blonde in silver sequins about to take the stage. The killer only a shadow in the blizzard, turns out to be his best friend. Except he didn't have any friends.

"Mr. Flynn?"

He still liked the way she talked, but he wasn't in the mood for the whip-crack aggression tonight, and he knew she'd come at him strong, cutting into his soft spots. "That might not be such a good idea."

"I've got a feeling about you."

"Yeah, what kind?"

"A bad feeling, which is good for me."

He hung up on her.

He went back to work on the Charger, refitting the headers. The cops watching him were out on the street, their exhaust pipe the only one smoking because they were running the heat. The windows were cracked to keep from steaming up inside. Flynn figured they'd keep an eye on him another two or three days and then call the surveillance quits. Raidin would probably brace him one more time just to squeeze out what last few drops he could.

Flynn had been at it over an hour when he saw the long, straight blond hair coming at him from across the lot. She was walking that same way as the last time he'd seen her in the hospital. With a forceful intent, as if heading toward an important goal. She had a natural grace. The heavy purse swung wildly, like David's slingshot picking up speed to take down a behemoth. He didn't like the intimations she'd made on the phone. He had the feeling she'd throw him under a train if it gave her a punch ending to her latest article. He tried to remember that she'd quoted him accurately when everyone else in the papers was making innuendos and implications designed to put him in the bull's-eye. He wondered if he could trust her.

The fact that he was maybe fifteen years older than her began to unsettle him. He was only forty but he recognized the dirty-old-man syndrome in himself. In some ways, she reminded him of Grace Brooks. In others, he saw Marianne. He watched her coming toward him, toward the car, the way he'd watched Danny's lovers swaying their hips thirty years ago. He couldn't shake the drift. He began to smooth his white patch of hair.

She hit a pose in front of him. Her dark eyes weren't all that dark at all; they were the color of nickel. That glimmer of bemusement was gone, which made him realize he'd been right to hang up on her. She knew she couldn't run roughshod over him. She couldn't cover him the way she could cover a school vote on healthier lunches. Now she'd have to try for a new way in. Whatever it was, he knew it was going to hurt.

"That was rather rude of you," she said.

"I'm a rather rude person on occasion."

"So am I. I should've been more sympathetic. That wasn't kind of me."

It wasn't an apology, but he figured it was about as close as she ever came. She must really be thrilled about his story's potential to be making such an effort. "So this is the famous Charger. Danny Flynn's muscle car."

So there it was.

The needle. The rise.

She'd intoned Danny's name with just the right emphasis. She'd wanted to find a way into him, and now she had.

You had to give her credit. She'd done a little digging. Thirty years—she'd have had to put some time in at the paper's morgue. She wasn't just sitting on a computer letting others do the deep work. She'd gotten dusty.

He stared up from the engine and said, "It's mine."

"You think you can get it running again?"

"I will."

"Some of the tabloids have picked up on the piece, you know."

"No, I didn't know."

"Covering it from a different angle. They're running 'Curse of the Deadly Car' stories. 'Murder on the Road,' that sort of thing. They've got photos so they're lurking about."

"I know," Flynn said, "I've seen them."

"Your bad guy might be posing as one."

"Maybe."

"It doesn't worry you much, does it?" she asked. She liked angling her jaw to the right. He wondered if she thought it was her best side. He liked them both.

"It worries me," he said.

"You handle it well." She hugged herself and stomped her feet against the ice. "Look, maybe you don't like me much, but I would like to talk with you further and I'm starting to freeze here, my nose hairs are starting to stick together. I hate that feeling. Can we go inside?"

"I didn't think ladies ever talked about things like nose hairs."

"We don't under normal circumstances, but if the situation calls for it, we can manage pretty well."

He threw his tools back in the box and slammed the Charger's hood. For an instant he thought he saw Danny behind the wheel, but he often saw that. It was his own reflection in the windshield.

Small clouds of her breath broke around the back of his neck as he led her up to his second-floor apartment.

She was, he guessed, the first person to enter the place besides himself in maybe a year.

He had no furniture in the living room except for a couch, a coffee table and a decent home-entertainment system. The apartment was small but because it was so empty it felt like you could do ballroom dancing in it.

She stared at all his film noir posters, gazing back at Bogie and Bacall, Dana Andrews and Gene Tierney, Tyrone Power trying to find his way back from *Nightmare Alley*, John Garfield and Lana Turner in a half embrace having just bumped off her husband in *The Postman Always Rings Twice*. A framed press book for *The Strange Loves of Martha Ivers* hung parallel to a lobby card showing Robert Ryan and Harry Belafonte about to end each other in *Odds Against Tomorrow*.

She noticed the seams and creases. "And I thought I was obsessive. These are originals?"

"You are obsessive, and yes, they're originals."

"You must've spent a fortune."

"Yeah, but they've only gotten more rare. I could sell them for twice what I paid. They're about the only things I ever really cared about. I let my ex have everything else."

"Don't you think at your age you should care about more than movies and fast cars?"

"It's only one fast car, and I'm predisposed to noir."

"How do you mean?"

"My old man got me hooked when I was six or seven. I was imprinted with a passion for them. I watch lots of DVDs but I prefer seeing them on the big screen. The Paradigm and a couple other theaters in Greenwich Village have revivals all the time."

"I'd love to go with you sometime," she said, as if responding to a question he'd never asked.

"Sure."

She moved off and looked out the window facing the parking lot. "And that imprinting, your predisposition, your passion . . . it's the same thing for your brother Danny's car."

He never wanted to see it that way, but it might be true. "I suppose so."

"You sound almost resentful."

"Do I?"

They sat on the couch together. He had nothing to offer. He kept no liquor in the apartment, and he didn't think he even had any soda. Asking if she wanted a drink of water was just too damn silly. It only served to remind him that he'd never been social and had only gotten worse with age.

Marianne used to climb out of bed at two in the morning, after they'd finished making love, and stand there watching him for a moment. He'd watch the shimmer of sweat drying on her belly, a light salt drift fading to the right, thinking, What'd I do now? She'd run her hands through her hair and shake her curls out of her eyes, the fire building in them until she'd say, "I want to go out." He'd look at the clock and she'd go, "Not now, just once in a while." He always promised he'd take her somewhere nice, whenever she wanted, but the only time she ever seemed to care was at 2 A.M. when she was pissed off at him. It got so he'd get a little tentative about touching her in bed, knowing beforehand how things were bound to end.

"You're my unique story," Jessie Gray said. "The one I need to tell."

Her expression seemed carefully conceived. It hit the right amount of self-confidence and dedication. She turned her face and gave him the entire good side. She was trying to work him from both angles—she could tell his story better than anyone, and he should allow her to do so because she was cute. Flynn realized he wasn't social for a pretty good reason.

"Actually, it's my story," Flynn said. "And I don't want it told yet."

"But why not? You've read my work, you know I'm capable of presenting you in an honest, positive light."

"You already know the reason," he said.

She leaned back and cocked her head, maybe reappraising him. He got a very real sense that she wanted to be a broadcaster one day and was practicing all her moves in front of the camera she imagined was always trained on her. "Because it's not finished?"

"Because a woman is dead," he said. His voice came down harder than he expected, sounding very much like the voice of his father. The voice of Danny when he got upset. He wanted to add, *There's more murder to come.*

"Don't you understand? That's what makes it so *fascinating.*"

"Not to me. I find it infuriating."

"Just as I find you, Mr. Flynn!" She'd stepped outside of the lithe, silky facade. He saw the real Jessie Gray there for a second. Miffed but with a hint of respect. Like everybody, she liked the ones she couldn't run roughshod over. She was interested in the men who gave her a hard time.

She gave a little-girl huff and tried again. "What's your personal journey been?"

His lips framed the words but it took a while before he repeated them. "Personal journey?"

"Yes," she said. She waited. They both waited. It was the kind of impasse that could keep warring nations at bay for decades. He didn't want to wait that long. "I'm not sure I know what you mean."

"How have you changed?"

"Since when?"

"Since the incident."

"You'll have to be more specific than that. My life is made up of incidents. So's yours, by the way. So's everyone's."

"I believe you know what I'm talking about."

He really didn't. She could mean the crash and the comeback or Angela Soto's blood in his face or getting Harry Arnold to cough up the truth about why Grace Brooks died. The world had grown more compact with episodes.

"Remember what I said about precision," he told her.

He stared at her. She was the kind of woman who always had guys sniffing around her but very few who ever made it onto her radar. He knew he wasn't actually there yet. The story was, but he wasn't. He could see why she'd had two bad marriages and why the husbands had both bailed in less than a year. He was already getting fed up with her, which was maybe why he was starting to get interested too. It was easy finding the wrong women when you went looking for them.

"Tell me about your brother."

"I'd rather not," he said, but he could feel the memories already surging forward. His mind buzzed with trying to put them in the correct order. Jessie Gray had opened the slit and now he wouldn't be able to hold everything inside. It was another weakness. The need to always think and talk about his dead brother.

She watched him, her features conveying a kind of incidental sadness. She was giving him the look that his mother used to give him every time his brother's name came up. It was encouraging and embarrassing. It put a stitch in his side.

"Tell me about Patricia Lee Waltz."

It had been so long since he'd heard the name spoken aloud that at first it didn't register. It took a couple of seconds to hit him. She was saying another name now but he couldn't quite hear. He knew she'd repeat it enough times that he'd eventually get it. He thought maybe he should get into therapy, he still had a lot of shit hiding out in his darkest spots. And that wasn't even counting the dead talking dog.

The other name was Emma. Emma Waltz. The girl flashed in his mind and he almost let out a yelp. Sometimes she came through right in his face, like she was about four inches from him. When she paid him a visit, she got way the fuck up close.

He said, "Why do you want to know about Patricia?"

"Your family went through a lot back then."

"Families go through a lot all the time."

"But—"

She finally noted the look on his face. He was glad she was starting to take things seriously. She tried another tack and continued. "Do you see that what you're doing for the CPS is in some way paying for his sins?"

"No one can pay for someone else's sins," he said. "We're responsible for our own. I do what I can to help because it's what I do. Not because I'm trying to make up for my brother's mistakes."

"He killed a young woman."

Flynn nearly argued the point, so strong was his love for Danny. The reality seeped into him second by second, growing larger until the truth of it nearly crushed the breath from him. Emma Waltz's nose was almost touching his own. Her eyes were locked on his.

"He got her killed," Flynn said, his voice hoarse, as if he hadn't spoken for weeks, "yes, he did."

EIGHT

He would never escape the smile of his brother. Danny drew him in. Danny would always draw him into the mysterious harbors of his own history.

Flynn struggled to contain his thoughts and keep them restricted to the safest memories. His mind would tentatively reach out along the avenues of pain, inching along, picking up speed, until he was racing toward them again.

Flynn awoke that morning to find his mother seated on the side of his bed, her hands resting lightly on her legs, shoulders slumped and her chin up. It was the position she often took when Danny called to say he'd been nabbed by the cops again. She'd hang up and sit on the bed and let loose a sigh that filled the house like a hurricane. For some reason, it always made Flynn smile.

Danny worked freelance delivery, finding jobs mostly out of the Pennysaver. So long as it would fit in the Charger, he'd haul it out as far as Atlantic City. He carried car parts, cases of sunglasses, vitamins, printing materials, birthday balloons, paintings and even shipments of live bait. Crates of nightcrawlers that he'd bring up to

City Island in the Bronx for the fishing tournament every summer.

Most of the jobs were sucker runs and hardly paid enough to cover gas, but it gave him something to put down on his taxes. At night, he'd race up and down Ocean Parkway, Deer Park Avenue, Sunrise Highway, dragging down at the beaches and out at Airport Road.

Danny must've been as gut-hooked by the past as Flynn was. What tied Flynn to his brother also tied Danny to their father. It was a part of their genetic makeup, this need to skip backwards a few decades. Flynn remembered their old man pretty well. A couple of images stayed with him all the time. A smiling guy always with a cigarette in his mouth, propping Flynn on his lap to watch black-and-white movies on the late show. Memories came at him sideways. He'd be at the Paradigm watching Edward G. Robinson on the screen, and his old man would be right there with him.

His father worked the graveyard shift at the L.I.R.R. train yard. He slept all day and got up as the sun was setting. The only time he had to share with Flynn was after nightfall. Something about the dark theaters brought his father close.

The old man had a call in his blood that turned him around to stare behind him. He had photo albums of his own father off the boat from Ireland. Pictures of a cop walking a beat in Brooklyn, posing in front of apple stands and playfully chasing kids through open fire hydrants. Danny had inherited that blood. After the old man went to the yard, Danny would page through the albums looking at photos of their father decked out in his fifties leather jacket, black boots, tight jeans and T-shirt, with a greased up D.A. and a cigarette hanging from his lip. A different girl slung across him on every page. Posing in front of a souped '58 Comet.

Anytime Danny talked about dying, he said it would be behind the wheel. The idea ramped him up, let him embrace death and stave it off at the same time. Too cool to go out of the game any other way but with the engine roaring.

He knew his doom was waiting for him in the Charger. Flynn knew his own death would be in it as well. He realized it even back then when he was ten. In school they'd ask what he wanted to be when he grew up and he'd answer that he didn't care so long as he could drive. In art class the teacher gave an assignment to draw something outside the window: the flagpole, the football field, a plane in the sky. Flynn would use up all the orange and yellow crayons drawing cars exploding into fireballs. The school counselor got into it. There was talk of taking him to a child psychologist. Flynn's mother sighed.

Common urges ruled the home. Danny would invite his straight-haired girlfriends back to the house while the old man was snoring and their mother was at work. Sometimes the girls were supposed to be babysitting their little brothers or sisters, and Flynn would have to entertain the kids. They'd watch television or play Wiffle Ball in the backyard. Flynn would feed them peanut butter and jelly sandwiches. If he really liked the kids, he'd let them read his comic books. Danny and the girl would come out of his bedroom and the old man's snoring would rattle the paintings on the wall. The girl would have pink cheeks and look proud of herself. Danny would look a trifle bored and expectant. They'd grab the little brother or sister and move out the front door like a family of prospective home buyers. Danny would give Flynn a wink that made Flynn's heart swell although he didn't know why.

Their father would wake up with a grunting cough that grew until he was spasming on the bed. Nobody knew, except maybe him, that he was already dying of lung cancer. He'd never spend a minute in a doctor's office.

Danny never got along with the old man, but at least there was no real tension. Just a mild indifference that every so often became barbed with a sneer or a sarcastic comment. Most of it went over Flynn's head. He knew discouraging words were being exchanged but since no one ever seemed to get upset he didn't know what was expected of him. Only his mother showed small signs of dismay. She'd ladle soup hard. She'd bang the dishes. She'd stare out the kitchen window into the backyard and call on saints Flynn had never heard of. She held a lot in her gut.

Danny brought a date to the old man's funeral.

He was decked in a black suit, thin black tie, white shirt with the cuffs shot, and she was in a mandarin red paisley dress. They were going out someplace afterward. She wore broad sunglasses that hid most of her face even though it was a cloudy day. She was black and had a pretty big fro. She held Danny's hand and frequently kissed his neck. There was a murmur among the elderly Irish. The priest didn't look happy. Their mother acted like she'd expected something like this. Flynn cried a lot and tried to understand all the mystifying rituals. He failed and it was a failure that would continue to rear inside him whenever he passed a cemetery. Danny and the girl dogged out the minute they threw their flowers in the grave. Flynn never saw her again.

The girlfriends and their little brothers and sisters breezed past Flynn in vague succession. He did the job he was implicitly given. He entertained the kids. Danny couldn't control himself, didn't even make an attempt to pretend that the girls meant anything to him. Flynn felt his brother was self-destructing through intimacy.

Patricia Lee Waltz was somehow different.

Flynn recognized her as having been to the house before, but Danny appeared to think it was her first time. She didn't just want to hop in the sack. She moved around the house asking questions. Pointing out photographs and saying, "Who's this? When was this taken?" It threw Danny off. He'd somehow forgotten and misread her.

He didn't know how to handle the situation and actually looked around trying to implore someone. Flynn was on the floor setting up Candyland. Patricia's little sister Emma was a scaled-down version of her, with the same straight, long hair they had to constantly keep parting like curtains so they could see out.

Flynn picked up on his brother's dismay. He didn't fully understand it but he noticed the tension in Danny growing. He wasn't answering any of Patricia's questions but that didn't stop her, so she just kept asking more. Emma started playing the game without Flynn. She was taking his turn to pick his card and move his piece.

Since the old man's funeral, the house seemed infused

with their father. His presence filled the rooms to an enormous degree, until you could smell his breath. Flynn found himself talking aloud, answering questions he thought the old man was asking him.

Patricia wanted to see Danny's room, really wanted to *see* it. She looked at his sports trophies, the local newspaper clippings yellowing on the corkboard, and asked why he didn't get a scholarship to college. She asked if it was his knees. He never answered. She checked the nicks and dents in his bedframe. She pulled novels down off his shelves and wanted to discuss themes, characters, ambiguous endings. Her favorite book was Albert Camus' *The Stranger*. His opinion seemed to matter. She had cornflower blue eyes that were bright with a monstrous attention. Danny drifted from her and she put her arm out to grab his jacket. He fought for footing and lost. She pulled him closer. She told him she was pregnant.

Emma turned a card and giggled. She rolled the die and slid pieces across the board, enjoying herself. Flynn heard his dead father cough.

In the front window, glare from the sun framed the Charger at the curb with a wreath of golden fire. Flynn had to turn his head aside. Emma glanced at him as if to ask what was the matter. He looked back and the day had dimmed. She touched his shoulder and some kind of protective urge overcame him. He gently took her wrist. He didn't know why.

Stumbling into the room, Patricia wore a look of amused irritation. She went for Danny's arm again and he shrugged free once more. Danny's hand moved like a beaten animal slinking closer and closer. He took her elbow and guided her through the living room, giving her little jerks and shoves. She smiled more broadly and let out a giggle.

Flynn knew it was time to leave. It had somehow become the only thing to do. He started collecting the cards and pieces even as Emma moved around the board. She didn't really mind and began to help him. He folded the board and put it back in the box and put the lid on. The old man was still coughing. Maybe he'd never stop no matter how long he was in the ground.

Danny said, "Let's go for a ride."

They drove out east toward the Hamptons, Danny opening it up on Sunrise Highway and hitting triple digits. The girls loved it and screamed with excitement. He squinted and brooded the whole time, occasionally catching Flynn's eye in the rearview.

Flynn felt a dark and trembling sensation thrumming through him like a black nerve. He put his hand on the back of Patricia Lee Waltz's neck and she half turned in the seat to smile at him. She gestured for him to move closer and she pressed her fingers to his lips, outlining them, smoothing them. Flynn thought he must be in love.

He knew the facts about sex and pregnancy. He didn't fully believe them, but he knew them. His father had given him the crude information one afternoon while they watched Rita Hayworth and Glenn Ford twisting through their love-hate relationship in *Gilda*. Gilda was supposed to be sleeping all around Buenos Aires while Glenn Ford kept the truth from her nutty husband. For some reason, the old man took this as the perfect launchpad for explaining the wet and awful realities of lovemaking and birth. Flynn was annoyed and wanted to watch the movie.

They picked up a cop somewhere in West Hampton, where Danny gunned it through the area making sure the engine was roaring and could be heard by everyone in their mansions. He kept glancing at Patricia's belly while she commented on the walled-in acres of the estates. Emma appeared oblivious to everything going on in the car and she continued a steady silence. The weight of it pressed in on top of Flynn. He told her to buckle up.

The cruiser fell in behind them and hit his cherry top. The siren was almost loud enough to drown out the Charger's rumbling cry. Danny burned rubber through a red light, narrowly missing a couple of well-dressed women in the crosswalk. Their hair swept up across their eyes and they spun on their heels. Everyone on the sidewalk stopped and looked. For a moment it felt like time had quit grinding across the world for everyone but them. A terrible rush of apprehension filled Flynn, but he didn't know what he was afraid of. It wasn't the speed. It wasn't because he thought Danny would crash. He'd never crash, he was incapable of it.

The cruiser peeled after them and Patricia braced her feet against the dash, biting back a groan of terror. Danny turned around, looked at Flynn, and grinned for the first time that day. Finally, he was having fun.

Patricia yelled for him to stop and pull over. She started rapping him in the arm as they sped around traffic, hitting side streets and careening up on lawns. Danny's lips were upturned in a small smile of desolate simplicity. It was their mother's smile. It was their father's smile.

Emma reached out and gripped Flynn's elbow. There was no expression on her face. She stared straight ahead between the front seats, through the windshield as the world raced by them. Danny kept glancing back at Flynn. Flynn knew he should probably say something to his brother, but he couldn't find his voice, couldn't find the words that might help him to discover his voice.

This all seemed to have been acted out many times before. Flynn could feel the wide turns coming up before they actually happened. He knew when they were going to take a left or a right, or when Danny would rip out on the straightaway.

Another cruiser joined the chase. And another. Every time a new siren went off Danny let out a thick laugh from the center of his chest. The Charger was filled with flashing lights. The police tried to close in and bump them, until one of the drivers spotted Emma and Flynn in the backseat. Flynn let his gaze drift over the police officers' faces and thought they all looked worried as hell but just angry enough to make drastic decisions. Danny let out more quiet laughter as Patricia begged him to slow down, to give up, to stop and think of the baby. Whenever she said the word *baby* the Charger would zag and the tires would squeal.

Flynn wondered what the baby would look like. With almond eyes and a buried temper that would release itself in strange but memorable ways. Flynn tried to calm Patricia by reaching forward and rubbing the back of her neck. She lunged from his touch and let out a small scream.

In the confines of the car the sound went on as if she was being slowly knifed.

Flynn sat back and stared out the window again. They were near the ocean. He watched the saw grass and cyclone fencing go by, the sand sweeping across the road. There were four cruisers behind them now, the cops no longer bracing the Charger but staying no farther back than two car lengths. Everybody really hustling.

He knew that Danny still had more to do. That his brother hadn't, in fact, done anything yet.

Emma stared at him as if to ask, *What's going on?*

"I don't know," Flynn answered, although he understood the wasted tension within his brother and inside the car. Deep in Flynn as well, and it had also lain within their father. The old man was still coughing. Flynn put his hands to his ears to drown out his father. The sirens couldn't do it. Nothing could do it. He wanted to yell for his daddy. He wanted to dig up the coffin and relieve his grief. He hoped Danny would drive into the sea. He wanted to go into the water with him.

There is a futility in having no enemy. Danny didn't hate the cops, he wasn't even angry with them. He had grown too lonely for fate. He could no longer bear the strain of their mother's sighs. His own second-rate failures had surmounted his capacity for belief. His regrets were shallow but numerous. His mediocrity had driven him out of his head.

He found an estate that had its sprinklers going. He let out a bark of real humor and jumped the curb, then downshifted to get enough traction to tear up the lawn and spit mud everywhere. The police followed across the grass. Danny didn't even hate the rich, it was just something fun to do.

They had the bullhorns blaring, shouting orders. They'd run his plates, and knew he was a speed demon and airport dragster. Everyone was shouting at the same time so that the sky filled with the rumbling, irritated voice of God.

Danny let out a nasty snicker. It held more meaning than anything else that day. He'd come to a decision, and Flynn, somehow knowing the sound—that laugh being in his own blood—sensed what was coming next.

Danny swung out behind some shrubs trimmed to look like lovers twined in each other's arms and got the Charger back into the street. He hit seventy on a groomed road of million-dollar homes that ran a quarter mile toward the ocean.

Flynn put his arm out across Emma Waltz, the way Danny always threw an arm across Flynn's chest whenever he was about to hit the brake. Emma put her hand over Flynn's and the sudden depth of feeling made his head swim. He shut his eyes and braced his feet, gritted his teeth against the abrupt lurching and halting of the car. Patricia screamed Danny's name.

A row of four cruisers were parked across the end of the street, backed by saw grass and sand. Twenty-foot-high wrought-iron fencing, stone lions, topiary hedges, clinging ivy, imported Italian-tiled retaining walls and huge sconce planters bordered the road. There were five police cars behind them now, all of them skidding and bashing bumpers. The tension was concentrated and insane. Rage wafted through the air, you could pluck at it with your fingers. It had happened so quickly, and all for nothing. There was no reason for it and never would be.

The entire day seemed like a dream Flynn had declined to awaken from. He kept thinking it shouldn't be so hard to change what was happening. The sirens and lights and shouting filled the interior of the car but nothing could drown out Danny's snicker. It was still going. It would always be going. Danny was going to take it into the ocean with him.

Tears filled Flynn's eyes but refused to fall. In the years to come, this would be the moment of his greatest guilt. That he did not cry. The fact would torment him at the oddest moments: the afternoon he lost his virginity in the back of the Charger; on his wedding night as Marianne sat on the hotel bed, pulling off her shoes; the day his boy Noel wasn't born; in the hospital the first time he visited his mother, carrying flowers, and she told him he shouldn't have gone to such trouble. You can deny nearly everything, but you can't dismiss your own failure to weep.

Patricia had blood on her lips. Flynn saw that she was trying so desperately to love and save his brother that she actually believed she could do it. That it could be done. Perhaps it was a function of her fear. Perhaps in her own way she was as reckless as Danny was. They both struggled against the clichéd unimportance of their own lives. He could never be a bitter, unemployed ex-jock sitting in a recliner sucking down beers in front of daytime television. She would not exist without the romantic drama of an *amour feu* between strangers. Flynn felt a strange respect for the wild courage of their stupid convictions.

Danny told her to get out and she wouldn't. She mentioned the baby again. He shouted that there was no baby and she screamed that there was, there was. Danny reached back and undid Flynn's seat belt with the barest brush of his finger and grabbed him under the arm. It hurt but Flynn didn't make a sound. Painfully, Flynn slid across Danny's lap until he was nearly behind the wheel. He took the steering wheel in his hands and Danny started to push him out the window. Flynn refused to let go. He struggled to hold on, biting his lip, clamping his eyes shut. Danny yanked and shoved and finally broke Flynn's grip. Danny kissed him on the top of the head, said, "Good boy," and threw him out the window.

The wealthy filled their windows, eased out onto their lawns, and watched with eagerness. The cops drew a bead on Flynn like he might be a lit stick of dynamite. When they finally realized it was a ten-year-old boy, they made whining doggie sounds and gestured to him, holding their arms out like he was a baby taking his first steps. He heard wind chimes and ringing phones. He held his ground and took Emma from his brother's arms, helping her to the ground. Together they walked away without another word. Flynn started up the street, with Emma Waltz close on his heels. She still appeared intensely calm.

The police rushed toward them with their guns drawn and Flynn managed to wag his head. They kept coming closer and he turned and bolted back toward the Charger. It was a moment of weakness. It wouldn't do Danny proud, seeing him like this, but Flynn couldn't help it. He called his brother's name and saw Patricia turn her head to peer back at him through the rear window. She smiled at him.

Danny had outfoxed everyone. He knew these roads well all right. He'd probably made love to Patricia or other girls out on the beach in the setting sun, the moonlight. With the silhouettes of the mansions rising up to scratch against the silver sky.

He hit the gas and swung the car out wide to the left, easing against a spear-rail fence. He knew that driving was more than just speed or power; it had to do with knowing the angles, understanding the vectors, describing the arcs. The police didn't know the area as well as Danny. They were close to the end of the street but not quite there. Danny sort of tapped the huge gates in the middle of the fence with the front grille, doing maybe 20 mph, just hard enough for the lock to spring. He ramped up the tremendous semicircular driveway and sprang out the other side right past the police, skidding past the sign that read: PRIVATE BEACH. NO ENTRY EXCEPT FOR RESIDENTS.

Like he could get away anywhere. Like he might actually be trying to escape.

That's what ratcheted the cops up and got them even more crazed for blood. The idea that this ballsy kid wasn't only making a run but really thought he might be gaining ground. Someone fired a shot. A gray puncture appeared in the trunk of the Charger. Flynn would fill and buff and repaint it himself six years later.

So close.

Danny would've made it to the water except the rear tires got hung up in some storm fencing set out in the nearest dunes. He tried to spin the wire off by yanking hard on the wheel, but the Charger bounced down the sandy slope fast and hit a deep wide hole dug by some kid. The tide had started to rise as if trying to reach the car. The left-front tire plunged and the shock absorber buckled. The Charger rocked hideously forward once, then jolted to an immediate stop and slowly angled to one side on the beach.

If he had gotten to the water, it might've been enough. The cops would've leaped onto him and busted his ribs against the hood of the car, and Danny would've laughed hard and long and it might've been enough for him to feel like he'd done one solid, outrageous act of defiance in his life. He could've married Patricia and had the kid, and no matter how many beers he drank in front of the television, or how fat he got or how hard he coughed, it might've been enough to keep him going.

Cops kept trying to grab Flynn. He dodged, and outran every one of them. He made it to the beach and an officer tackled him. Flynn let out a grunt of pain and it wasn't until three days later that his mother discovered his left femur had been fractured. He struggled, but the cop lifted him easily and carried him back to the street.

It didn't matter, he'd seen enough.

He'd seen Danny with his forehead resting propped against the steering wheel, lifelike but utterly lifeless. No charm, no hipness, no cool, no breath. There wasn't a mark on him except for one small blemish on his chin. All because of the goddamn busted shock. His neck had been broken.

Patricia's head had gone through the passenger window. Jagged glass had sheared her right ear off. A small splash of blood trickled down the door in a thin line that thickly dripped into the sand.

The tide crept up the beach, inch by inch, but Flynn never got a chance to see it reach the Charger.

The cops offered soothing empty words like the crooning of pedophiles. They offered candy bars and juice and comic books. They threw a blanket over Emma's shoulders and led her away. She glanced back at Flynn once and they never saw each other again.

NINE

The icy morning wind blew angel-wing patterns of frost against his windshield. Flynn saw Sierra walk the kids to the bus stop at the corner, then stomp back and get into her red '91 Civic and drive to work. He watched Kelly interact with the other foster kids, talking animatedly as her breath bloomed around her face. She had a tendency to smile brightly, then close up her face as if embarrassed to have found something worth smiling about. It would be a while before her own grin didn't shame her.

He found himself wishing that Shepard would get the hell out of his coma already. He had a daughter who still needed him, no matter what his troubles. Flynn had the urge to rush to the hospital and smack the shit out of the guy until he woke up. Flynn needed answers.

"Turn on the heater," Zero said.

"You're dead," Flynn told the dog. "How can you feel cold?"

"You tell me," the dog answered. "You're dead too. Don't you know that?"

Flynn thought maybe he did, but he started the car and popped on the heater. He sat back and hit an oldies station while the school bus passed by. It slowed at the corner and the kids proceeded on. Kelly took a seat toward the back on the side closest to him and Flynn watched her hair gleam beneath the sheeted ice on the window. Emma Waltz got right the fuck up in his face again, so close he fell back in his seat.

Zero said, "Who is she?"

"Who's who?"

"The girl in your head."

"If you know about her, you know who she is."

"I don't know about her, I know about you."

Flynn was starting to feel a little insulted. "Don't you think it's time to go on to doggie heaven?"

"Whenever you're ready to go, I will be too."

When the bus pulled away from the curb and disappeared down the road, Flynn shifted and glanced back at Sierra's house.

"The cops are going to pick you up, sitting around here all the time, acting suspicious," Zero said, digging at the passenger seat, turning in circles, trying to get comfortable. "What are you looking for?"

"I want to see Nuddin."

Flynn got out and slammed the door. He walked across the street, up onto Sierra's front lawn, and peered into the living room window. The wind trilled through the trees and icicles rang above him. He moved around the yard until he got to the kitchen window. He saw the teenaged Trevor clearing away breakfast dishes, cereal boxes and a container of milk. Flynn got a good vibe from the kid. He seemed responsible, always cleaning up after his foster brothers and sisters. Nuddin sat staring off happily at nothing, humming. He was dressed in workman's overalls and thick boots. He looked like he was getting ready to go work the docks. Sierra must've had some leftover clothing laid away by the exes.

Nuddin's misshapen, scarred head appeared much more normal now that Sierra had allowed Nuddin's hair to grow out a little. He had a handkerchief that he used to wipe the drool from his chin. Trevor was saying something Flynn couldn't hear, but Nuddin seemed to ignore the kid. His gentle brown eyes found Flynn in the window and filled with joy. He appeared healthy and happy. He smiled and started out of his seat, but Flynn was worried about Sierra hearing he'd visited. She might give him hell.

He retreated fast over the lawn, got in the car and punched it to the Expressway. Zero was still sleeping in the passenger seat. He yawned once and rubbed his booted front paws across his nose.

Flynn went to the office and discovered his desk piled with case folders. Every one of them a threat to a child. Seeing them stacked like that got his bad mood cooking. Sierra was out on a call. He read through files most of the morning, then went out and visited four families. He picked up a bad vibe on only one of them and faced down the rude roughhouse without throwing fists. Barely noon and the guy stunk of gin and cheap weed. The stereo was on loud, and so was the television. Flynn figured the complaint had more to do with noise pollution than anything. A seven-year-old girl with a broken leg was in bed laced up in traction. He asked her questions while her father glowered from the bedroom door. Her room was the cleanest in the house. She said she slipped in the kitchen on a slippery floor. Flynn found no suspicious bruises. He checked out the kitchen. The floor was wet with melting ice cubes. The father had been drinking gin and tonics. The daddy was stoned and had that look of strain, but he hadn't hurt his kid. He just couldn't keep his kitchen floor dry.

Flynn got back to the office right after lunch. Sierra was at her desk on the phone reaming out a high-school nurse for sending a girl to the shower after she'd claimed she was raped in a stairwell. Failure to immediately garner a rape kit could ruin a criminal case. Who knew how much evidence had been washed away. Sierra's naturally tight grin was notched a little higher than usual.

He turned on his computer and stared at the screen for a minute. He was surprised that after three decades he'd never tried to find Emma Waltz. Despite her haunting him in her own way, he'd never given her much thought. But suddenly the urge to see her again was growing inside him.

It was the kind of thing that would consume him if he couldn't get it locked down. His hand drifted over the keyboard. He started to hunt for Emma through the agency's database and affiliate intergov networks.

Women were tougher to find. They got married, changed names, used hyphens that weren't picked up by some directories. He grabbed the phone book and started checking under *W*. He stopped before he got to *Waltz* and tried to run it out. What he would say to her, and exactly why he would be saying it.

He could see how the meeting between them might

go. Each with the same immobile memory fixed in their childhoods, emanating outward to touch them every day since. His imagination fritzed when he tried to hear her voice. He'd never heard her speak. He ran through possible opening statements, comments, questions, but nothing held enough weight. It all sounded empty and silly. He saw himself trying to take her hand and Emma pulling away in anger or fear, overcome with emotion.

His thoughts started getting dumber. She comes flying into his arms, presses her lips to his, because it was always meant for them to be together. Because no one else could understand. Because blood pulls kids together and keeps them bound through the years. Because you need to think things like this about someone you only knew for a couple of hours on the worst day of your life.

Before the day you died, of course.

A shadow crossed Flynn's desk. He eased shut the telephone book.

He'd really lost his edge. Sierra had on her three-inch heels and he hadn't even heard her. Her new wig was a bright blonde with pageboy bangs. It hung a little too far to the left. He got the feeling she did it on purpose, just daring somebody to say something.

She checked around the room and said, "You didn't bring the cactus to brighten this place up."

"It's at home."

"I'll get you another."

"I'm not responsible enough to take care of two cacti."

"You could've said 'cactuses,' you know, it's also considered proper English."

"Really? I had no idea."

He looked at her and thought, are we really talking about fuckin' cactuses?

Sierra's left eye really hung low today, a sure sign that she was exhausted. He hadn't been pulling his weight lately. She'd been working a lot of his load. A spear of guilt hit him low and he resolved to get on the ball. The commitment wavered an instant later when his gaze crossed the computer screen and he saw the search for Emma Waltz still in motion.

"Glad you decided to come in today. We've been short-handed thanks to the flu. You work any of these cases so far?"

"Four this morning."

"That's a good jump. You break anybody's head?"

He hadn't told her about Grace Brooks and decided not to get into it right now. "Thought about it, but no."

"Good, you need to control yourself. The cops are still watching."

"They'll have to pack it in shortly unless someone makes another move soon."

She reared over him. "Knock on some goddamn wood, would you? Don't go calling down the whirlwind."

He said, "No, not me."

But maybe that was the only way to get from here to there, to shake loose the figure hiding out in the snow. No move he made seemed to be the right one. For all he knew, he was endangering Sierra just by showing up to the office. He thought about running. He thought about staying put. Nothing hit him as the smart thing to do.

"You're edgy," she said.

"Yeah. It's the cactus. I feel bad about it."

There he went again. No cool, man. Danny would be ashamed.

"You can't bring a gun in here, Flynn," Sierra said. "I can tell you're packing by the way you're sitting."

He unclipped the .38 from his belt and stuck it in his bottom drawer. It didn't appease her, but he knew she wouldn't push it. He wanted to ask her about Kelly. He didn't think the house was safe with just a teenager looking after Nuddin. He imagined somebody breaking in and killing the boy and torturing Nuddin with a branding iron right in the middle of her living room.

"I think you should see Dale," she said.

"Oh hell, Sierra, come on now." Dale Mooney, head CPS shrink, and a total bore. Flynn had been semiexpecting her to suggest it for a while, but still it hurt. Sierra was losing her confidence in him. "A basic component of the patient-doctor relationship is trust. Mooney's slippery and soft and I don't like him."

"He's better than you give him credit for. It's nearly time for the second psych review of the year anyway. You might as well go and get it done."

"That's a cakewalk. But now, you've prepped him for me, haven't you?"

"I mentioned you might need some help shouldering your recent freight."

"He's a serious asshole."

"So are you. I hire my crew based on competency, though, not personality. If I did, I'd have to clear all the desks out of this place and take up ballroom dancing."

"And just why do you think I need to get into treatment?"

"Therapy. Treatment is PC for rehab nowadays." She ran her tongue alongside the dry teeth that her mauled lip could never close over. "I don't have all day long, but I could give you the highlights if you'd really like. Should I bother to lay it out? You've got too much coming at you from all directions, that's part of the reason why you need to talk to someone."

"I'm not going to see that prick."

"You are or you can start hitting the Help Wanted pages tomorrow."

She had the staunch expression of his mother. Her eyes were hard and dark and brimming with pain and disappointment. Every woman he'd ever cared about in any capacity had finally smacked him with that look. Unlike his mother, he knew Sierra would do a lot more than sigh. She didn't bluff or bullshit. She really would kick him out.

Doing the job was all Flynn really had, it was everything that mattered.

He nodded and said, "All right."

Sierra let out a small, tight smile. "I'll let you make the appointment. Do it this week. Leave the gun when you go see him."

"Sure," he said as she retreated up the hallway. "Don't want to make myself a slave to temptation."

The search for Emma Waltz had turned up nothing, but he didn't have top clearance and wasn't as computer-savvy as Sierra. He started another on Angela Soto. Maybe she was in the system. Maybe he'd been wrong and he'd crossed Angela Soto somewhere along the line. She'd died for him, but had she been a complete stranger? He waited while the screen flickered through names and dates and information, hunting a match. There wasn't one.

The phone rang. It was Jessie Gray. She even knew his office number.

"So," she said, "how about taking me to the movies tonight?"

"I prefer late afternoon. Five o'clock showing. I don't know what's playing."

He should've known she'd be ahead of him.

She said, "That's okay, I do."

TEN

The 1948 version of *The Killers* starring Edmond O'Brien and Burt Lancaster was showing at the Paradigm. Jessie Gray left her car at Flynn's place and together they took the L.I.R.R. in to Penn Station, nabbed the A train down to the Village. She liked to walk a step or two ahead of him. She had a fast gait and he sensed she was worried this might not all pan out. He hoped she wouldn't ask about his personal journey again.

They got to the theater and she started to ease her way down an aisle toward the back. He said, "Sixth row center, always."

"I thought that was just for plays."

"It's for everything with a stage."

He sat and she made herself comfortable beside him. She laid her handbag on the seat next to her and the thing landed with the weight of a barbell. He tried to figure out what was in it beside the usual lipstick and tissues: a microcassette recorder, iPod, cell phone, a couple of books on film noir so she could get a clue on his hobby, a can of Mace (the hard-core stuff, no pepper spray for this one) and probably a file with his entire history tamped down into it. Something she could study and read on the train.

"I know you come here often," she said.

"Every chance I get."

"Do they only play film noir?"

"No," he said, "but they mostly show classics from the forties and fifties."

"The kind they don't make anymore? The place is completely empty. How do they stay open?"

"The hard-core movie buffs show up here for the later showings on the circuit."

She was a writer. Words triggered her interest. This one made her stir. "Circuit?"

"Yeah. Most of them either live out in Queens or Brooklyn or way uptown at the north end of Manhattan. They live on social security, welfare and their pensions. Most of them are elderly or social misfits. They live for nothing besides film. Not movies, but film. The classics. They project themselves in and think Bogie's still alive. If they're coming down from uptown they hit the Aleister for a first show, then the Courant and then the Twin Golden Revival. They'll get here around nine o'clock. If they're swinging in from Brooklyn, they'll hit the Bowery Headlight and then the Paragon Twin and the Marquee Classic. They'll show up for the seven o'clock and later showings. But that's mostly on the weekends."

"So you get the theater to yourself every time?"

"Pretty close. If I come directly here from the Island."

"I never knew there was such an underground movement of film fanatics."

"Write it up for *Parade*."

"Perhaps I will," she said. "I still find it surprising theaters like this can exist. How's a place like this make money? I only saw two people working the front counter."

"Two's all you need. The guy who takes the tickets, he's Huey. The lady who sells the candy, she's Hazel. They've been married for twenty-five years. There's a projectionist up there I've never seen, but they refer to him as Gramps. He probably is. Three people run the whole thing."

"They do it for love?" she asked with a subtle jab.

"I doubt it. Huey and Hazel don't seem too happy most of the time. But nobody who's been married twenty-five years does."

"I noticed alcohol on his breath."

"Scotch. He runs up the block and has a snort between pictures."

"So not everyone is entranced by the magic of Hollywood?"

"No one who has to grind a living off it."

She sat straighter and said, "That sounds like it might actually be profound."

"Don't fool yourself." The door at the back opened and Flynn angled his chin. "Here comes another true believer now."

Florence was an earthy, straw-haired lady with a dented face hard as oak. She had a short, squat body that looked like it was ratcheted too tightly at all the joints. She carried a tub of popcorn and a couple of boxes of candy, kind of trundling along. She stopped at Flynn's aisle, peering at where he sat hunched in his seat. He stood and when she saw it was him she cried, "Flynn!"

"Hello, Florence."

She jittered excitedly, a few kernels of popcorn falling to the floor. "It's Edmond again, they're giving us Edmond."

"It's been a while since Edmond has dropped by. Last one was, what, *D.O.A.*?"

"*The Hitch-Hiker.* Nine weeks ago, I believe. The best film directed by the star Ida Lupino. Oh, it's so lovely to think that film noir even worked its magic on Hollywood starlets. The ones normally known for gala events and high-drama vehicles. Before she became queen of the B's."

"You're right, and Ida knew her business too. She knew how to get the best out of O'Brien and Lovejoy and Talman. And she cowrote the script too. Ida knew her way around a rough story."

"Ida, when will they give us Ida again?"

"I don't know, but she'll turn up again for a visit. I haven't looked at the schedule, but it looks like next week is *White Heat.*"

"James and George! How wonderful it will be to see them again."

"It may be my first time seeing Jimmy shout, 'Top of the world, Ma!' on the big screen."

"Get the quote correct, dear. 'Made it, Ma! Top o' the world!' You're in for such a treasure."

"I know it. What's brought you in this early, Florence? You usually don't show at the Paradigm until the nine o'clock."

"My daughter Vicki moved back in with me. Her third marriage hit the skids and she's back home, bartending, complaining every minute. My granddaughter Maggie is seventeen and I worry about her. She runs with a fast crowd, but she's not stupid. She knows it's going no-where, and she's fighting the pressure. I like to get home early so we can talk before she goes to bed. It's the best time to get through to them, at the end of the day, before she tries to sneak out while her mother is still out work-ing the bar crowd. Vicki can't help herself, she takes after her father. There's still time to keep Maggie from going down that dead-end alley. I'm doing my best, but it's a struggle."

"You'll get the job done," Flynn said, believing it.

"I hope so. Maybe I can talk her into coming next week when they give us Jimmy and George."

Flynn ushered her to the other side of the theater, where she liked to sit in the third row near the fire door and see everything on a slant for some reason. She handed him one of the boxes of candy without a word, and he took it without looking. When he got back to his seat, Jessie Gray was staring at him with a lot of deep thought playing across her face.

"You like Dots?" he asked.

"Good Christ, do they still make those? I can't believe anyone ever ate them."

"Nobody does, but they're part of the moviegoing ex-perience."

"She talks like they're still alive, those actors," Jessie said quietly. Her voice was heavy with sympathy and a touch of distaste.

"They are," he told her. "In a very necessary way. Alive on the screen. As a part of history, a communal fantasy. It's the kind of thing you hear all the time—*they're alive on the screen*—it sounds stupid and maybe a little crazy, but it comes from an honest place. Few people take it to heart the way the real fans do. Everyone likes movies, but some folks, they're a whole other level of fan."

"She probably has nothing else in her life except these fantasies."

"Don't be appalled, Jessie, it's not fair. She's actually a pretty sharp lady. She's gone through a lot. You're right, she doesn't have much else except these movies, but if you're going to be disgusted—"

"I wasn't disgusted, for heaven's sake."

"—then don't forget to be disgusted about the guy putting in a twelve-hour day, stuck in a loveless marriage, who'll probably take a header when he's fifty and his arteries are as hard as high-tensile steel."

"I wasn't being judgmental." Her hand reached out and clamped over his own. It was an urging grip, unusually strong for a girl, trying to invoke validity.

"You were," he said, "you just didn't realize it. Don't let it bother you. We all discriminate."

"I was not *discriminating*. You are so infuriating! I could crack you one."

It made him laugh. They settled in to watch the movie. Burt Lancaster gets his ticket punched ten minutes in and the film unfolds through flashback. Jessie Gray's hand brushed against his arm. This didn't feel like a date, but it had been so long since he'd been on one, he couldn't quite grasp the dynamics. The dirty-old-man syndrome continued to throw him off. The fact that they were arguing a bit was comforting to him. He felt the way he had toward the end of his marriage.

Burt is led off the straight and narrow by Ava Gardner,

a world-class femme fatale. Edmond O'Brien searches backwards through Burt's life to discover why he left an insurance policy to an old cleaning lady he barely knew. The script had some nice zags to it. Flynn had never read the original Hemingway story, and he promised himself he would.

Halfway through Florence got up, hugged her mostly untouched box of popcorn to her chest and hurried back up the aisle and out the door.

"Is she leaving?"

"She always has to go to the ladies' room at the halfway mark. A while back they discovered she had colon cancer and took out a significant part of her small intestine. She probably hasn't made it through an entire movie the last five or six years. She can't go the full two hours."

"The poor woman." Jessie Gray's eyes were large and moist in the flickering light of the film. "But all that popcorn and candy . . . why does she . . . ?"

"Because it's a movie. You do certain things out of love for the entire experience, even if they cost you. It reminds her of Saturday nights at the theater with her family when she was a kid. It reminds her of her husband back when they were dating."

"That's why she gave you a whole box of Dots?"

"And that's why I'm eating the goddamn things," he said, swallowing another.

"My God, I would never leave the house if—"

"She's tough. She slugs it out every hour of every day. She's going to show her granddaughter the right way out of that alley too, I bet."

"You've got a lot of faith."

"In some things. You want to do your *Parade* piece, you can start with her."

"I'm starting with you."

"I still don't know what my personal journey is. Okay, watch this, Edmond is closing in on Ava and the crew that did Burt wrong."

They watched the rest of the movie. Edmond tracked down each member of the gang until he had the full story of why Burt got bumped off. He showed up Ava for what she really was and he sneered while he did it. Flynn had to get to a Barnes & Noble and find a collection of Hemingway's fiction.

Gramps turned on the lights. Flynn stretched out in his seat and tried to keep from yawning. It was six thirty. He wondered what the protocol was now. If he was supposed to take Jessie Gray to dinner. If she expected him to pull a few moves. If he could get over his fear of ever showing off the gray hairs on his chest. If she'd Mace him in the face for leaning in too far and making a dive for a kiss.

Jessie said, "She never came back."

For a second he thought she meant Ava. It stymied him. Ava didn't go anywhere at the end. Then he realized she was talking about Florence.

He scanned the theater. Florence never left a movie. She had to use the bathroom a lot, but she never spent more than five minutes away from the film. She never would've quit on Edmond.

Flynn stood and started up the aisle. The box of Dots spilled around his feet and the candy rolled under the seats, loud as ball bearings. Jessie Gray followed him closely. He wasn't sure if she should. He wanted to send her away but didn't want her to go anywhere alone. He got that intense feeling again that everything he was doing was the wrong move.

They got out into the lobby. It was empty. Through the wide glass doors he could see Huey and Hazel out on the sidewalk sharing a cigarette. The sun was down. It looked like it might snow again.

"I'll check the ladies' room," Jessie said.

"I'll go with you."

"You can't."

"Consider me an escort."

"You're starting to scare me."

The black nerve began to bang around inside him. Every step took him farther along the midnight road. He pushed in the ladies' room door. Jessie Gray came in behind him and let out a brief scream.

Florence sat on the floor, near the sink, with her blouse torn open and her breasts exposed. Her hands lay on the tile beside her legs, palms up. They looked youthful and soft. Her chin rested on her chest. Her eyes were half-open in an endless gaze. Her breasts were what he thought of as medium-sized, drooped and wrinkled. But there was something else. Her chest was pink and slightly puckered over her heart. Her nails were cracked. Half-moon indents scored her palms. Whatever had happened, she'd felt it.

The uneaten box of popcorn was propped in her lap. Set on top of it was a neatly typewritten note.

I CAN'T STAND THIS ANYMORE. CAN YOU?

ELEVEN

No, he couldn't. And he wanted to climb a tower in the center of the city and let everybody know it. Sometimes the scream inside you needed out, and it was all you could do to keep your teeth champed.

Jessie was talking to the cops, smiling and looking very sincere and cooperative. She'd upped the charm factor and somehow looked even more attractive. She'd slid into reporter mode. It was just her way, he knew, as she hounded out a story. It activated her, brought out her best.

Flynn hoped she'd do the *Parade* article one of these days and make Florence's love of film, rather than her murder, the centerpiece.

Raidin was on the scene even though the city homicide dicks had caught the squeal. They kept up a steady stream of questions that Flynn answered as well as he could.

It wasn't long before they started implying he'd killed the old lady himself. If Flynn hadn't been expecting it, he would've been sickened, or maybe he would've laughed in their faces. The Manhattan police made up the dumbest reasoning he'd ever heard. Flynn had wanted her money. He'd killed her in self-defense. He did it for the

media coverage. Grinning and telling him he was a murderer in an amiable matter-of-fact manner, as if they were
all good friends, like they might go out and grab a beer afterward. He thought if this was how they ran every investigation, it was amazing that anybody ever got put in
prison.

They had no one else to cling to. Things were going to
be even rougher now. They were going to turn up the
heat on him.

Huey and Hazel stood huddled together in the lobby as
Raidin questioned them. Huey's breath reeked so bad
that Flynn smelled it from fifteen feet away. He was drinking the cheap stuff nowadays. Four Roses, the same shit
Flynn's father had downed toward the end. Huey admitted he'd been up the block having a couple of shots. Hazel
had been in the back going through yesterday's receipts.
Nobody ever came into the Paradigm halfway through
the film. She hadn't seen anyone.

Raidin didn't believe it, or acted like he didn't. Nobody
left an entire theater unattended for any length of time.
Hazel said it wasn't unattended, Gramps and Flynn were
here. Raidin had no idea how houses like this worked.
How few people came for the early show. It didn't matter.
The stiletto was determined to give everybody a hard
time. Flynn didn't have much faith, but he decided that
Raidin might work the case hard enough for something
to shake loose.

Flynn finally got his first look at Gramps. He was a
hard man, maybe seventy years old, clean-shaven, bald,
with hip, fashionable glasses that changed tint depending
on the light. He didn't like the way Raidin spoke to his

son and daughter-in-law and let the detective know it. Flynn loved older folks who didn't take shit off anybody. He didn't think he was ever going to be one.

Gramps was acting like he was about to throw down. The other cops started to move in a little closer. Huey tried to calm his father and eventually the old man had his last say and stood there breathing deeply, the tendons standing out on his wiry arms.

The stiletto turned to Flynn and did a short skinny guy's dance over to him. He was decked in the same black outfit as before: black raincoat with heavy lining, gloves, three-piece suit. A different tie today. His hazy gray eyes appeared even more lifeless in the dim lighting of the Paradigm.

Raidin said, "Okay, please tell it to me from the beginning."

At least he wasn't going to waste any more of Flynn's time. Flynn told him everything. His brief exchange with Florence. He explained about Flo's colon cancer and how she still bought lots of candy. Every detail he could remember. When he got to the end of it he should've stopped but couldn't keep his mouth shut. He said, "He's bringing it closer to me now. Florence always had to run to the ladies' room halfway through a show. If he's targeting people around me, she fell into his lap. If he was waiting out in there for me to go hit the head—" Flynn thought about it, wishing it had happened. "He's slick and steadfast."

"He couldn't plan on the owners being out of the theater."

"It was a safe enough bet. Huey always goes for a bar

run. There's always something for Hazel to do in the office. She's busy. She doesn't just stand in the lobby. If he's been watching, he knew that. If not, he got lucky."

"Things run a little differently here than at the multiplex."

"Oh yeah."

Raidin ran his thumb under his chin. He stared through Flynn, then through the wall, his gaze brooding and steady, seeing how it would've gone down. "By his own admission, he's in pain. At his breaking point. Why? What does he feel that you've done to him?"

It always came back to Flynn hurting the poor killer in the snow. "I don't know."

"Yes, you do," Raidin said, assured and calm. "Somewhere. You've got to think it through."

"I've been doing nothing but."

"You've got to make more of an effort."

It nearly sounded like encouragement or faith. Flynn knew it was neither. Raidin would always be suspicious, he had to be. It was the way he went at the world, probably what made him a good cop if he was one. He'd always have one finger ready to tap Flynn for murder.

"I've tried," Flynn said.

"Not hard enough."

"How the hell would you know?"

"The only one I can think of is Bragg. That's when this all started."

"Bragg's dead."

"Maybe."

"Forget him. Guy like you, with all your natural charm, has got to have plenty of enemies." He drew several creased pages from his pocket and handed them to Flynn. It was a lengthy list of names. He recognized some of them. All the real hardasses and violent offenders from his past cases.

Flynn said, "You've been checking them out?"

"Yeah, so far it seems like everyone's got a firm alibi for the Angela Soto murder, and now we'll go through them again to see where they were all at this afternoon. Any name on there jump out at you?"

Flynn scanned the list, remembering a lot of rough scenes, some fisticuffs, a couple of serious threats. A couple of the folks jabbing knives, waving guns. Seeing it all laid out before him now, the names stacked up like this, he was surprised to realize at least half of the real scary times he'd had were when he was dealing with women.

He said, "Miriam Welby." He recalled a vicious woman who tried to brain him with a meat-tenderizer.

"She's in prison."

"For hurting her daughter?"

"No," Raidin said, "for capping her husband. The daughter's with relatives and flourishing. Anybody else?"

They were all loose cannons, he tried to put them in order of the loosest. "Don Charrier. Guy pulled a .22 on me. Shot his house up, tried to chase me out."

"What'd you do?"

"He was ranting and drunk, nearly out on his feet. He could barely see. He fell on his face and I took the pistol away. In court he said he was stressed because his mother was sick, but when he lost custody of his kids he swore he'd get even. With me, with the judge. He was just letting off steam. It was over two years ago. What was his alibi?"

"He's dead. His mother was terminally ill. He shot himself in the head on his ex-wife's lawn."

"Jesus!" In Flynn's hands, pages of misery, like all the files and records of pain he dealt with every day. "Not for nothing, but if they're no longer viable suspects, shouldn't they be crossed off the fucking list?"

"I wanted your unbiased opinion on your past case-load."

"Yeah right." So, not only checking them out, but checking him out too, Flynn thought. He got out a pen and put a check next to three more names. He didn't think any of them would come at him in this way, killing folks around him, but it gave him a feeling that he was doing something proactive. Even though, for all he knew, they were dead or in prison or comatose too.

Their gazes locked, and they had a brief stare-down. You could learn a lot from a person during those five seconds. Flynn kept trying to look into Raidin's brain and see what lay behind the steel-gray front.

"Are you married?" he asked.

The cop cocked an ear, and his brow furrowed like he couldn't quite believe he'd heard what he'd heard. "What did you just ask me?"

"I asked if you were married. Do you have children?"

Raidin's features flattened and hardened until he seemed carved from stone. Absolutely no emotion showed but Flynn sensed Raidin's rage growing by the second. Flynn had crossed a line. You could do a lot but you had to know when to ask about somebody else's personal journey and when to keep quiet about it.

Okay, bad call. Erase it, make like it never happened.

"The notes," Flynn said. "What can you tell me about the forensic testing? Fingerprints? The ink?"

"Tell you?" Raidin's lips moved, framing the words like he didn't fully understand them. He looked Flynn up and down, allowing just a minimum of annoyance to enter his eyes. "Who are you? I've got nothing to tell you." Saying it quietly, but with his usual edge.

The EMTs wheeled Florence out on a gurney to an ambulance parked at the curb. They hadn't fully covered her face. Flynn thought they always draped a sheet over a corpse's face, but there Florence was for everyone out on the street to see. The vultures were out, excited, angling over the police line to get a better glimpse of the dead. The M.E. had searched inside her mouth and left Florence's lips skewed in an unnatural manner, skinned back over her brown teeth. Flynn watched them load her body into the back of the ambulance. The paramedics sat across from her talking. One of them let out a laugh. It was a normal thing. She was dead. There was no implied insult, but Flynn wanted to bounce the guy on his ass up and down the block. You could get angry at anyone for anything.

"What did he do to her?" Flynn asked.

"She's got burn marks to the chest."

"I saw that. What kind of burns are they?"

"Maybe a taser."

"She was fit. Hard, strong."

"She got zapped repeatedly, and the ordeal brought about fibrillation and heart seizure."

"Jesus Christ," Flynn whispered. The black nerve tore through him, on fire.

He held his white-knuckled fists down to his sides. He drove them against his legs. It didn't hurt enough to dampen the ache that continued to grow inside him. While he'd been watching Burt and Ava getting it on, his friend was being murdered in the bathroom. He swallowed down a meaningless noise.

Raidin said, "Now he's inflicting himself upon people you definitely know."

"Where were your men? You had them tailing me for weeks."

"We pulled them off four days ago. Didn't you notice?"

Flynn's tongue got away from him. He couldn't help himself. No style, no composure. Iced, but no cool. "You stupid bastard."

Raidin chopped Flynn in the throat with the side of his gloved hand. It was a fast and efficient move that hurt like hell. Flynn fell to one knee and tried to suck air but nothing went down his windpipe. The panic rose and began to overshadow his thoughts. Sweat slithered through his hair. He was going to die again. Jessie Gray would have to rewrite the story. Scratch out the last paragraph and substitute, *And then, in a deadly twist of fate—*

Abruptly he managed to gasp through his tears. No one else had seen Raidin's move. It looked like Flynn was having an anxiety attack. Jessie was on her cell phone calling in the story. She stared anxiously at him but didn't come over to help. She turned away so she could focus on what she was telling the copy desk.

While Flynn was down, Raidin reached in and un-clipped the .38 from its holster on Flynn's waist. He pulled out the pistol and held it up admiringly, cracked it and checked to see if it was clean. It was. He nodded and stuck it back on Flynn's belt. "You think you'll be able to use it when the time comes?"

Flynn couldn't even choke out an answer. He tried to get to his feet again and couldn't make it. All at once he felt a warmth and respect for Raidin, even though he still wanted to throw down and smack his little face in. It had been a cheap fucking shot.

He wasn't going to get the chance. Raidin looked at the poster of Burt Lancaster on the wall behind Flynn and said, "*The Killers*. I've never seen it." Good time for a com-ment about murder, but Raidin passed it up. Flynn knew it was coming. He held on, waiting for it, his chest heav-ing, breathing painfully through his teeth. "Lancaster was impressive in *From Here to Eternity* though. Regardless, he paled in comparison to Montgomery Clift, but still excel-lent for what he had to do. Besides all the rolling around on the beach. Did you know he started out in the circus?" Raidin noted Flynn's furious expression and said, "Cheer up. Maybe your bad guy will finally put the tap on you next time and stop killing these other people."

TWELVE

Jessie Gray sprang for a cab and Flynn stared out the window at the frozen city around him. They got out at Penn Station and walked downstairs to the L.I.R.R. waiting area. Their train wouldn't be here for another twenty-five minutes. They hadn't exchanged two full sentences since before finding Flo's body. For the first time since he'd met Frickin' Alvin, Flynn wanted a drink. He tugged Jessie along with him and hit the nearest restaurant that served liquor.

The Wall Street shakers of the universe were out in force. Their suits and smiles and flash haircuts offended him. He leaned up against the bar, slapped some cash down and threw back two double shots of rum. The bartender gave him the eye, picking up the moody vibe.

Jessie sat beside him and ordered a stinger. Flynn downshifted to beer and the bartender lightened up. Anybody could have a bad day.

Emma Waltz got right up in his face again. He stared into her eyes. He couldn't get rid of her. She went around and around in his head now, making up for lost time. The note was from somebody who had a connection to him, who was suffering and expected him to be suffering in the same way. Maybe he was. He couldn't think of anyone else from out of his past who might be tied to him through such a shared, important agony.

Jessie Gray sat with a kind of satisfied but grim set to her lips. She'd broken a major story first. He had no doubt she'd reported the facts perfectly, with a literate quality to her write-up.

"You certainly know how to show a girl a good time," she said.

It took him a while to look up from his glass of beer. His jaw tightened. The veins in his throat snapped so hard they brushed his collar. He swung around on the barstool to face her. He gave her a dismal smile even though he couldn't feel his lips. His eyes were no more than glimmering slits.

"Is that a joke?"

"I'm sorry," she said. "I shouldn't have been so casual. That was terrible of me. It was foolish."

She meant it, but didn't mean it quite enough. Some of the yups were staring at her, passing remarks Flynn couldn't hear. He could guess the comments. What's a babe like that doing with an old creep like him?

"It's all right," he told her. His anger had subsided and left him worn-out. "You shouldn't be with me."

"I know what I'm doing."

"No, you don't. You can't. You should stay away. You're in danger."

"I don't think so. He's already given you his message for today. Now he'll let you live with it for a while."

Flynn said, "Or die with it."

"He doesn't want you dead. He wants you alive. He wants to keep communicating with you for some reason. He has a tale to tell, but he only wants to tell it to you."

"And you want to be there when he does?"

"Yes," she admitted. "I *am* a reporter. It's my job." She took a sip of her drink. He waited for her to finish the minor speech he knew was coming. He'd heard it before and given it before. Everyone had. It was a part of how people defined themselves. They couldn't help speaking it aloud. "It's what I do. It's who I am."

"I see," he said.

"It's sweet, you being frightened for me. I'd almost think you cared."

"That's a rotten thing to say."

"I say a lot of rotten things around you. Maybe that means I like you. I tend to marry men I speak rudely to. Of course, they don't put up with it for long."

You wouldn't think it was much of a romantic opening, but there was just enough of an honest invitation.

Without fully meaning to, he parted the curtains of her long straight hair and reached for her, reaching for something else. Maybe his youth, or all his lost love as she wound against him, and they kissed.

It went on for a while. Plenty of need in it. Heat, lust, but no passion in any real sense. He still couldn't feel his lips. With their tongues still pressing together he opened his eyes. In a few seconds she did the same. They stared at each other and finally broke apart. It was the best and worst kiss he'd ever experienced.

They made the train with half a minute to spare, and they moved against the crowd to find an empty seat at the back of the car. They were holding hands. He didn't know when they'd started doing that. A surge of confusion began washing through him, so absolute that he was even confused about what he was confused about. Some days you couldn't get the ground back under you.

"Let's go to your apartment," she said, slipping into his arms again. He'd always been rather stupid about acknowledging a woman's lust, but this time there was no mistaking it. Getting the story had turned her on. Seeing death reinvigorated you for life. He felt it himself. Aroused but unsettled. He supposed it was normal, or as normal as it could be.

"How have you changed?" he asked.

"Changed? In what way? Since when? I thought you were a man of precision."

"Since before you got the story on Florence's murder."

"You're still angry with me," she said.

"Maybe. But see, I—"

"You're a naturally cautious person, and you're even more sensitized because of your wife and because of what's been happening to you. You don't trust me. That's all right, I can accept that. I'm not after a wedding band. I just thought I could comfort you. I thought we could have something . . . distinctive."

It was a good word. *Distinctive.* It bestowed no emotional content except what someone was willing to give it. He still didn't think he was entirely on her radar. He might never quite make it even if he did get her into bed.

The train pulled in and out of tunnels and Jessie Gray slumbered contentedly against Flynn. His gun pressed against her, but she seemed to find it comforting. Eventually she fell asleep. He turned his face to her hair and stared out the window at the Queens townships rolling by.

On the floor, seated between his feet, Zero looked up and said, "You're never going to figure this out. It's going to keep happening until someone walks up behind you, taps you on the shoulder and stabs you in the eyes with an ice pick."

Flynn thought it might be true.

When the train pulled into his station he gently awoke Jessie Gray and they disembarked among the rushing yups. He looked out over the parking lot and saw the rental car. He was having a little trouble remembering the early part of the day. It took him a second to get back to it—Jessie had met him at his apartment and they'd driven to the train station less than a mile away together. He held her close while they walked down the stairs to the lot.

"You're worried about me," she said.

"I'm worried about everybody."

"I mean, you're bothered. You're ill at ease. I came on too strong for you. It's all right, I do that sometimes with certain men. I chased my first husband around the university campus for almost two years. We met as freshmen in a journalism class, and even though he didn't like me much, I eventually wore him down. I have a habit of doing that. I told you I'm compulsive. I'm very self-aware. My therapist has reams of notes on the subject; but for some reason, despite my understanding, I fall back into the same pattern."

"It's what makes us who we are," Flynn said. "Our

habits and methods. Our ruts. The ineradicable flaws in our character."

"You remember me saying that."

"Yeah."

He unlocked the car door for her. She didn't want to get in, she wanted to talk. "And this relationship is already tangled enough."

Is that what they had? Did they skip into a *relationship* on the first date? A date that could be considered somewhat tainted, what with a murder occurring in the middle of it.

"What'd you do to your second husband?"

"Ran after him too. I got pregnant a couple of dates in. We shotgunned it. I lost the baby a few months later, and him a few months after that. I missed the baby more, even though I'd make a terrible mother. I know that. I shouldn't have children. But I probably will, isn't that awful? Of course it is, you see that all day long."

She slid into the seat and he closed the door, got in, started it up and waited for the heat to get going. She got up close to him again and he turned his face to her, went in for another kiss. It was sweet and friendly and altogether meaningless. She drew away and smiled at him.

"You don't really want me, do you?" she asked.

He didn't know how to answer, which was an answer itself. She seemed to take it in stride. She must've expected it. It was part of her rut. She liked men who turned her down. It fired her obsessiveness. He should say he loved her and watch her run for it.

The complexity of his own emotions had never been

quite so obvious to him before. He wondered if he'd always been like this, even with Marianne.

"It's going to snow again, I think," Jessie said. "They're going on and on about how it's the worst New York winter in thirty years. I'm friends with the Channel Two weatherman, the guy who does it at eleven o'clock, and he says people aren't paying enough attention. Cases of frostbite are way up. The homeless are freezing in the streets. You don't hear about it much."

Flynn drove back to his apartment. She got out without a word but gave him an expressive look.

He didn't know what the expression was supposed to mean, but thought his own face might mirror it. Interested, excited, a little wary. She came in close for a last kiss, and he turned his face to her, his lips parted. She drew away and left him like that, got into her car, started it up, and hauled out of there.

Flynn had to be honest. He was glad she was gone. He wanted to work on the Charger some more before the next snow came. Driving the rental weakened him. He needed to get back his horsepower.

That night he called Sierra and told her everything that had happened. He laid it out with more detail than he meant to and was startled to hear himself discussing Jessie Gray's kisses.

Sierra made gagging noises on the line. "You couldn't listen to me. I told you to knock wood, right? Didn't I tell you?"

He didn't pick up on it. He thought it was a sexual reference. "You told me to knock wood?"

"When you talked about whoever making another move."

He remembered. "Yeah, you did. You told me not to call down the whirlwind, but it's here anyway."

"And she was a friend of yours, this lady."

"Yeah. Feels like he's getting closer."

"He's been close. He could've aced you either time. But don't worry about me. He tries to get close to me or my crew and I'll put a bullet in his ass."

"I think the proper street slang is *cap.*"

"*Cap?* Where the hell have you been for the last fifteen years?"

"Okay, so what is it now?"

"How the fuck should I know? You think I stand on street corners talking about shooting people?" She covered the phone and shouted something to one of the kids. He thought it was late for them to be up. She called Kelly's name and said something about putting on pajamas. "The media been hounding you again?"

"They keep calling, but not so many this time. Jessie broke the story. It's already out of their hands. I also kind of think they care less because the victim was an old lady this time."

"Warms the cockles of my heart to hear that."

"Have you been taking Kelly to see her father?"

"Once. It was enough for her. She didn't cry, but the image of Shepard with tubes going into his chest, the machinery damn near devouring him, was enough. It gives her nightmares. I hear her. She doesn't say anything."

With the volume way down, the television whispered about the latest celebrity breakups and hookups, our overseas successes and failures. Jessie's weatherman friend said little about the snow. No wonder people were freezing. Flynn waited to see what they covered on Florence's murder.

"What are you carrying?" he asked.

"A .45."

"You know how to use it?"

"Who in the hell do you think you're talking to anyway?"

"My mistake. I revoke the question."

"The bigger stuff is out in the garage locked up. A twelve-gauge, a little wussy derringer, a Luger and a Mauser without firing pins and I think there's even a broken-down Remington too. One of my exes was a gun nut, as if you couldn't guess."

"I could guess."

"He robbed a bank with the Remington, him and three of his friends, all of them wearing dusters and ten-gallon hats, hooting and hollering like old-time outlaws, can you imagine?"

"I can imagine."

"They got caught twenty minutes later and he tried to get rid of the gun in Ronkonkoma Lake. He went away for eight years, then stabbed a guy in prison and got another five tacked on. He's still got a while to go. The police gave the rusted parts back to me and I locked them up with the rest. I wonder if I should pawn it."

"A piece used in a bank robbery? I'd say no." He wondered how good she could be with a .45, which could break your arm if you didn't hold it right. "So you can nail a beer bottle at fifty yards with that pistol of yours?"

"No, but I can blow somebody's head off. It's got a kick but I'm not exactly delicate. You should seriously consider vacationing in Bora Bora."

"Don't think it hasn't crossed my mind."

The soft hiss of her breath streaming through the corner of her mouth filled his ear. He heard the subtle movements of the plastics in her reconstructed face as she grinned over the line. "But you don't want to run."

"No."

"You want to stay close and try to catch the guy. Now it's a matter of pride with you."

"Call it what you want."

"I'll call it what it is. I can hear it in your voice right now. You want to pop this guy. Cap him. Ice him. Ace him. What do they say in film noir? Plug him. Better yet, you want to do it with your hands, if you can."

He thought he could. He thought he could get the job done, whatever it cost. Someone had to make it happen, and soon.

"You don't have to admit it out loud," she said. "I know it. You need to quit feeding that beast. Even if it makes you feel righteous. You have to turn your back on it, Flynn, do you understand me? The more you feel like you deserve to take someone's life, the more you forfeit your own. I've been there."

"I know you have," he said.

"No, you don't, you just think you know. There are things I've never told you. Things I'm still not going to tell you. But trust me on this one."

The story was on Channel 2. They were holding back the fact that Florence had been tasered to death, if that's what had happened. They said she'd been bludgeoned, which was a word you didn't hear much anymore. They were going to weed out the confession nuts. It wasn't going to matter. The killer wasn't going to call the cops or the news stations, but Flynn held out a little hope that maybe the spook might give him a ring.

"Are you still there?" Sierra asked.

"Yeah," Flynn said. "Do me a favor and run a check on the name Emma Waltz. I tried but got nothing. You're better at digging up info than I am. She's about forty now."

Sierra waited for a moment. "That's it? That's all the information you have?"

"Yeah."

"Why are you after her?"

"I think she's part of my personal journey."

Sierra's hiss shot out the corner of her mouth again. "Please tell me you didn't just say that. Please. Did you just say 'personal journey'?"

"I did," he admitted.

"You've been watching too many daytime psychologists, that's what you've been doing. Don't you know some of those guys don't even have degrees? They just know how to work the audience and the camera. Don't get hooked into that. What personal journey are you talking about?"

"I'm not quite sure."

"You talk, I'll listen."

He lit a cigarette and stared at the burning end of it for

a moment. She already knew about the day Danny died, but he'd never gone in depth with her.

He went further than he'd ever gone before, surprised at himself for saying so much. The details of his brother's death, which he'd run through his head ten thousand times, sounded foreign to him in his own voice. What he recalled embarrassed him.

The *Candyland* board, Camus' *The Stranger*. His preoccupation with Patricia's belly, Danny's small smile of simplicity, their mother's smile, their father's smile. Danny having no control over his foot whenever the baby was mentioned, the blood on Patricia's lips. The way his brother told him, "Good boy." The tilt of Danny's neck. Emma Waltz glancing back at him.

"And you think she has something to do with what's been going on?"

"No," he said.

"Then what's it about?"

"I'm not sure." Maybe if he could put it into words and explain it to her, he could understand it himself.

Flynn got up and started pacing around the room. Zero sat in the center of the floor watching him, his head cocked.

"She's a piece of my life that got away. She went through the same loss as me, the same depth and width and size and scope of it, on the same day. Saw her older sister crap out of the game ... the person she was going to be someday. We don't grow into our parents, we grow into our older siblings. I've become my brother. All I have to do is look in the mirror to remind me. I'm who he would've become. I'm older than him now. I'm more of a father to him than our father was." It was heaving up from him too quickly, he was losing control of what he was trying to tell her. "She watched her sister die bleeding on a beach. I bet she can't look at the ocean anymore without thinking of that last run toward the water...a failed run, a last run that never even made it off the sand. It stays with you, it carries on. It has with me." He hoped to Christ he didn't start talking about Zero or Danny under the ice waving him in. But it felt like he might. "I keep thinking that, somehow, we're connected in a way that can't be explained. That we always have been." He waited for Emma Waltz to get in his face again, but she was nowhere in sight. He missed her. It was true, he needed her. He had to find her. He'd come back for a reason. He knew his name but he still didn't know his purpose. Maybe this was it. "That if we can get back to each other maybe it'll clear my head, give me back what I've been missing."

Sierra waited a full ten count and said, "You seen Mooney yet?"

It took him a second to find his voice. "That's what you have to say to me?"

"That's what I have to say to you. Have you seen him?"

"You know I haven't."

"That's right, I know you haven't. Get it done. You need to talk with a professional. Don't listen to the guys on television, all right? This has been bottled up inside you for too long. You need to do something about it. Or do you disagree?"

"I don't disagree. But—"

"There is no but. There's never any but. You think you're wasting time and that you should be out there sleuthing, detecting, being the Continental Op, Sam Spade, all those guys from your favorite films. That's a bad road to go down. Your head's stuffed with black and white."

"All right, I'll go see the pain in the ass."

Sierra pulled the phone closer to her mouth, so her words, spoken plainly and quietly but with real muscle, would get through. "I don't think you're going into this with an open mind."

"I'll go see him," Flynn said and hung up.

Zero turned in circles before finally settling on the throw rug. He rested his chin on his booted front paws. "This guy any good? You need a competent psychiatrist. I think you might be starting to come a little unglued."

THIRTEEN

Flynn did everything he could on his own for the Charger, replacing parts, banging out dents. There was still more to do. The insurance companies were still thrashing it out. Until the case was settled, all he had in the clear was his rental. The rest came out of his pocket. He got the Charger towed to a friend's garage and cut a pretty good deal that still drained most of his savings account. The mechanics got it cleaned up and running, but that wasn't good enough. He needed it tuned, refined, perfect. He didn't have the money for it and had to sell some of his collectibles. His friend took it as a personal challenge and made it his priority.

A few days later he went to the hospital and sat in on Shepard. The man lay there wired to machinery, catheters and shunts and tubes leading to bags all around the bed. His breathing was regular, his face full of healthy pink. Flynn thought he appeared to be pleasantly sleeping like a man who'd earned himself a good long rest.

Flynn said Shepard's name twice, first quietly, then much louder. Flynn started talking but wasn't fully aware of what he was saying even while he said it. He seemed to be apologizing to the man. Flynn suspected that he owed Shepard his life. If the guy hadn't walked in when he had, his wife Christina would've blasted Flynn out of his shoes and dumped him in the Sound anyway.

It started snowing on the drive back to his apartment. He got home and took up station at the window. He kept a watch on the lot, eyeing the cars growing white as the snow swept the area. He was backlit. A sniper could nail him. He half hoped somebody would try. The snow and the window might be enough to throw off the shot. He might see the muzzle flash and make a move, get on the run, find a clue he could follow. He didn't move for hours.

Sierra phoned him at nearly midnight and said, "She likes the bad boys."

"Doesn't everyone?"

It came out wrong. There'd been a barb in his voice. Sierra went silent and he could feel the mood chilling over the phone. His ear started to freeze. She was going to take it as a wiseass comment about her own love life. He really had to watch what the hell he was saying.

"Is that a crack?" she asked.

"No."

"I asked you, is that a crack?"

"No, I'm sorry if you took it that way."

"You think that's funny?"

"It wasn't a crack at you! Even Betty Grable liked the bad boys. She dated George Raft. If I didn't know better, I'd think you were getting sensitive."

"Things aren't so great at home," she said.

He asked, "Does it have to do with Nuddin or Kelly?"

"No. My oldest, Trevor. I told you about him. I think

Nuddin's been keeping him up at night. They play video games too late. And they're always on that damn computer. Or out in the garage fixing up my old clunker. Trevor hasn't been sleeping, and those early hours, they can be killer. He helps me get the kids ready, makes breakfast. I think he's fixating on his parents. He's actually been writing to them, trying to reestablish contact. He's backsliding. His therapy sessions aren't going so good."

"He's not seeing Mooney, is he?"

"No, and stop insulting the guy. Maybe I'm giving Trevor too much responsibility too early, but it seemed to be good for him."

"You said he might be picking up on Nuddin's damage."

"Yeah, because of the abuse in their histories. Seeing Nuddin's scars might be doing a lot to remind him of his own. He still handles the younger kids well, washes clothes and the dishes, cleans the house. But I worry that I'm taking advantage of him, putting so much on him. It could be my fault. We all might do better if I hired someone to watch Nuddin and the others and let Trevor just get a part-time job somewhere he can meet girls, socialize a little more."

"Do his parents write him back?"

It took her a second too long to say, "No."

"You pull the letters, don't you."

"You want to hear about your little girlfriend or what?"

Flynn wanted to hear and he didn't want to hear. He tried to shove away images of Bragg sneaking into Sierra's house and tormenting his son all over again. He wondered what kind of abuse was in Trevor's life that such hideous scars as Nuddin's might invoke his own pain. The dead past came surging in again. It would never stop hunting for him, he might as well go meet it.

"Yeah."

"Emma Waltz, married three times, divorced three times, always kept her maiden name. No kids. Plenty of domestic disputes, lots of cops over the years, more than her share of battering. Spent some time in the hospital for various contusions and broken bones. The usual damn pattern, but nothing too serious, so far as I can see on her sheet."

"Her address?"

"I think you should stay away from this one."

"Duly noted. What is it?"

"You're backsliding too. You need to face front."

"You didn't hear a word I said about her, Sierra."

"I heard you, all right, and I've been watching you, and that's why you ought to listen to me."

"Her address?"

"One Twenty-one Dolan Street, Massapequa."

"Thanks. I'm coming in to work tomorrow," he said. "I have cases."

"You just want to bounce the bad daddies on their ears. You're coming in to talk to Mooney. You never did get it done even though I told you to. So here it is. The appointment is for 9 A.M. Sharp. You understand sharp? Sharp. You miss it and you're fired. You've walked up to the line. I let you do it. It's been my fault too. I backed up for you. That's done. You push anymore and you'll break. You want to catch this guy, get well first. Don't tell me you're okay because you're not. See Mooney, that's step one. Maybe see somebody else after him, someone you like, but you need to sit down with him. And don't beat him up, you hear me? Unless he talks that 'personal journey' crap. Then you have my permission to smack him in the mush."

You could tell the trouble surrounding Flynn frightened, intrigued and kind of turned on Dale Mooney. It got under his skin and made him think of sex and murder. His eyes burned in his doughy, placid face.

This wasn't your common neurosis and tendency toward OCD. There was blood on the ground. Mooney's eyes gleamed and he kept wetting his lips like a nervous starlet getting ready for her close-up. He was obscenely fascinated. You could see Mooney thought it added a certain street cred to him as he sat there in his leather wingback chair, ballpoint pen in his hand, clicking it over and over against his hairy chin. Freud would have something to say about that, definitely.

Mooney had some of his own issues. He went three hundred with a shag beard and a Hitler haircut. He squinted and sniffed like a coke fiend. Somehow he had a strong presence. Folks at the CPS rallied to him. Even those who didn't like him admitted they found him fascinating. Flynn couldn't get it into focus.

Flynn had refused to lie down. He didn't like the disadvantage it put him at. Mooney staring down at him, Mooney fully aware of his surroundings, and Flynn there on the couch with his eyes shut, waiting for somebody to put a letter opener in his ear. No, he'd meet the guy eye to eye, and, if he thought he might actually get anything out of this, he might even tell the truth. Some of the truth. About some things. Probably not the talking dead dog.

"It would be much more beneficial for you if you could lie on the couch and try to relax a little," Mooney said.

"I prefer not to."

"To relax?"

"To lie on the couch."

"Why, if I may ask?"

"You may ask indeed," Flynn said. His phony smile cut into his face like a thumbnail gouged into a piece of clay. He gave it a three count before continuing. His voice had a lilt to it that it didn't normally have. He should never be amenable, amenable and him just didn't go together, but he was still trying. It was a weak effort, but it was still an attempt. "The reason is that I've been feeling quite vulnerable of late, and although I'm 'among friends,' as it were, lying on your couch, even though it is a nice rich leather, would make me feel even more insecure and so less forthcoming."

"I see. I assure you, you're quite safe here."

"Your assurances aside, I don't feel safe anywhere lately."

"Yes, well, I suppose that *is* understandable."

"Your supposition is correct," Flynn told him. "But take it on faith that I'm trying here, Dale. I didn't even bring my gun in."

"You wear a gun now?"

"Yes."

"Loaded?"

Probably the stupidest question ever. Flynn stared at Mooney, waiting for him to acknowledge his misstep, his folly, but he didn't. The shrink just kept waiting, his eyebrows on the rise now, climbing farther up his forehead, his whole face saying, I am inquisitive, I am curious, I anticipate an answer.

Flynn said, "Yes, the gun is loaded."

"Are you—"

"Yes, I'm licensed."

"Have you—"

"No, I've never shot anybody."

"Please, would you kindly—"

"Yes, I'll allow you to finish a sentence."

Mooney put down his pen and pad and hit a new pose, raising both his hands, steepling his fingers and resting his chin on them. Flynn wondered, If there'd never been a film featuring a psychiatrist in it, would anybody in real life make that move? Would they ever stick their fat chins on their fingers like that? He looked like a buttercup about to fly away in the wind.

Scenes from *Shock Corridor* started going through Flynn's head. Reporter goes undercover into a madhouse to get the real story and winds up losing his mind.

Mooney said, "Before we begin—"

"We've already begun."

"—I'd like to say, Flynn, that despite our rather antagonistic relationship in the past, which I've done everything I could to avoid and amend, I'm going to make an extensive effort to help you in whatever manner I can. Is that all right? I hope you'll at least give me the benefit of the doubt that I can possibly be of some assistance to you. Especially during these awful, dangerous times you're experiencing, which I doubt anyone could, or should, endure alone. Otherwise, we're both just wasting our time, regardless of what Ms. Humbold would wish for us. I don't think it's too much to ask for, *vis-à-vis* the fact that first and foremost we are coworkers, and that we labor in the same system to the same ends. We are colleagues, comrades who seek to aid those who are losing their own personal battles, ergo we're not so different. Your recent distress being at the eye of this...this storm of brutality, if you will, and the guilt you must feel due to these senseless murders, and even those difficult events occurring before this recent, ah...downturn in your life, *par example* your divorce and various familial issues, the stillbirth of your child, difficulties with your temper and your tendency toward violence, all of these are snarled together, and it shall take an enormous struggle on both our parts to untangle the knot. I hope to get at the root of some of these matters, and, I should think, help you to become a higher-functioning individual in both your personal life and in society at large."

Flynn's face had paled considerably, his breathing shallow now. But he said, "Sure."

"Sure?"

"Yes, sure."

Mooney had been disarmed. He wanted his speech to receive a greater validation.

He licked his lips and sniffed. He smoothed down his hair and fluffed his beard. "I'm glad."

"I'm glad you're glad."

"Are you ready to proceed?" Mooney asked.

"I am."

"Well, good, I'm very happy to hear that too. And you still won't lie down."

"Still, I won't."

"All right then. Let's proceed."

Flynn imagined scenarios that focused on evil psychiatrists hypnotizing their patients and sending them off to do their ill bidding. The *Testament of Dr. Mabuse, The Cabinet of Dr. Caligari*, the German expressionist films that predated noir but gave them their look. He pictured Dale Mooney as the great degenerate brain behind all his recent troubles. Dale Mooney, secret supergenius out to conquer the world *vis-à-vis* an asylum full of robotlike madmen. Flynn would out-think him and outfox him somehow, and prove his superior intellect and noble heart. Dale would wind up pinned to his chair by a letter opener, a derringer clenched in his fist. Raidin would shake Flynn's hand and call the mayor of New York. Lana Turner or Veronica Lake would fall into Flynn's arms at the end, and just before planting one he'd say, "I knew it from the way he talked, baby. Never trust a shrink who says *ergo* and *par example.*" The pinup girl would titter. He'd cock his hat and fix his tie and they'd walk off down the gloomy, water-slicked cardboard sidewalk on the back lot of 20th Century Fox. It would be all right.

Flynn's grin made Mooney frown at his notes. Flynn's file was stacked on the desk atop other folders, at least twice as thick as the rest in view. Maybe Mooney did that on purpose. You could get paranoid about being paranoid. Christ knew what personal comments and reports were in it. All his write-ups and commendations. Sierra bitching about him and the cactus. Some of his cases had been failures. Some of them became failures years afterward. Grace Brooks. Children had died because he didn't delve closely enough. He'd been late, he hadn't been rough enough on the right people. He'd been too rough on the wrong ones.

Mooney started clicking his ballpoint pen again, stared deeply into Flynn's eyes and said, "Tell me about your mother."

Flynn hopped up, said, "Oh for the holy love of sweet baby Jesus Christ in a shit-strewn manger," and walked out.

He didn't answer the phone the rest of the afternoon. He'd given it a shot, maybe not his best shot, or maybe it was. There were other things that counted more. Let Sierra fire him. She shouldn't be pointing any fingers. She had her own troubles, still. Reading your foster kid's mail, destroying letters from his real parents, even if they were jailbirds, it was a felony.

He put his gun back on.

Three days later, just before they closed, Flynn got the Charger back from the garage. It looked exactly like it had the day Danny had died in it. Newly repainted, buffed and waxed. Flynn got in, fixed the seat and angled the rearview back into place. He snapped on the radio, tuned it to an oldies station and sat there listening to the music hum and the engine growl. The sun began to set and threw slivers of gold across the hood even as the shadows thickened.

He opened his eyes and Zero was in the passenger seat, turning circles, his white outfit as clean as the day they'd died. The dog told him, "Try not to get us killed again, all right?"

"I'll do my best."

"Oh hell, we're in serious trouble then."

Flynn put his hand on the gearshift. He could almost feel Danny behind him, breathing on his neck. Smiling, with a cigarette hanging off his lip, looking hep cat hip and beautiful with cool, his dark eyes meeting Flynn's in the mirror. As if to say, Listen to that engine. Let the horsepower into your heart. You've still got a lot to do, a ways to go, but it's going to be all right now. Except for this fucking dog.

FOURTEEN

He tried to imagine what Emma Waltz would look like now, but he could only see her sister Patricia standing framed in the front window, and only in black and white. He wasn't quite himself either—not Danny, but not entirely Flynn. Flynn with the smoky inner power of his brother. Not Flynn at all, but somebody wearing his face, standing outside Emma Waltz's house. The two of them having been parted too early.

She liked the bad boys. Maybe it stemmed from Danny. The worst of the worst boys, the one who killed her sister. She could be cross-wired. Sex and death might be linked in a way she could never be freed from. Perhaps that was Flynn's problem too. The nerve kept stinging, throbbing, burning through him. It moved up his chest, trying to get even deeper into his brain.

121 Dolan Street was a single story corner house in a run-down, tightly packed residential area. Flynn parked across the street on the diagonal, which gave him a clear view of the house. The garage door was open and a young tough in tight jeans, a T-shirt and work boots smoked a joint while he replaced the exhaust on a Harley. He had a

patchy beard and long hair he had to sweep out of his eyes every few seconds. It was twenty-five degrees and the kid acted like he couldn't feel the cold.

Flynn scanned the garage and saw a glowing heater propped on a shelf. Dumb as hell. The guy was not only smoking around gasoline and oil but also standing there with red-hot open wires behind him. One spark into a pile of rags and the whole place would go up.

A blue '89 Capri puttered into the driveway. Flynn's pulse started kicking faster. The Capri blasted a cloud of burning oil as it came to a rest. Sure, the guy spends all his time fixing up his motorcycle but won't even change the oil in a car he doesn't drive.

A woman got out and went up the walk carrying two bags of groceries. Her unruly blond hair draped across her features, and Flynn couldn't get a good look at her face. These people, how did they stand it, always having to peer through a web of hair?

She walked into the garage and said something to the tough, who was on his knees at the back of the Harley. She said more, probably about the heater. Not only idiotic but a total waste of money with the garage door open. Burning electricity for no reason. She seemed to be repeating herself. The punk didn't respond. He didn't offer to carry the groceries. His features folded into a child's petulant expression. Bottom lip out, eyes hooded, his chest beginning to heave. He looked up and gave a single retort. Probably called her a bitch. Emma walked inside without showing Flynn even the side of her face.

The punk finished his joint, drew a cigarette box from his back pocket, pulled another J from it and lit it. He was a stoner. Flynn hadn't seen a real stoner since high school. Plenty of hard drug users and worse, but not the white-trash mutts who stayed lit all day at the expense of their parents or others. Who sat around with no style, shivering in their dirty T-shirts.

Zero said, "Go kill him."

"I'm not going to kill him."

"You want to."

"I don't want to."

"Your hands are trembling."

"No, they're not."

"You've been walking up to the line for a while, and now—"

If only it wasn't his own voice he had to listen to. Always making the fight harder. "Now nothing."

"It'll win her over. She'll sweep into your arms and you can plant one on her lips and she'll kiss the blood off your hands."

It was a reference to the worst-titled noir of all time. "Don't you have a rubber bone you need to go chew on?"

"Think how good it'll feel to finally get it done. Reach for the .38 and shoot him in the forehead."

"That's not how it's going to go down."

"First one's the roughest. Then? It'll never be as hard again. You'll get what you've always wanted, you'll be a completely new person."

"It's your fault all this happened," Flynn said. "If you hadn't run after me, Kelly wouldn't have followed, and the mother wouldn't have freaked as badly."

"I was only trying to help!" the dog told him. "And she wasn't going to let you take her baby brother."

Flynn watched the tough for a while, wondering how this kid fit into his own life. He narrowed his eyes trying to see the thread that connected them together. This punk was here only because Danny had gone into the water. One event led to the other, directly, down through time and covering uncountable waves and ripples of life. There were no coincidences, everything tied together in the end. You couldn't keep the door shut if someone was destined to walk through and find you.

He shut his eyes and listened to the tide of his mind. The past continued to pound away at the shore of the present.

Zero had been right, Flynn's hands were beginning to twitch. He grabbed hold of the steering wheel and held on until his knuckles cracked. The Charger flushed him with cool.

The tough finished his second joint. Flynn could see him thinking about lighting another but the mutt decided not to. He leaned against the Harley and glanced back at the door and then shook his head, swept his hair from his eyes again, sneered and followed after Emma.

It was the sneer that did it. Flynn could've let the rest of it slide, figuring the stoner was too high to get his blood boiling. But you pull a face like that and it's because you're letting the monster out of the cage.

Flynn unclipped the .38 from his belt and locked it in the glove box.

"You'll just use your hands," Zero told him.

"No, I won't."

"Or the base of a lamp. Or you'll break off a table leg or..."

Sometimes you couldn't keep your dead dogs quiet.

Flynn walked up the driveway into the garage. The heater was still on. He flipped the switch and shut it off. The tough's angry muffled voice heaved against the wall. Flynn went to the door and didn't knock. He walked in and followed the shouting to the living room, where the smell of blood was already in the air.

Emma Waltz sat on the floor, her coat still on. She had red trickling from the back of her head, dribbling over her ear. Wrapped meat sat defrosting at her ankle. One of her sleeves had been yanked up past the elbow and an Indian burn welt was growing purple. A line of cans and food products led from her feet to the open freezer.

The tough had started in on her before she'd had a chance to put the groceries away. He'd slapped her and she'd struggled. There was still some heat in her. He'd clasped on to her arm. She'd torn free and made it three steps away. He'd hauled off and clocked her in the back of the head with a frozen round steak.

Emma's mouth bled. She glanced up at Flynn without surprise or interest. She looked exactly like Patricia in the car at the end, with blood on her lips. The ripple from thirty years ago was finally reaching them in full force.

Charging with his muscular arms raised, the punk screamed, "Who the fuck are you? What are you doing in my house?"

Flynn waited, and the punk hit the brakes. He'd grown used to Emma running from him, so he expected everyone to do it. He didn't know how to face someone down, he was only good at throwing shit at them. Flynn wanted to smile but couldn't. The icy air from the freezer blew across his back.

He studied the kid. He thought he could see what initially attracted Emma. Broad shoulders, real fire, his eyes smoky and with a hint of pain. No deep intellect, this one ran on his instincts and moved with the flow of the moment. Slim and trim, exactly how all women liked them, with his long glossy hair shaping his blunt face like a mane. The wild child, a little feral. He was much younger than Flynn and Emma, maybe twenty-five.

His muscles and good looks offended Flynn. Damn near everything about him did.

Flynn figured it was a case of opposites attract. Emma was looking for whatever she felt she wasn't. She was hoping to find someone to shave the veneer off, to strip away the insulation.

Standing behind the punk were all the men who were just like him, who'd made the same mistakes and compounded them daily with their anger, their ignorance and weakness. Flynn had met this guy a thousand times in a thousand homes with thin walls that never stopped vibrating with fury.

The sneer again. The punk couldn't help making the face. His features naturally folded into it.

He stood tall, rearing now, trying to broaden himself into a more imposing figure. His eyes darted around the room as he searched for any kind of leverage he could find. You could look in his eyes and see his thoughts wheeling. It amused Flynn. The tough had no idea what to do next. Try to fight, make a run for it? He never once looked down at Emma.

"I said who the fuck are you?"

"I'm Flynn. Who are you?"

"Get out!"

"What's your name?"

"I live here!"

"It doesn't sound like you do. It sounds like you're free-loading."

"I'm what?"

"Sponging off Emma."

Flynn walked to her and held his hand out, but she ignored it. She thumbed the blood from the corner of her mouth and stared at him through her hair. Here he was, two feet away, and he still couldn't really see her.

"I pay my share!"

"You take more than your share, though."

"What? Get out of here!"

"It's not all your fault. Some people are just wired in a way that leads them to the worst possible choice. She's got to work on that. Maybe we both do."

"What?"

"You heard me."

"You're crazy! You can't be in here, nobody invited you! I don't know you! I'm calling the cops!"

"Yeah, you do that. We'll bust out your cigarette box and have them crawl over this place looking for the rest of your stash. What's your name?"

Like he had to think about it. "I'm . . . Chad."

"Chad?"

Even the name offended Flynn. He glanced at the frozen round steak and thought of what it would be like to smash a man's skull in with it. Then, the old Hitchcock ploy. Cook the murder weapon and serve it to the investigating homicide dicks.

"Chad, get the fuck out of here."

"I live here!"

"Not anymore."

"You can't—" Chad began doing a little boy gotta-piss dance, sort of hopping in place, his knees bent. "You can't!"

"You're moving out. Go crash with one of your burnout buddies."

This was it. Sometimes you ran up to the moment of truth and sometimes it ran up to you. Here they were. Chad had to jump left or right now. Either come rushing at Flynn or leap on his Harley, he had no other choice. It all depended on whether he had a real reason, in his heart, to fight. For his pride or his home, his woman or his action, or just to protect his pot. If anything pushed him forward, it would probably be the pot.

Chad did his dance some more, swung close like he might take a poke at Flynn, didn't, then hit the garage door and was gone.

Flynn sighed and went to one knee beside Emma.

He could only see the subtle glimmer of her eyes and a hint of her bloody mouth. Not much else as she peered through her sweaty clinging hair at him. Flynn wanted to reach out with both hands and tenderly brush her hair back, pin it up, tie it in a ponytail, do some damn thing with it. But he kept his distance.

A strange urge to pick up the scattered cans filled him. Put them away in the cabinets, cook her a fine dinner, light a few candles. He thought, This might be the place to start again. Move in, remove the bad memories one at a time, like buffing away fingerprints. Cleaning up someone else's house was so much easier than cleaning up your own.

He'd come back from the dead for a reason. Maybe she was it.

"Emma?" he said. "Do you remember me?"

He'd been waiting thirty years to hear Emma Waltz speak to him. He hoped they would be words of power and wonder. He hoped that, broken as she was, she would recognize his own cracks and flaws and know how to aid him. He hoped. It was something new.

You got a lot of weird thoughts in the night that picked up speed through the day. His chest heaved and he felt light-headed. He hadn't killed anybody, he was still in control. He waited for salvation from a woman who'd been knocked down by a steak.

Motion at the window drew his attention. Flynn spun to his feet and got between it and Emma, thinking it was possibly Chad, outside on the lawn with a shotgun, having finally steamed himself into action. Or the shadow in the blizzard making another effort to insert himself into Flynn's life.

But it was only falling snow weaving across the glass.

He could feel death out there waiting in the wind. Danny outside with Patricia, watching to see what would happen next. Not holding hands, showing no love for each other. Aloof and tied through eternity. Her baby too. His baby as well. His parents in the freezing alley, angry, defeated, disappointed. All the dead cases, his mistakes pooling together.

His hands trembled again, the nerve more alive than he

was. The snow blew harder, urging him faster down the midnight road.

"Emma?"

He let his hand slowly waft toward her. She stared at him. Her mouth hung open, tears filling her eyes. They didn't fall. Perhaps she'd twisted through life full of guilt because she too had never cried when it was most important to do so.

Emma Waltz leaped to her feet, turned, and fled through the front door.

The freezer blew cold air at the back of Flynn's neck, the open door at his face. He moved to the doorway and watched her get into her car, tear out of the driveway, skid in the street and rapidly advance into the oncoming whiteness.

Flynn still hadn't heard her voice or seen her face.

FIFTEEN

Shepard's fresh-faced, delicately featured doctor, making his rounds followed by eight even younger med students, played to the girls and kept showing off his inhumanly white-capped teeth.

He spoke with flourish and seemed overly aware of his glossy curls, constantly fingering and primping them. Flynn didn't blame him. You couldn't help preening before beauty, even in a hospital room stinking of astringents and bedsores. Flynn felt the need to do the same thing, tug at his gray hair, try to appear younger than he was.

No matter how close death got you still wanted to look good.

The doctor flashed a light in Shepard's eyes and ears, pulled back the sheets and checked the shunts and stints in Shepard's chest. The suture bisected him from his sternum to his belly button, a painfully pink line of shining flesh. Flynn expected to get thrown out or told to wait elsewhere, but no one said anything to him.

The doc made inside jokes about medical procedures and serums that Flynn didn't understand. He didn't mind. He tried to be amiable. He grinned a lot. It wasn't helping.

Flynn's hand flashed out and gripped the doc's wrist. The kid—he was another kid, they were all kids, this one worth maybe 400k a year—stared down at Flynn's hand, then looked in his eyes, then looked back down at the hand, then again checked Flynn's eyes. The students milled out in the hallway uncertain of what to do, what to say, what the next move might be.

"When's he going to wake up?" Flynn asked.

"It's impossible to tell."

"An estimate."

"I don't have one."

"I thought he wasn't in a coma but only nonresponsive."

"He is."

"How can that be? It's been six weeks."

"Yes," the doc agreed. They were always agreeable, terrified of lawsuits, unwilling to say anything of value. "Are you a relative?"

"Yeah, I'm his twin brother. Billy."

The doc had no file to check, no paperwork in his hands. He glanced over at Shepard and back to Flynn, still not seeing, truly seeing, either of them. An expansive ache filled Flynn's chest as he thought of his dying mother in a room no different than this, a doctor no different than this, a hopeless situation much the same. Flynn equally helpless, ready to hurl a chair out a window just to see someone scurry.

The doctor said, "I understand your frustration."

"I don't think you do. I need to talk with him."

"I'm sorry."

"It's important."

"I'm sorry."

Trying to shove off again, almost putting some muscle into it this time, but not really, the doc looked back at the prettiest girl in the hall. He was going to make his move on her soon, cross a line, help her with her exams in the Commack Motor Lodge. Flynn kept his grip tight on the doctor's wrist, thinking, a couple more foot-pounds of pressure and I could ruin his career. They'd put pins in the joint but it would never be the same.

Sometimes it helped to make a silent threat, to understand your own power in the face of other storms that brushed you aside.

Sometimes it didn't. He released the kid, who apologized without meaning again. "I'm sorry."

The others sensed potential action but had already acquired an M.D.'s carefully established enamel of noncommittal expression. They stared. They said nothing.

They all left and Flynn found himself seated on the edge of Shepard's bed, wanting to thank him for making the final move that put him in the way of his own wife's bullet. The man had saved Flynn's life, at least until the big dip. Flynn owed him something, even if it had taken the guy six months to make the right call to CPS.

He put his hand on Shepard's arm, trying to make contact and reach past the slow death. He'd done the same thing with his mother and failed, watching her dwindle, day by day, until she was out of sight. Until the morning he walked in and the bed was full of more machine than Ma, and he couldn't even catch a glimpse of flesh beneath the metal and plastic.

"Open your eyes, Shepard, talk to me. Give up your secrets, it'll lighten your load. You took a stand but you didn't rise quite high enough. It's time to try again. Your conscience isn't clear yet, and neither is mine. I know you can hear me, damn you. Think of your daughter. Whatever's coming after me might hit her on the way. How do I get us out of this?"

Shepard continued to sleep, floating in some safer harbor, too afraid to come back to the blood.

Saturday morning, Flynn parked in Sierra's driveway, got out and walked to the front door.

He hadn't even knocked yet when a child opened it for him and skirted away toward the side of the house. All he saw was a flash of dark eyes and pale skin, coming up to about his belly button, and then it was gone.

He followed. The side gate was open and he walked through, hearing laughter and yelling and whining and crying. It sounded like recess at an elementary school. A vague upset clambered through him because the gate had been left open, because anybody could step into the yard. But you couldn't expect children to always lock the doors and shut the gates and live in fear.

He passed the garage. The door was down but through dirty, cracked windows he saw the teenager, Trevor, in there pulling plugs out from under a dented, dust-covered hood. Nuddin sat on a stool in the corner, bobbing his scarred head, apparently humming. Trevor seemed to be talking animatedly, showing Nuddin how the engine worked. Flynn was glad the two of them had each other to help them get through whatever it was they'd been, up until now, forced to brave alone.

A girl howled nearby and Flynn turned and narrowed his eyes, checking around. He shouldn't be here, but he had to see Kelly Shepard and Nuddin again. The need had swelled within him until it forced him here knowing Sierra was going to give him high octane-fueled hell for it. After the fiasco with Mooney, he knew he might really be fired. He hadn't shown up yet to find out. Whatever she did to him now, it was probably going to hurt.

The yard sprang alive. It was a snow-choked whirlwind of children. They were in the trees, they were charging around igloos. They were throwing snowballs and wailing because they'd lost their mittens. They swirled past him without noticing.

Kelly Shepard, out in the snow again. Wearing the same bright white ski outfit as the first time he'd seen her. She stood chattering with a little black girl about her age. How did Sierra play it? Did she tell them they were sisters now? Cousins? How did she bind them into a family, or did she even bother? Were they all just pals? Was she Mommy?

He couldn't believe he'd known her for so long and knew hardly anything at all about her home life. How had he messed up so badly that he'd been to his one friend's house only two or three times over all these years? His mistakes were becoming more obvious. The things that had driven Marianne away more prevalent.

He couldn't get a count of the kids. There seemed to be more every minute. There were slides and swings and a covered aboveground pool. Neighbor children must pour in and out of the yard in varying numbers as the day wore on. He could see Sierra through the back door storm window. She was making sandwiches and pouring grape juice. Kids clumped in and out, in and out.

Trevor got the engine to almost turn over before it died. The clapboard siding of the garage rattled where it was loose and rotted black.

Flynn heard his name and angled his hip with the holster out a few inches in case he had to pull the pistol.

He turned and Kelly Shepard rushed at him with her arms open and before he knew what he was doing he was moving toward her. She slammed into him and he went to one knee in the snow.

He held her, smiling, going, "Hey, hey there!" like an idiot. "Heya!" He thought, This is what it would've been like if Noel hadn't died. If the world had come down a little differently for me and Marianne and we'd gotten the important things right in the beginning. I'd be holding my child, and the shadow in the blizzard would have a carrot nose and be wearing a top hat. Wouldn't that be nice?

He wondered how close he might've come along the way. If there'd ever been a point when he could've cut a half inch left instead of right and everything else would've fallen into place. He could maybe blame a lot of it on Danny, his father, and the other dead, but not everything.

"How are you?" he asked.

Her cheeks were bright crimson circles. She smiled and he saw she'd lost one of her front teeth. "I'm very fine, thank you," she answered, under her breath, knocking the answer out with the unusual poise he'd noticed that first night.

"Look how big you've gotten. You in college yet?"

"No, not quite."

"Ah, not quite, huh? You sure? I was thinking you were a freshman."

"No, not yet. I'd like to attend Harvard. My daddy went there."

"How are things here? You get along with everybody? You like Sierra?"

"Miss Humbold is very nice to all of us. I've made some friends."

"You have, that's great. I bet you're the belle of the ball."

"I don't understand what that means."

"It means you're the most liked one among the crowd."

She let out a giggle. "You're silly."

He wondered how she'd take the news that her dog was still around, talking to him, urging him to murder. He felt like telling her, Your bulldog, you feel like taking him off my hands? He's got a bad attitude.

"How's your uncle doing?"

"Nuddin loves it here," she said. "We get to see all the storms, standing out here. Miss Humbold lets us. Even if it's icy, we stand under the patio . . . me and some of the others, we enjoy it."

"That sounds very . . . social."

"Oh, it is."

Icicles clattered in the trees overhead. Flynn got a wonky déjà vu feeling, knowing this had happened before, standing out in the snow with this little girl, talking of storms.

She still seemed like a regular, happy kid. He didn't know how much Sierra had told her about her parents, if she understood what had been wrong in that house. He knew she'd seen her father in the hospital, unresponsive but, they said, not in a coma. The guy hiding within himself. Maybe a few more visits from Kelly could change all that, but Sierra would never let that happen. She had her own hang-ups and it was time for Flynn to address them, to put a few things on the line.

"Flynn, why haven't you visited sooner?" Kelly asked.

Now there was a tough one. He thought of her mother, Christina Shepard, saying to him on the night she died, the night she killed him, *Would you like to speak to my daughter? Ask her questions? Foul questions, no doubt. What kind of man wheedles his way into working with children every day, Mr. Flynn? What thoughts go through your piggy mind?*

What kind of thoughts were in his head when he was more worried about this girl than he'd been for his own wife? As worried for her as he was for Emma Waltz, another complete stranger? Maybe it was just easier caring for people who didn't know you.

"I meant to," he said.

"But you've been busy?"

"I've been . . . distracted. Does Miss Humbold ever mention me?"

"No. She said you worked together but that was all. I've asked a couple times but she doesn't answer. She says we should make peanut butter. So we do. There's a lot of people to feed. I help out, a little."

"I bet you help out a lot."

"Not really."

"Do you need anything? Can I get you anything?"

"Like to buy me?"

"Yes," Flynn said. "Or anything else. Whatever."

"No, I don't need anything."

A slight tinge of sadness invaded her words and Flynn thought she might ask him, confidentially, when she might be going home. How much longer she had to stay here with these people who weren't her family. But then she looked at him and her eyes brightened again and the moment passed.

He said, "Kelly, has anyone tried to contact you since you've been here?"

"Contact me?"

"Get in touch with you. Anybody saying they were your family? Any letters or notes? Any phone calls?"

"No, no one. Nothing like that. Nobody calls me. There's nobody to call me."

"You're sure?"

That made her laugh. "Well, I wouldn't say it otherwise!"

He had to keep reminding himself this girl was only seven no matter how she talked or how much maturity she projected. The weight of his useless sympathy strained his chest. He could think of nothing to do to help her when the time came when the truth of the world flooded into her. When she visited her mother's grave and when she met with her father's dainty-featured doctor and had to watch him flashing that vapid, white-capped smile at her.

The garage door opened and Nuddin loped to Flynn with a wide smile, his eyes alive with joy. He held his arms open and hugged Flynn, stroking his back, patting him. Flynn clasped Nuddin and rubbed the top of his scarred, battered head.

Nuddin went, Whoo whoo whoo.

The teenager, Trevor, sauntered out as well, wiping his hands on a rag. He shut the garage and gave Flynn an uneasy smile. He said, not unpleasantly, "Who are you?"

Flynn reached over Nuddin's shoulder and held his hand out to the boy. "I'm Flynn."

"You work with Sierra."

"That's right."

"You're the one who brought Nuddin and Kelly to us," Trevor said. "It's good to see him so happy."

"From what I understand you're mostly responsible for that. You've helped him out a lot."

"I don't know how much gets through to him. I try to show him about cars and games and downloading music. It makes the time go by."

Kelly said, "Trevor is his best friend."

Nuddin hummed and murmured his childish tune. Flynn held him and sorta danced with him in the snow for a minute. As he circled around he spotted Sierra framed in the back door staring at him, munching absently on a bologna sandwich, her expression pure hellfire.

SIXTEEN

He stepped inside and sat at the kitchen table. Today Sierra wore brown hair with thick curls coiling all over the place. She said, "You're fired."

"I figured that."

"You figure everything, Miracle Man, and you get it all wrong. You purposefully threw a wrench into that meeting with Mooney."

"What makes you say so?"

"He gave me a full report."

"That's supposed to be confidential."

"Not from me."

He shrugged. "I gave it a shot. I gave him a chance. I did my best. And I didn't smack him in the mush."

"You've got no right to be here, I told you to stay away."

"They seemed happy enough to see me."

"It wasn't your call to make."

"I think it was." He locked eyes with her. "You're not their mother, Sierra. They're as much my responsibility as yours. Maybe even more so."

"God, I hope that's not true."

The tone hit him hard enough to lift his chin. "Oh, that's nice."

It was self-righteous judgment. Was she taking him to task now, saying he'd botched the Shepard case? Or was it a mother's instinct to stand up against anything that might bring trouble to her house? He searched her face and saw strain and fatigue there. He hadn't picked up on it before. He'd been too wrapped up in his own troubles to be interested.

"You're blaming me?" he asked.

"You could've handled things differently."

"How so?"

"You know what I'm talking about."

She was being petulant, something Sierra almost never did. Sarcastic, sharp, even embittered, you could expect that from her, but not this. It was a kid's game, and she never fell back that way.

"Tell me how."

Sierra said nothing. She was trying to flatten her lips together, but that never worked, the scars pulled them apart.

"What's this about?" he asked.

One difficulty he had with her is that he couldn't read her face very well. The plastic shifted in ways he couldn't fully appreciate or understand. She was annoyed all right, but was she also scared? He couldn't lock it down.

"What's going on? Did someone threaten you?"

"No."

"Tell me, Sierra. What's happened?"

"Nothing happened. Don't turn this around."

"Something did. I know you."

A draft rolled in behind him. He turned and children were walking in, circling around the kitchen, laughing. The door opened and shut, opened and shut.

He stood and he and Sierra moved to the living room. She lowered her voice. "You don't know shit about anything. You had to go and start something with that Emma Waltz girl, didn't you?"

"What?"

"I did another check. She went to the emergency room Wednesday night. You went over there and got her boyfriend riled up, didn't you? You bulled your way into her home and with your usual charm you heated him to his boiling point and he took it out on her. Not you. On her. After you left."

"Jesus Christ."

"He filed a police report on you. Got your name wrong as 'Finn,' which helps you out in a big way, but I wouldn't be surprised if they track you down and drag your ass into court sooner or later. You never think things through. You don't give a damn about consequences, who might get hurt along the way."

"I do care," he said, and his voice sounded weak even to himself.

"You said she was a piece of your life that got away, with the same loss as you. That perhaps you're both connected, and that if you could get back together, maybe it would help you both."

"I know what I said."

"But you didn't think it through. You barreled in."

"I was trying to help her. I made him leave. I didn't know she'd take him back and he'd hurt her even worse."

"You haven't learned a damn thing about people in all the years you've been at the job. You think you can so easily unknot somebody's wiring when they've got their signals between love and pain crossed? If you could do that you might not be so fucked up yourself."

"I thought she might be ready."

"Yeah? Why? You don't know her. You don't know a thing about her. You don't even know yourself."

He didn't have to admit to it. He understood she was right. He'd gone to set Emma Waltz free from her past and he'd simply imposed more of it on her. He went to ease her pain and she'd taken another beating for it. Goddamn it.

The door opened and shut, opened and shut. Flynn wanted to snarl like an animal. Nuddin walked up behind him, ready to fling his arms around him again. But instantly sensing the mood, Nuddin began to moan.

Flynn turned and said, "It's okay, buddy. It's all right. This isn't about you, everything's fine."

Nuddin tottered forward and rested his face on Flynn's chest, then rushed out the back door to join the others.

Flynn stepped to the window and stared at Kelly out there surrounded by foster kids. Most of them had come from poverty and middle-class bitterness. From unemployed parents hitting the bottle too hard. From crackhead daddies and cocaine-heeled mommies who went in and out of rehab or jail.

Her story was different. Kelly would someday inherit millions. He didn't know the legalities of it. He didn't know how long each night Sierra spent talking with attorneys trying to help and protect the girl. What her attorney fees might be, how closely she dealt with Shepard's doctors.

"Is Kelly all right?" he asked.

"She still hasn't cried. I thought it would've happened by now. She's seeing Mooney, and he's helping a little. But you're right, when it hits, it'll hit hard. I hope it's soon, so I can help her."

And if it takes thirty years, he thought, she'll wind up like me.

"You're not fired. Go back to your desk. You've got cases."

"But—"

"Shut up. Don't argue. Maybe you've learned a lesson, maybe you haven't. I'll be watching even closer. You'd think a guy who'd come back from being dead for a half hour would learn to appreciate his second chances more."

"I do. What about my psych evaluation?"

"Forget about that."

"But then why did you—"

"Don't give me any more lip. Just go. Kelly and Nuddin seem to really care about you. I was wrong keeping you separated from them. I can learn from my mistakes. Can you?"

That was the question all right. Flynn lit a cigarette and stood there thinking about it, the laughter and screams of children filling the yard and the house and his head.

SEVENTEEN

Jessie Gray showed up at his door while he was watching the seventies remake of *Double Indemnity* with Richard Crenna and Lee J. Cobb standing in for Fred MacMurray and Edward G. Robinson. It was an interesting failure, lots of flair cuffs, porkchop sideburns and shag rugs replacing the cool smoky shadows and Venetian blinds, but it still held Flynn's attention. He had his .38 out in his hand, the barrel pressed to the door in case he had to fire through it.

She stood there smiling, slid inside followed by a swirl of falling snow, held him in her arms and turned her lips up to his. The gun didn't bother her.

Her nose and lips were cold and she toyed with his tongue until her skin heated. She pressed a palm to the side of his face and kept it there rubbing back and forth. He had no idea what to say to her.

She threw her jacket on his kitchen table and asked, "What happened to your apartment?"

"What happened to it?"

"I mean, your walls. They're mostly bare. Where'd all your rare original posters go?"

Like digging into a tender spot, it made him wince to focus on the empty walls. "I sold most of them," he admitted. "I needed cash to get the Dodge fixed. The insurance hasn't come through yet."

"Your brother's car."

"Stop saying that. It's my car."

"But it has meaning to you because it was your brother's."

"So what?"

A shrug and a flutter of eyebrows was all he got. It was her way, to keep him on his toes, always aware that anything he might do or say could end up in ink. He had to face up to the fact that he was a little scared of her.

Jessie met his eyes, grinned at him, and said, "You're the 'Finn' guy that Chad Rocca of 121 Dolan Place put a complaint in about, aren't you?"

She watched him. He thought he kept his features expressionless but her grin grew wider. He was really bad at this game. He had to stop letting her in.

She put her hand back on his face while he finally got around to holstering the .38 and said, "Emma Waltz's boyfriend. You stormed in there to kick ass. Why? What's this got to do with her?"

She was a better reporter than she'd originally led him to believe, all that crap about her father pulling strings to land her a job, making it seem like she didn't deserve her position. Maybe it had been true at the time, but not anymore. She was first-rate. He wondered if the rest of them at *Newsday* worried about her working her way up the ranks, nabbing their jobs.

Every time he turned around somebody else was coming at him, aware of something he wanted to keep secret. As if he wasn't backed against the wall enough. Knowing there were people out there digging beneath the floorboards of his life was getting to him.

"It has nothing to do with anything that might interest you," he told her.

It was the wrong thing to say and he knew it the instant the words were out of his mouth. Her smile broadened. He thought it was beautiful, or would've been if it wasn't always aimed at him like a high-powered spotlight.

He champed his lips shut and sealed his tongue to the roof of his mouth, wondering why the fuck he ever talked to anybody.

"You're wrong," she said. "It's layering, it's back story. It fleshes you out, that's what makes this such a hot item. It ties together, it's the reason why you're who you are. That's what people like to read about. And who knows, it may even have something to do with the Shepards. With Colonel Bragg maybe."

Pleased with herself for a job well-done, she eased through the apartment like a woman deciding if she wanted to move in. She looked at the high corners. The empty walls gave an impression of space. She opened the blinds and his pulse picked up speed. He came up behind her quickly and shut them again. It made her giggle. The little girl's voice slid into him like a fishing blade. He hadn't shaved for three days and knew the white in his beard was showing. You could drive yourself crazy with your petty embarrassments in the light of major tragedy. Nothing could make you live with yourself any easier.

"You really should leave this case alone," he said.

"Is that your way of saying you don't want to see me anymore?"

He hadn't been sure they were seeing each other anyway, but she certainly knew how to work herself into his life and take different tacks whenever she thought they could help ease her forward. That's what the kiss was all about. He thought she might even take it into the bedroom, throw him a tumble just to see what else she could use to flesh him out. It both aroused him and really irritated the hell out of him.

"Are you still mad at me?" she asked, genuinely surprised.

"I told you already, you shouldn't be with me."

"And I told you I know what I'm doing."

"But you don't."

She shrugged. "Well, nobody knows as much as they want to, right?" The idea seemed to inspire her. With a lot of loose action in her hips, she sort of sashayed to the kitchen. "The only plant you have is a cactus?"

"I have it for warmth."

"It doesn't look too good." She scoped the nearly empty fridge and said, "Not even a beer? You may be the only guy I've ever met who doesn't stock beer."

"I don't like it much."

"Is that because of your father?"

Flynn flinched. She'd been talking to Marianne. Marianne was the only one alive who knew anything about Flynn's father.

He waited to see where she would take this. If his feelings meant anything to her or if her emotional compass was so off that she felt she could push against all his black doors until they buckled.

She checked his eyes and her grin froze there and flaked apart. He thought she would apologize, but she didn't. Perhaps she didn't understand she was supposed to. She simply stood there with a sorrowful expression that lasted only as long as it took her to walk up to him and put her hand on his chest.

She patted him there, a sign of understanding but nothing more. Things with this girl, he thought, could go very bad very quickly.

"I interviewed Detective Raidin," she told him. "I think he likes you."

"No, he doesn't."

"He didn't say so, but I sensed his respect for you. What they call a grudging respect, no doubt, but it's there."

"I know what they call it," Flynn said, "and no, he doesn't feel that. He can't afford to. He's a cop. He doesn't know where I fit in. He has to reserve judgment. It's what makes him such a difficult bastard."

"Are you still mad because he hit you in the throat?"

It made him frown. "You saw that?"

"Yeah, but I pretended not to. I didn't want to embarrass you. And I didn't want to irritate him."

Of course. He clearly remembered Jessie Gray talking into the phone, glancing over at him anxiously but not coming to help. "No, you wouldn't have been in as good a position to interview him then."

"That's right."

He could only stare. It was what he found himself doing more than anything else in his relationships with women.

Standing there watching, seeing Frickin' Alvin climbing off the bed. Looking at his wife. Looking at Emma Waltz. Looking at Jessie Gray. An inability to comprehend.

"You still don't trust me," she said, "which is good."

"It is?"

"It means you're smart, but I already knew that."

"You did."

"Yes. That's why we're having something distinctive."

There was that word again. It sounded even more hollow and cold this time around. The fact that she said it while showing her teeth gave him greater pause. She flipped her hair aside and a slash of light coming down from a bent edge of the blinds highlighted her face.

He saw the soft down beneath her left ear and, somehow, it drew him to her. Anything could do it. You never knew what was going to reach out and grab your guts and pull you forward. Here he was moving toward her again, understanding that it was stupid, that it would end badly. She would smooth his mysteries all over the headlines, and he wouldn't be able to do much besides watch.

Swaying around his apartment like she was dancing, she moved around him in tightening concentric circles. He didn't turn when she slid behind him, then slipped in front. Maybe it was just her game of seduction, maybe it was something all the kids did.

She pressed against his chest and they kissed. He twisted her in his arms and this time there was more passion than before because he was angry. Just as much heat and lust. He was hard and starting to feel a little crazy. Crazier. He knew if they broke apart now she would say something he would regret, and he wondered what it might be.

Flynn pulled back and eased a step away from her.

Jessie Gray, her lips pink from the force of his own, said, "Would you mind if I interviewed your wife?"

There it was. You had to give it to her, boy.

"My ex. You mean you haven't already?"

"I tried your wife's place, but I got some guy named Al."

"My ex. And her new beau. So you talked to Alvin."

She was digging again, reaching for the deeper story. He wondered why in the hell he'd let her in. Why he'd kissed her, why even now he wanted to take her to bed when he knew she cared nothing for him. When he realized he hardly liked her. Her shallowness must be attractive to him.

He still wanted Marianne, for Christ's sake. He seriously needed to sit down and examine these bent romantic urges soon.

"Al likes you," Jessie said. "And your wife discusses you a lot with him, so you're very much a topic of conversation."

"Terrific."

"He talked about your father to me, told me you were very angry about him. He didn't know anything about your brother though."

So Marianne told him about the old man, but not Danny. Why would that be?

He stared at Jessie as she continued. "Al follows you in the papers and on the news. He actually turned red when I mentioned your name."

"Alvin got caught in a bad situation."

"Yes, I could see that. He mentioned how—"

He cut her off and said, "Do you really think I want to discuss any of this with you, Jessie? My father? My ex?"

You could get backed into a corner and spend all week with people trying to get you to talk about shit you didn't want to talk about. They acted like you owed it to them, coming clean on every last little feeling. Your secrets were only yours so long as they let you keep them. The dark nerve skewered through him. Jessie Gray was sharp but couldn't read a person's face. If she could, she would've shut up by now.

She looked confounded. At the zoo or the circus it would've been cute. Surrounded by the dead it wasn't.

She asked, "Why not?"

"Because it's more rotten, rude things. And don't tell me that means you like me or want to marry me."

She took his hand and immediately dropped it. The movement had meaning. Every movement did.

"You didn't beat him up, though. You didn't hurt Alvin but you hurt this other guy, Chad Rocco."

"I didn't hurt him either. I just kept him from burning his garage down."

"He reported that you struck him."

"I didn't."

Either Chad was lying to get Flynn in worse trouble or he was covering up for the fact that maybe Emma hadn't taken a beating without dishing some out.

"I did some checking on your Emma Waltz," Jessie said. "The sister of the girl your brother killed. She hasn't led a very happy life."

"I know."

"And you want to save her. You want to save her to make up for what Danny did to her sister."

No point in lying. "Yes, I think so."

"It's a very simplistic attitude and it's set you on a hard-line course."

"That's me."

"You didn't think it through at all. You just run in and bounce the guy around and you didn't expect him to take it out on her?"

"I didn't bounce him. I even introduced myself."

She shook her head, disappointed in him. "Chad Rocco told the cops you beat both of them up."

"He's covering his own ass."

"And she let him, that's my point. She didn't see you as a white knight." Jessie frowned, really giving it to him the way his mother used to. "Did she even recognize you? Your name?"

"I don't know."

"You have some truly goofy issues."

"I'm well aware of that," he told her.

She walked to the bedroom and stood in the doorway, checking his bed out. The room was spartan at best. He had one pillow. He had one winter blanket and one comforter. Marianne had taken away all the softness, the comfortable lived-in look of the place. Except for the bed and a single dresser, he'd never bothered to replace any of the furniture she'd taken. Or the once-abundant niceties and color and blithe aesthetic. He didn't know how.

Jessie turned, hit a nice pose with her hand on her hip, leaning against the jamb, her hair angling over one eye. He'd seen it in five hundred movies, but seeing it now with her it was something totally new. He wet his lips. The area between his shoulder blades began to feel clammy and itchy.

"You still worried about me?" she asked.

"Yes."

"I'm still coming on too strong for you. I can't help myself. I'm attracted to you. My therapist isn't helping me at all with you. I talk and talk about you. He's fascinated by you as well."

"Maybe you should fire him. He sounds a little nutty."

"You're starting to want me, aren't you?"

She sat on the bed and swung her legs up onto the mattress. She was a little too young to make the come-hither look work, but there was a heat coming off her now.

He scratched at his stubble and she said, "What if it's true? What if I do like you?"

"I think you need to untangle your wiring and find a husband you'll stick with. You should stop running after the wrong guys."

"Sound advice," she said. "I wonder if anybody's ever taken it. You only go after the right women?"

"No."

"Like I said—"

"It's another of my goofy issues."

She pulled a face. "Stop obsessing with your white hair, Miracle Man. Jesus Christ, you're worse than my mother." She started unbuttoning her blouse and got the smile back into place. The fever in her eyes passed into him.

Still, he didn't move until she told him, "Now come over here, Miracle Man, and fuck me."

EIGHTEEN

In the night, Flynn got up and checked the front door, the windows, all the locks. He opened the blinds and stared out at the glowing silver snow, willing a sniper to put him in the crosshairs, thinking he might see the bullet coming and just step aside. Then run out there, his crank hanging, rushing through the ice that had killed him once and saved him once already, hoping it might happen again.

If only he could get his hands on the figure out there, waiting, anguished but holding on.

The empty white walls burned in the darkness. He no longer had the decades of the cool and the hip protecting him in here. Bogie no longer gave him the knowing eye. Betty's cheesecake that got American GIs through the Pacific Theater wasn't going to get Flynn through anything anymore.

Sliding back under the blanket, he smoked in the dark and waited to get smart enough to figure out his next move.

He thought Jessie was sleeping but she stirred beside him. He'd left the bathroom light on and it threw just enough illumination for him to see the outline of her lips as she spoke. "I like older men. You all screw like you have something to prove."

Talk about a left-handed compliment. "We do."

"I'm glad."

She couldn't seem to help herself. Every statement out of her mouth left him sort of cold. He thought she probably planned such comments carefully just to see the reaction. He saw a lot more ex-husbands in her future.

He'd been handling his involvement with Jessie Gray all wrong. She'd been digging into his life when he should've been getting her to help him. He'd been saying it since he'd first met her. She was a good journalist. Maybe she could teach him something.

"What do you know about Bragg?" he asked.

"He's dead."

"They never found his body."

"That's not as uncommon as people are led to believe. You figure if someone throws themselves into the river, they'll float to the surface and get fished out sooner or later. But the Chatalaha runs into deep swampland and morass. Plenty of people are lost to the gators and other animals in the bogs."

"Christina Shepard spoke of him like he was alive."

"Maybe she had a daddy complex. I have one. A lot of my friends do too. They're pretty common."

He didn't want to think about where she might be heading with that and tried to focus on Bragg. He lit another cigarette.

Christina Shepard, the girl who'd once been Crissy Bragg before making it all the way to a million-dollar house on Long Island, had said, "We take such things seriously in my family. Our name is important. Our history." The husband had said, "Your father's never been right about anything in his life, that crazy son of a bitch." Treating the man like he was alive. Unable to believe he was dead. Was it just the incapacity of two people to forget a forceful personality?

Flynn played it out. Christina Shepard flying down there to maybe care for the man while he was losing his mind? Keeping Nuddin locked up to protect him from the world? Protect the family name? A name already tainted with a bizarre history and a crazy colonel running around shooting up a playground? He thought of what Sierra had told him about autistics. How they had difficulty understanding the contours of their own body. Therapy included weighted vests and special shoes to help keep them from floating off into their own heads. Is that what the beatings were about? Was it possible that Nuddin had done it to himself just to feel something? Jesus. Maybe the cage was their way of continuing with the therapy.

Jessie was still talking. "I did an article once on a woman who slept with her father. They hadn't seen each other in twenty years, since she was eight or nine years old, and she hunted him down and seduced him without his ever realizing he'd been to bed with his own daughter. She wrote a book about it and did the talk-show circuit. Everybody wanted her at their parties, colleges paid big money to have her lecture."

Flynn wondered what in the hell a woman who'd fucked her father could possibly say in a lecture besides the fact that she had fucked her father.

"She used a pseudonym to protect him, but I found out their names and tracked him down. He was living in a little burg in North Carolina, but by the time I got down there a couple other journalists had cracked the story and he'd killed himself. Got drunk, climbed up onto a roof and threw himself on one of those wrought-iron weather vanes."

There it was again, the need to shock. Flynn looked at her. "This is the goddamnedest postcoital discussion I've ever had."

"Well, anyway, I do hope you realize I'm not here with you because you're older than me. It's not that kind of complex, not for me anyway. My dad was always away, traveling, chasing stories all over the world. Christina Shepard's father was one of those guys who put in his time to the Army, rose quickly and distinguished himself early on. He took his family with him everywhere but who knows about Nuddin. That guy could've been in a school for years down there, or off with some other family member. Some great-uncle out in the swamps."

All these investigators, all this wealth of facts at everyone's fingertips, and when it came down to it nobody really knew shit about anything.

Jessie went on. "He retired a colonel after he was diagnosed with cancer of the brain. He refused to check himself into a hospital or accept any treatment, possibly because he'd seen his wife slowly dying from cancer as well. He started going crazy."

"Yeah, shot up a playground."

"You know this already."

"I know this already. Did you manage to find anything at all on Nuddin?"

"No. And I searched. I should've come up with something. Maybe she was lying. Maybe he's not her brother at all. The police checked to see if there were any missing mentally challenged men but they came up empty. Nuddin's prints didn't match anything they had on file."

"So what's it mean?"

"I don't know, but it bothers me." She said it with some bite, as if finding the truth was a challenge that prodded her ego. She'd missed out on the guy who fucked his daughter, but she didn't want to get scooped here by anyone. Not the cops, not by Flynn.

She touched his chest, wafted the back of her hand across his belly. Sweeping back and forth, drawing her fingernails lightly all over him in patterns he tried to read. "Do you think you could get me in past your boss to interview Shepard's daughter?"

"No chance."

"I could get Kelly's story."

"It's not her story."

"Or Nuddin?"

"Nuddin doesn't talk."

"You don't even want to try?"

"No."

"You should," she said. Her voice took on a harder tone that made him turn his chin to her. "The papers, the media, they're not just a bunch of animals picking at the living. Headlines have real power. You could turn them to your advantage. We might be able to draw your bad guy out, lead him into a trap."

"I think you should sit back and be my go-to man," Flynn told her. "I'll front run this thing, you be the behind-the-scenes gal who actually solves the crime. Let me be the Neanderthal."

"You're not that tough."

"You're right. But help me to figure this out anyway."

He slumped back on the pillows and Jessie Gray unwound her body across his, running her lips against his throat.

"I'm a beautiful young thing lying in your bed on a snowy night, wanting you, needing you, throwing out all kinds of damn signals so you'll roll over and screw me again, and you want to keep talking about murder. You want my therapist's number?"

NINETEEN

After they'd made love again, Jessie fell asleep with her head resting on his belly. She semisnored, puffing quietly through her lips, a strand of hair wafting and falling and drifting again. Flynn lay there watching it, trying not to breathe too hard so he didn't jostle her, his thoughts turning redder while he knocked out his second pack since midnight.

The phone rang at 2 A.M.

He eased her aside. Jessie didn't wake. He padded into the kitchen and answered. "Hello?"

He heard nothing, and he almost repeated himself. But the silence soon emerged into the room with him, a great atmosphere of emptiness. The silence stretched on for ten seconds, twenty, thirty, then more than a minute. And then, in a great leap it became some amount of time he couldn't guess at. He moved through the years and the years moved through him.

This is it, Flynn thought. He's on the line. If the cops still have me bugged, maybe this is the mistake that'll reel the shadow out of the snow and into the fire.

But he knew the cops had packed it all up. Maybe for a

second time, maybe for a third, but they were gone and Flynn, for all his ghosts, was alone.

Behind him, his dead brother stepped out from some black corner, coming closer until he was nearly next to Flynn and yet somehow still hadn't reached him.

Zero sat on the rug and stared solemnly at him, his nub of a tail twitching. Flynn shut his eyes and urged himself deeper into the receiver listening for any sound.

His mother came in and put her hand on his shoulder.

His old man, where the hell was his old man? Figures his father wouldn't show. He was haunting some other family in the house where he'd died, sitting in their recliner, in front of their television, staring down some exorcist hurling holy water at him. The old man just sipping his beer, cursing out the Jets quarterback.

The phone wanted to fly out of his hand. There was a dark power in it, either from the killer or from Flynn or maybe because of them both. You could never tell if the evil urged you forward or if you cajoled it toward you. Flynn thought perhaps God Himself was calling to discuss paying off some old debts.

He clenched the phone tighter. The plastic groaned in his fist. There was only an immense swelling of despair and desolation. So great he never would have believed it before his death.

He almost spoke Emma's name.

Zero said, "Who is it? Is it for me?"

"It's you," he said into the phone. The waiting continued. "You want to tell me what this is all about? Is it Christina Shepard or something else?"

He was there again, in the Charger, watching the water

swell across his face, feeling himself dying with numbness first and then the pervasive nothingness that followed. He wondered what it would be like the second time he started down the midnight road. If it would happen in a similar way, in the car, or if would just be a bullet to the head, a taser to the heart.

He started to tremble in the cold, aware of his own weakness. He embraced it because it humanized him. He didn't take such things for granted anymore. Not after experiencing that instant *before* he returned to life, when he did not exist, and never had and never would.

"Well?" he said.

"*I am afflicted,*" a whisper told him.

He couldn't tell if it was male or female. That wasn't so easy to do. You always leaned one way or another, but Flynn really couldn't get any kind of bead.

There was anguish in the voice. The deep sorrow that literally tore people apart, gave them pneumonia, shattered their teeth, sent them to the madhouse. Flynn got the sense that the voice itself had no name, that the thing the person had now become had never been identified. It lurked unseen and unknown, perhaps even to itself.

"What's that got to do with me? What do you want from me?"

Zero pawed at Flynn's ankle and said, "Tell him I said hello."

Maybe Bragg really had hit the river and been smashed against rocks by the rapids. He could've started off crazy and gotten steadily worse. Maybe Bragg was out of his mind, all right, but Flynn couldn't put the voice together with a military man, no matter how far out of his tree he may have gone. Maybe this was Frickin' Alvin's doing. Maybe Chad's. Maybe Shepard had a brother out there blaming Flynn. Flynn had gotten under somebody's skin and had infected the hell out of him.

"Thanks for giving me a ring," Flynn said, a little light-headed. "I appreciate it." His lips squirmed across his face, he couldn't be sure what they were doing. "Now listen up. I'm going to put a hot knife through you. I'm going to spit in your blood."

The connection broke. Flynn waited, still listening, afraid to move. His mother left him. Danny faded back. Zero sat on the couch peering down at the open newspaper. He was checking the Dow.

Flynn touched his mouth and realized he was grinning. He couldn't help it.

He'd outwaited the bastard. He'd been able to stand it longer than the spook in the shadows. He didn't have to chase anybody, the bad boy was going to keep coming after him, to him. But that would take time, and Flynn hoped no one else would get murdered.

One way or another it would be over soon. Flynn went back to bed, wrapped his arms around Jessie Gray and had his first good night's sleep since he'd died.

TWENTY

Mooney sat behind his desk in his leather wingback chair and had a whole new tic going. He toyed with his shaggy beard, brushing it outward from his neck, then smoothing it back into place. Out and back, repetitively, consistently. Giving Flynn the professional cool eye the entire time he jacked his beard.

Flynn tried to ignore all the things he mistrusted about Mooney. He forced himself to look through the man's issues—layers and webs and veils just like Flynn had himself—and simply see someone who might be able to help him find out what he needed to know about the shadow in the snow.

Mooney stared at Flynn and said nothing. The moment lengthened, the mood remained cool but not altogether cold. Mooney was warming to the idea that Flynn had come back on his own. The initial obscene fascination that Mooney had shown wasn't there this time around.

"I won't ask you to lie down," Mooney said.

"Good, see that? We're making progress already."

"I notice you're wearing your gun today."

"Yes, I am."

"I'm not comfortable with that."

"I don't blame you," Flynn said, but he didn't unclip the .38.

Again steepling his fingers, Mooney rested his chin on them. Flynn wondered why Mooney found the position so comfortable and why he himself found it so irritating. Why everything annoyed him in here, even the smell of the leather furniture polish. Somebody had really given the place a serious dousing.

"I'm surprised you've come back," Mooney said.

"Me a lot more than you."

"But I can appreciate that you're trying to get to the root of your problems."

"Actually, I think I need your help with something else."

"I see," Mooney said. "All right then. You seem to be under less strain."

"I know I'll catch him now."

"The killer? Why is that?"

"I can outlast him."

Flynn mentioned the notes and the phone call. The fact that the shadow in the blizzard was unraveling just a little faster than Flynn was himself. Mooney wavered between fascination, self-interest and a genuine desire to help. Flynn knew Mooney must be in analysis himself and wondered what the man's psychiatrist thought of him.

But he couldn't let himself become distracted. He caught Mooney's gaze, looked deep and thought he made some contact. If Mooney was going to be able to help him at all, now was the time.

Flynn asked, "What's he trying to tell me?"

"On the face it's self-evident. The subject is in pain."

"Sure, but what can I do with that? How do I draw him out?"

Mooney quit it with the tics and just sat there, centered, confident. Sitting with Flynn like two guys taking in a beer, watching a ball game. "I'm not absolutely certain that's applicable. We already know what draws him. You do."

"Yeah."

"And he uses others to send his messages. So to bring him forward is to endanger others. We don't want to urge him out in the same fashion as before."

Flynn had to rethink it. "No. How do I get him to focus all of his attention on me?"

"You're assuming I know all the details. I don't. Start at the beginning."

You could go back and back and never quite get to the beginning. Flynn decided to take a chance and laid it out, starting with Shepard's tip. Nuddin in the cage, scarred. Christina Shepard holding the gun, the talk of her father, her husband's betrayal, the escape into the ice, the wipeout in the Long Island Sound. The murders. He still kept the dead talking dog to himself.

"Do you have specific questions?" Mooney asked.

"First, why this aggression toward Nuddin? The beatings, the cage?"

"There's no clear-cut answer of course. The family may have felt humiliated by the fact that they had a mentally challenged person in the family. Or it may have been an attempt at some kind of rehabilitation. Autism is still a vastly unknown disorder referenced with a great many conflicting theories and contradictory forms of treatment."

"She said she was protecting him. Saving him from the world."

"Typical of such personality disorder, the need to 'overprotect' to the point of harming the individual. It's fear-related, I believe, not instilled anger, evidence to the contrary. We think of one person hurting another as an act of rage, but it can be an act of love as well, misguided or not. A simplistic example is of a father spanking a child to teach him not to play with matches. A more pertinent illustration might be a mother terrified for her teenage daughter's safety when the girl doesn't return all night. In the morning, when the daughter returns home safe and sound, the terrified and frazzled mother smacks her, perhaps beats her mercilessly. The motivation is love and fear entwined. Self-hatred projected outward but catalyzed by you. Implemented through you."

Flynn whispered, "But what did I do?"

"The subject's rage at himself...it's escalating. He's losing control, the phone call proves that, but he remains immensely patient. Killing the old woman in the theater ladies' room demonstrates that."

"He started off by shooting a woman in the head, and *now* he's losing control?"

"That's not where your lives intersected. He chose you before that point for some unknown reason. But in essence, yes. The killer is calculated and involved with your life. Collected, dedicated, forbearing. But his direct communications with you—the letters and the phone call—that is the subject emotionally uncoiling. That's him

at his weakest. He values your participation in these situ-
ations. Your opinion must matter to him."

"Jesus Christ. Why?"

"Perhaps it is someone you know very well."

Mooney was great at stating the obvious, but hearing it
again, out loud, made Flynn think about it even harder.
Did he already know who the killer was? Had he seen a
glimpse of a face but just wasn't getting it?

On film they slowed down the movie and did a nice big
close-up of the single frame where the killer can be seen.
Maybe some people really could remember like that, if
they focused and tried hard enough, but Flynn just couldn't
get there.

"I don't understand how it's all connected. The suffering and the rage, and the love and the fear."

"Perhaps it's not," Mooney said, throwing it out while
stroking his beard again. He was onto something. He felt
proud of himself. "Perhaps you're actually dealing with
two individuals here."

Two shadows in the snow. Two figures bracing him on
the road. Getting bumped on either side and squeezed
down the middle of the lane.

Frickin' Alvin and Marianne. Chad and Emma. Mooney
and Sierra, teaming up to wipe Flynn out of the game for
reasons he couldn't understand. Sure, why not, you never
knew anyone the way you thought you did. You didn't
even know yourself. Maybe Shepard had two brothers.
Maybe Bragg had picked up a partner. Flynn saw himself,
brain-damaged and bisected, a split personality doing all
this to himself, then forgetting about it. *Sure, why not, you
never knew—*

Flynn slumped in the chair and said, "Ah shit, don't tell me that." He turned to the window and thought about who might be out there and how many of them there were. Why stop at two? Maybe three. Maybe ten. A hundred cars following the Dodge under the ice. A fucking gridlock on the midnight road.

TWENTY-ONE

The snow kept falling. Flynn worked his cases. The winter got worse. Sierra watched him and made sure he was doing his job, that he wasn't coasting too lost in his own troubles. She didn't fully trust him anymore. The wedge was there and might always be there now, and the idea of it saddened him.

He knocked back the files and folders. He worked in a frenzy. He chased down bad dads and mean mommies. He kept his eyes open, wondering when the folks in the snow were going to make their charge. Every time someone passed him in a hallway he looked for a note in their hands. Every time he stepped into a men's room, he wondered if he'd find a body zapped in the stall. He hounded abusive fathers and stupid mothers and he called in the Suffolk cops more than he ever had before. Maybe he was worried his judgment was off. He was worried about being worried.

Sierra triple-checked his paperwork to make sure he wasn't fudging details. She held semiclandestine meetings with Mooney and other coworkers. If he'd taken better care of the damn cactus, things might be altogether different.

He read through files at home and spent his off-hours checking on kids. A greater number of bad tips and false leads came in. The rotten weather shook people up. They saw bundled children running into each other with sleds and figured something awful was about to happen. The more ice that layered across their lives, the more bored they got and the more they needed to serve their drama and pained intuition.

Flynn worked through the cases at redline speed. He cleared his stacks and went looking for more. He caught a couple of religious loons who belonged to the same cultish church, a converted two-room schoolhouse that had been around for nearly a century. The whack jobs picked it up for loose change and hammered up a crucifix that showed Jesus even more skeletal and hairier than usual. They were big believers in not sparing the rod. One Sunday Flynn slipped inside to check out the services. He wasn't there forty minutes when he saw the preacher pick up an eleven- or twelve-year-old boy, shake him violently in front of the congregation for no reason Flynn could see, and toss him hard to the wooden floor. The whole antique structure shook with the force of it. The preacher went into a bout of tongues. So did the boy. It was all very weird.

Flynn was careful about his hands. He waited until services ended and everybody was milling around, waiting for Armageddon. He approached the leader and wrote him up and had everybody in the place screaming except for the boy, who stared at him in mute shock and wonder.

More of them started in with the tongues. It almost made him laugh. Somebody got pushy in the name of God and Flynn knocked him down. That really got them tonguing. Somebody tongued 911.

Two cops showed up ready to throw Flynn in the slam until they checked the logs and found a lot of complaints about the place. The creepy congregation slinked off and Flynn made an on-site inspection of the boy's home the next day. He called two Suffolk cruisers in to park out front for a little extra leverage. He waited for the preacher or somebody to press charges but nobody did.

Sierra triple-checked his report two days later and gave him the stink eye, but didn't say anything.

The next afternoon he had to haul all the way out to the Hamptons, and every inch of the way he thought of Danny. He refused to go over fifty the whole ride, forcing himself to make it feel leisurely while he waited for his brother to appear in the rearview. He waited for the dog to snap off a caustic comment. He waited for Patricia to make a move and give him the clues to saving Emma. But the whole drive he was alone and couldn't figure out why.

Once out there, in a beach house built on an eroding coast, with the shoreline moving in on the foundation and probably costing the family everything they owned, he found the father edging into oblivion.

Drunk with his insurance papers and bank statements and two calculators laid out on the living room table, the man refused to take Flynn's hand. A fireplace designed to perfection for roasting marshmallows burned and crackled.

Inside, the place vibed millionaire, comfort, class, style,

home on the heath, beautiful people united against the peasants of industry. Outside, the house was maybe a year from tilting into the ocean.

It would tear anybody up, investing in a castle that wouldn't last until next Christmas. All your poor cousins laughing at you. Having to crash on your sister's couch because you blew a few mill buying a disaster area. Flynn could see the guy about to fall into the sea himself.

His name was Kenton. Flynn had done a quick background check and liked that the mook had worked his way up from the bottom of the construction crew world. He'd spent years at a cement mixer and breaking rock with a jackhammer. Kenton's powerful, muscular body tightened under Flynn's questioning.

The wife and daughter seeped from the living room corners. Flynn saw plenty of shadowed bruises and black fingerprints on them as they cowered beneath prints of Dutch masters' paintings. The girl's left arm had been wrapped in a sling. Flynn stood there wondering why the wealthy had it so bad.

Kenton's angry talk eventually shifted into threats and devolved into worse. Flynn waited for him to jump. It would happen soon. He didn't even have to meet another man's rage head-on, all he had to do was stand there and the poison would pool on the floor.

Flynn just kept listening to him while the snow piled against the windows and the thermostat maintained a perfect seventy degrees and you could feel the place sinking by atoms. The smoky smell of the burning logs filled his mind with childhood memories that weren't his own. He thought of his parents feeding each other pumpkin pie, laughing as they held each other and swung beneath mistletoe, and he and Danny sat opening presents in front of the fire. The whole family going outside to build an igloo and make snow angels. It was never too late to dream about a happy childhood.

Finally the little girl started to cry and the shushing sounds of her mother filled the room and Kenton started blaming Flynn for making his daughter cry.

"See that!" the man shouted. "See what you've done now!"

It was so ludicrous that Flynn couldn't help letting out a little disgusted laugh. It got Kenton's eyes bugging, the thick veins in his temples slithering. Flynn shot the mother a sympathetic glance, went to the table, grabbed up a couple of the financial forms and threw them into the fire.

A tidal roar fluttered Kenton's lips as his face went purple. You'd think he'd have been happy. Flynn had just done what Kenton had wanted to do for months, maybe years. For a large, furious man he moved slowly, warily, knowing he was about to cross a whole new line now.

He stomped forward, waiting for Flynn to throw a punch or dance away, totally confused when Flynn didn't move at all. Kenton drew back his fist.

The wife let loose a plaintive cry and the girl mimicked her, then they turned toward each other and held on, resigned to death.

Seeing his mother and father on their backs in the snow, waving their arms making wings, Danny going by on a sleigh, it was enough to make Flynn shake his head and realize how carried away you could get no matter the circumstances. The shadow in the blizzard must've had plenty of happy fictitious memories veering around his skull while he electrocuted Florence. Maybe seeing himself with Angela Soto, loving her and ringed with happy fat children, even while he shot her face off.

Kenton's swing still not even fully drawn back to the shoulder. Flynn's mind and muscles were light-years ahead, warping around the sun. He could go home, take a nap, drive back here, get back in place and Kenton's massive fist still wouldn't have reached him.

Flynn wanted a wild drag-out. He wanted to take off his clothes and dive into the ocean. He wanted somebody to tell him if his life was making any difference to anybody at all except the shadow in the snow, who was the only one who seemed to give a shit.

The girl hiding her face behind the sling, the mother trying to do the same thing. Both of them terrified of Kenton's raised arm.

Flynn wanted to match wrath and righteous pain.

He wanted to behold the cosmic scales of outrage and misfortune and see how he and Kenton stacked up against each other. Who hurt more. How many dead brothers did Kenton have in his backseat? How many talking ghost dogs knocked out quips and urged him to let go with his worst potential?

Flynn still had plenty of time. He wanted to drag the lug by the ear and dump him in front of his kid. He thought about handing Louisville sluggers to the wife and daughter and letting them pound the crap out of the thug. It would take some creative manipulation of the paperwork, but Flynn figured it would be worth it.

Here came the fist.

But before it reached Flynn it veered and fell and Kenton sank to his knees.

This huge man just hunched there, his eyes wide and seeing some of his mistakes and the extent of his actions, turning to look at his wife and kid. He probably hadn't cried in more than thirty years either.

Kenton seemed to be meeting himself inside himself. His shoulders sagged and began to shake. The sobbing began down in his throat with a childish wail seeking escape. It rose and he looked puzzled, as if wondering where it was coming from. His rheumy eyes closed as if against a great wind, and when they opened again they were full of tears. Flynn felt a strange and sudden rush of jealousy.

The mother and daughter took a step forward as Kenton held his hands up in front of himself, waving them like a baby in a crib. His mouth opened wide and his tongue flopped loose as his cheeks reddened and glittered wetly.

The family piled together in the center of the room, crying and hugging and begging forgiveness. Their murmurs at once heartened and sickened Flynn. He wanted to steal the girl. He didn't want to offer second chances. He wished the fist had continued on its trajectory so he could have been within his rights to have shattered the bruiser's collarbone.

Sometimes you allow yourself to feel remorse and mercy. Sometimes you don't.

He went to the fire, threw another log on, and left them there.

The cool air hit him like the force of his own twisted, backward envy.

He was starting to think that maybe he wasn't going to outlast the figure in the blizzard after all.

Flynn was afflicted too. Whatever happened next had to happen fast.

TWENTY-TWO

The next morning Patricia Waltz, thirty years dead, pregnant with Danny's baby, stood at the door with snow in her hair.

No blood on her mouth now, just a plum-colored bruise at the corner of her lips. A shadow high on her cheek under her eye was carefully concealed with makeup. It had been a bad shiner a few days ago but was healing up nicely. She held a folded piece of paper in her hand. She said something quietly under her breath. Flynn thought it might've been his name, but he couldn't be sure.

He reached out and wrapped his arms around her, wishing he had the time to truly feel and hold her but already knowing the moment was up as he yanked her sideways, turning so he could block her with his body even as they fell.

A gout of wood and metal exploded from the jamb.

Two more shots tore minor scuffs out of the floor. He purposefully left the door open instead of kicking it closed just so he might see muzzle flash or the gleam off a rifle barrel. He wasn't smart enough to figure this out without putting his life on the line for it, but that didn't matter now. The snow helped him. He saw the black figure in the distance at the end of the parking lot.

Finally.

Time had been on hold ever since Kenton had lifted his fist. Now it began to whip-snap along again. Flynn lay on top of Emma Waltz for a moment, enjoying the human contact. She looked so much like her dead sister that she'd spooked him for a second. Her hair had fallen back across her face. He brushed it aside. Her mouth twitched but her eyes were dead. She was in shock and probably had been since the day Danny had thrown them both out of the Dodge.

He only had another half second to waste. He had to get moving, his chance was here.

She said nothing. He wanted to tell her that everything would be all right soon, that he would figure out a way to get them both back into the world. The moderate irritation he had felt knowing she'd folded for Chad and lied about Flynn to the cops now disappeared. He leaned down and gently kissed her bruised lips. She didn't respond and he didn't need her to. She'd brought the killer out of hiding. She'd delivered the bad boy to Flynn's door. It was an offering of love and redemption. She'd saved him.

The note fell out of her hand. It read:

I AM YOUR BROTHER

Flynn was on his feet then and out in the storm. He watched the black shape trickling away at the corner of his view, fading like everyone who'd ever meant anything to him. It could be his father. It could be Marianne. Maybe the kid he and his wife never had. Any or all of the medical students watching over Shepard, Mooney's patients, Sierra's foster kids, the other bodies floating around the Long Island Sound. It could be anyone alive or dead except maybe his brother.

He couldn't see much because of the snow. Another blizzard. It would keep coming down killing the homeless and causing wipeouts on the LIE until Flynn finished this. He would get the bad boy or the bad boy would get him, and as soon as one of them finally breathed his last the clouds would part and the sun would break through and the fucking flowers would bloom.

Flynn ran to the Dodge, got in, keyed it and felt the rush of power as the engine kicked over with a silky throaty growl. The car was in his blood, and his blood was in the car. He realized with only a touch of muted regret and surprise that he loved the Charger more than he had loved anyone in his life since Danny.

He eased it into reverse and hauled out of the parking spot, aiming for where the black blur had slid away. He wasn't worried or anxious. His pulse remained steady, his head clear. He pressed on the gas and bolted through the blizzard, aware of every element around him.

A couple of kids were playing in the yard diagonal from the parking lot exit. Behind him, his front door remained open. Emma Waltz was no longer on the floor. Her blue '89 Capri blew out a cloud of burning oil smoke as she started it up. He thought, There she goes, I'll never see her again.

He had questions but they were in the background,

quietly whispering. How'd Emma become involved? How had she been talked into handing Flynn the note? Why would she bother, what was she expecting? She had said something to him that might've been his name but he couldn't be certain.

Flynn hit the street and saw a black, souped '67 GTO hauling ass west, heading parallel to the service road of the Southern State Parkway. Flynn couldn't make out much in the whirling snow but he could hear it had a quadrijet four-barrel carburetor, 389 Ran Air engine, much quieter than the '66 Tri-power with its distinctive sound and fury. The enemy was showing Flynn that he had a car with muscle but was smart enough to park in the distance and come in almost silently. Sharp enough to weave his way into Flynn's past and trick Emma Waltz. The shadow in the blizzard had heard her voice and Flynn still hadn't.

He was chasing himself, another version of himself. A guy who had put a lot of time and money and love into a muscle car to prove he could be gentle with something carrying a lot of action and style. The car was covered in ice but Flynn could clearly see it had been well waxed. It shone. It burned black. Hours of elbow grease and ten chamoises had gone into it. So much love.

They tore along the streets in tandem, Flynn following at a nice easy pace, pouring it on when the Goat tried to make a break for it, twining along.

The roads, slick with ice and snow, tried to shake them both loose. Flynn skidded and slid whenever he had to hit the brake and ease into a turn as they jockeyed to the parkway. There was so little traffic out that it seemed the world had folded up and hitched back to the sidelines, everyone standing there in the wings waving little American flags as the Charger and Goat sped by, clocking another lap.

Zero leaped into the passenger seat, stood on his hind legs and perched himself on the dash, staring out as the wipers whipped to clear the snow.

He said, "You'll never catch him."

"He's already caught."

"You sound like an idiot when you say things like that."

"You're an irritating little shit, you know that?"

"Yes," the dead French bulldog admitted.

The Goat roared up to the entrance of the parkway. Flynn wondered if he wanted to try for it and got up to within two car lengths, struggling to see the driver. In the back window he thought he could make out the barrel of a rifle. The Goat swerved as if to hit the parkway ramp, started to pull out and then dug back in, slewing slush across the Dodge's hood. Flynn had a fair idea what kind of stunt was coming next as the Goat tried to shake him.

The bad boy was a runner. He didn't have the chops for serious driving. He was trying to make up for in nerve what he lacked in skill. Flynn put it together and could see what kind of stupid move the driver was going to make next even before he did it.

"Here we go," Flynn said.

Zero went, "I'm still dead, it doesn't matter to me."

"Glad to fuckin' hear it."

"You're still dead too, don't forget."

"Hey, Little Mr. Ray of Sunshine, you ever have anything nice to say?"

"I hear the Jets are only two games out, that's pretty good."

The Goat peeled away from the ramp, crossed the ice-choked curb and barreled across the broad expanse of deep snow piled on the median, churning west along the eastbound shoulder of the Southern State. Flynn shook his head and gave a disgusted smile. He pulled hard on the steering wheel and followed, the Charger jouncing wildly as the tires slammed across the brittle layers of ice-covered grass bordered by mountainous snow piled up by the plows.

All the traffic that had been held at bay on the side streets swarmed the parkway. Rush-hour traffic, everyone heading back from the city. Behind the shattered, dirty peaks and buttes Flynn saw cars whipping by in the opposite direction. In less than a mile the Goat would come to the first bridge and have nowhere to go except crash through the piled snow and hit the parkway straight into oncoming traffic.

The other driver knew it. Flynn could feel him worrying up there but enjoying the chance to go out head-on. Flynn sort of liked the idea too. Zero showed his fangs and said, "I always knew it would come to this. He didn't have to take you out. You were bound to do it to yourself sooner or later."

"What do we care, right?"

"Right."

The blizzard grew worse

Flynn stomped the gas, the tires sliding and the back

end wagging and fishtailing. He had to hold the wheel tightly to keep from flipping over. The channel tightened and the midnight road loomed ahead.

Fuck it. Back into the freeze.

TWENTY-THREE

You had to give the enemy some credit, he had balls. Just because he was insane and a killer didn't mean he was suicidal, so it took a lot of guts to twist the wheel and pancake out onto the parkway, crossing two lanes thick with traffic. The bridge loomed above them.

The Goat hit his horn and blasted through the three-foot-high wall of packed snow and ice, caromed off the back corner of a Ford pickup, and wriggled toward the median. Cars slammed into one another with heavy metal crunches and thunks. Horns blared but only few panicked enough to dare hit their brakes at such high speeds. There were a couple of fishtails but most cars just coasted and bumped one another, thumping along.

The GTO hopped up over the opposite curb, bottomed out on the cement median but managed to shake loose.

Traffic in the westbound side saw him coming and slowed up, skidding and sliding and also doing a little banging and bouncing but able to make a hole for the Goat to clamber into. It was some very nifty driving by everyone involved.

Flynn wasn't so lucky.

He couldn't loop the Charger through the same hole in the wall of plowed snow because the traffic had slowed down and backed up, covering his outlet. He had to floor it or he wouldn't be able to bust through the ice.

Zero said, "You know, I think you ask for it."

"I don't believe I do."

"You just want to be dead."

"Not so. Any suggestions?"

"Did you pray last time?"

"No."

"Then don't do it now either."

"Sounds good to me."

He jammed the gas, got up some speed, then slammed on the brakes. He saw an old Buick and aimed for it. There was a lot of Detroit steel in that baby. The Charger ripped through the snow and ice and the front end slammed hard into the side of the Buick, both vehicles pushing over onto the median. Flynn couldn't even see the driver through all the snow built up on the passenger window of the car.

The whole day seemed very muffled. Nobody was screaming. It felt like this had been rehearsed many times before until now the moment had come to do it for real.

Traffic had stopped for him. He backed up and saw he hadn't damaged the Buick that much. The rear passenger door was severely dented but Buicks were built like tanks and could take a little smashing. The driver was out, his face twisted in an expression of disbelief. Flynn rolled his window down and said, "You all right?"

"Yeah."

"You alone in there?"

"Yes! I need your insurance. The hell is going on? Who are you people?"

"CPS!"

"What's CPS? That a delivery service?"

Flynn backed up but was stuck on the median. The opposite lanes of traffic were rubbernecking, watching him. He couldn't tell where the Goat was, but he still had time, he knew he could still make it, if only he could get off the cement.

"Get out of the way," Flynn told the other driver.

"What?"

"Move!"

"I need your insurance!"

"Get the fuck out of the way!"

"I'm suing CPS!"

Flynn threw the Charger into drive and jammed the gas, the back tires wheezing and the Dodge scuttling for purchase on the ice. He pushed the Buick a couple inches farther up onto the divider. He wasn't going to make it. What a ridiculous situation to be in, wiped out in the middle of the parkway with maybe a thousand people staring at him, having no idea what was going on and not caring, hardly bothered at all. But nobody moving.

Even the guy getting his car fucked up didn't seem to give that much of a damn. He just stood there watching, his hands in tiny fists. What the hell had happened to New Yorkers?

Furious, Flynn kept grinding gears into reverse, into first, third, fourth, trying to rock himself free. All that bodywork and he'd messed the Charger up again. The front end mangled, one headlight smashed, the hood twisted. That was all right, he'd fix it. The back left tire started to catch. He reversed and spun, threw it into second, caught a little more, reversed and spun. He flipped the steering wheel hard and to the left, finally got enough ground under him to move, swung around the Buick and floored it across the iced divider.

Rubberneckers had been watching him, curious and amazed. Only a few cars were still moving with any speed. Flynn slid into traffic among them, barely avoiding getting wrecked by an SUV riding up hard on him. That was all right, he was in control. Nothing could stop him now. He sat there with his face blank but smiling a little madly on the inside.

"He's heading for the Robert Moses Causeway," Zero said.

"Yeah," Flynn said. "The beach."

The water, everyone always had to run to the water. Maybe we all still had some lemming DNA tucked away in our double helices.

Zero lay there with his nose nuzzled between his front paws, staring at Flynn the same way he had the night they'd drowned. Flynn felt it again, the water rising over the dog's nose, the eyes on him, the cold clenching his heart.

Zero said, "You're going to lose him."

"I'm not going to lose him."

"Yes, you are. You want to."

"No fuckin' way."

"You want him to come at you again and finish the job."

"If I die, what happens to you?"

"We're both already dead, I just happen to be wise enough to know it."

"No kibbles for you tonight, Fido."

"There's only hell. No purgatory. No paradise. Only hell."

"I'm wise enough to know that."

He hit the southbound exit and slid over the curb, heading back into the snow but compensating, coming off the loop doing nearly sixty as he tore for the Robert Moses Bridge. He wondered if the shadow in the blizzard was really going to do it, go to the beach, or whether he'd try to make it to the Ocean Parkway and head west, try to shake Flynn and gun for the Wantagh or the Meadowbrook.

Flynn saw the lights of the Goat up ahead and stamped the pedal even harder. The GTO had slowed because of the miserable driving conditions. Things were even worse here on the water. The snow swung in off the ocean winds and pounded down, relentless and diamond-needle-tipped.

They made the bridge with hardly any visibility at all. The Goat's brake lights burned red. He was slowing. He was scared. Flynn was ecstatic.

Zero said, "Wouldn't it be ironic if you went off the bridge and hit the water again and died pretty much like your own brother did, like you did, in the same car—"

"No, it wouldn't be."

"He's trying for the Ocean Parkway."

"He won't get the chance."

The Charger roared up behind the Goat and Flynn bucked the rear bumper. He closed in on the passenger side, trying to block the driver's escape onto the next exit. They were going too fast to make it anyway. From here on out it was nothing but off-roading and family beaches and frozen inlets where the old men liked to go ice fishing.

The Goat blasted off the road toward one of the parking fields for Robert Moses beach. He hit the toll and smashed the semaphore arm. Flynn was riding his tail but the shattered wood came up off the back of the GTO, landed on the Charger's hood and bounced into the windshield. Heavy cracks appeared, and the windshield wipers got stuck in the down position, hung up on the thick wood splinters.

In seconds Flynn couldn't see much of anything at all and he veered left toward the bathrooms and snack bar area on the far side of the lot, hoping he could find some cover. He rolled down the driver's window and stuck his head out, knowing he'd already made a mistake by slowing down, giving the other driver the opportunity to pull over and get the rifle out.

The killer was good in high wind. He'd taken out Angela Soto from a hundred yards away, in a storm.

Flynn hissed beneath his breath, his hair and face already covered with a sheen of ice. He searched the other end of the lot and saw nothing but white. With a growl of frustration Flynn turned his head left, wondering if the Goat had backed up or broken through the exit gate. Instead he saw the car parked less than fifty feet away, out in front of the women's bathroom. The tire tracks slewed up to the wall, then veered and wrapped around. Why?

The driver's door was open. Flynn cautiously rolled up on the GTO. The rifle lay propped in the empty backseat.

Why didn't he take it?

Flynn got out. He'd been insane to drive here the way he had, crazier than the killer, who'd slowed down, who'd wanted to live. Maybe that gave him an edge. Maybe it proved the dead dog was right.

Zero hopped down out of the Charger and sauntered through the snow. Flynn drew his .38 and approached the Goat, thinking of movies where the PI crept, slinked, lurked and serpentined to keep from getting blasted out of his socks. The shadow out in this blizzard would probably be on the other side of the snack bar. If he'd taken the rifle, he could have plinked Flynn off with hardly any effort. Why hadn't he taken it?

A styrofoam box, weighted down by what appeared to be hamburger, flapped its top near the front-left tire. The bad boy had gotten out of the Goat so quickly he'd knocked some of his trash out of the wheel well. Flynn kneeled, extended his arm and stuck the .38 inside the car as he checked it. Nothing. He kept low, blocked by the car door.

He squinted into the storm, the wind burning his eyes. He shielded his face, looked down and saw footsteps leading away.

"What's that smell?" Zero asked.

She's got burn marks to the chest. Maybe a taser.

No, not a taser.

A defibrillator. Zap paddles.

*They wheeled Florence out on a gurney and put her in an
ambulance parked at the curb.*

Flynn picked up the styrofoam box, sniffed it and his
features, already white and cold as deep-cut ice, hardened
further.

He said, "Tabasco."

TWENTY-FOUR

So what the hell.

No reason to play it safe or go in smart or quiet. He didn't know how to do it anyway. Flynn started off toward the snack shacks, pressing down the rising memories of summers when Danny would take him out here to body-surf the waves and dig holes down to where the sand crabs crawled. The very early days when Flynn was maybe three or four, riding his father's shoulders, his mother dressed in a white one-piece suit and a rubber bathing cap. The old man chugging beer even though it was illegal, always getting into a shouting match with the lifeguards and se-curity.

The footprints grew more visible in the thin snow cov-ering the cement, protected from the driving wind by the angle of the showers' brick walls.

Despite it all, Flynn felt safe. Stupid but safe. The killer had never come at him head-on. He'd always put the tap on someone else. Always hung up the phone, always run at the first sign of possible confrontation. Never wanting to stand toe-to-toe, always rabbiting as quickly as he could.

So what the hell.

Flynn rushed around the wall, head down, following the tracks. The waves crashed a hundred yards off down the beach. The force of the snow straightened him up for a moment as he struggled against it. Turning, the storm battering him like any other enemy, so that he kept wheeling, waiting.

You had to put the dare out there just to make the other guy jump. He held his pistol up so there'd be no mistake, so the fucker wouldn't think he was helpless or just coming out here to talk, to get answers.

There.

A shadow in the blizzard, down by the water.

Flynn made for it.

"Hold it!" Flynn shouted, pointing the .38. His hand was so cold it felt welded to the gun metal.

A blur of black motion cut a swathe through the white as the bad boy hurled something out into the water.

Flynn thought, There it goes, the one piece of evidence I'll need most. I don't know what it is but because I was a step too slow, the whole thing is botched.

Then he saw the face of God.

The round, eager puffy-faced lord of all creation who smelled like hamburger and Tabasco sauce. Divinity with a gap-toothed smile and an uncivil tongue. Who spoke in a voice of thunder saying that Flynn was the luckiest son of a bitch he'd ever heard of.

Dressed in dark blue, wearing a knitted hat, gloves, his coat zippered up to the collar, insulated.

It was the EMT who'd saved Flynn's life, the guy who'd brought him back.

"You," Flynn said as pellets of ice tore at his lips. "You. What the hell did I ever do to you?"

A pudgy-faced god of hurt, perhaps even shame. Flynn got up closer and read it in his eyes, seeing the guy's embarrassment at having been caught, but trying to keep a cap on it. Sort of calm and resolved about the moment, but thinking of deeper things. No guilt or prodding conscience, nothing like that, just disgrace and loss. He stared back at Flynn, full of grief but almost glad that they'd finally come face-to-face again.

"You let my secret loose," the guy said, and let out a sad chuckle like he knew it sounded stupid as hell.

"Me? I did?"

"You did."

"What secret?" Flynn said.

"I met someone as sick as me. Sicker than me."

"Who?"

"The Devil. He whispers. I've done a lot of bad things. I let people die. It's my job to save them and I let them die. You want to know why? Because I could. No other reason! I just let them fade. I let them go, just because I felt like it. You know how many? Dozens! Dozens over the years! I let them die. Sick, right?"

Flynn said, "Right."

The EMT let out a broad smile that filled with snowflakes. "But you, I fought for you. Harder than I ever fought for anyone before. I wanted to save you."

"Why?"

"I don't know. I let some die, and I try like hell to bring

others back. I told you, it's sick. That's the way I do it, that's the power I have. And he knew it. He saw through me and he knew it the second he looked into my eyes. The Devil knows what you do and what you hide."

"Sister Murteen told us the same thing in Catholic School."

"He speaks to you in your own voice. With your own words."

It made Flynn back up a step. He swallowed thickly, couldn't speak for a moment. Zero, the devil in him, with his voice. Was this guy talking to dead dogs too? "What the fuck do you mean?"

"He knew it immediately. He noticed my hands, saw it in my eyes, the very first minute. He let me know and I was afraid. He didn't have to tell anyone. All he had to do was whisper it to the world and let my sins out. Do you understand that? That was it, that was all. My evil was down deep where I could pretend I controlled it, instead of it controlling me. My evil was down deep where it was supposed to be, and he unlatched the cellar door. Once that happened, I couldn't stop. I liked what we were doing too much."

"Who?" Flynn asked. "Who else is a part of this?"

"I loved Angela. I wanted her dead."

"What?"

"I loved her so much, you could never understand. She was mine. I could do what I wanted with her."

"You sick bastard."

"His voice comes from hell. You can't resist. It feels too good to let go."

The EMT pursed his lips and his eyes flitted, his lashes

flecked with ice crystals, not looking for a way out but completely focused on some internal dialogue with himself. Maybe seeing how it would all look laid out on the six o'clock news. What he'd have to say to his girlfriend, his brothers, his parents, his aunt Edna, the people he graduated high school with who'd be saying things like *I always knew that one was sick in the head*. All the girls who ever turned him down realizing what a narrow miss they'd had.

And more than that, but Flynn still didn't know what it was. The EMT's eyes cleared and he stared over at the water and then at Flynn, his features sagging like he wanted to cry.

Flynn struggled for another question and asked, "What's it all about?"

The guy wetting his lips, his mouth working but refusing to answer. He was resisting something, trying to overcome it. Flynn wondered how a guy with this much funky wiring had managed to bring him back from twenty-eight minutes down the road.

"Why did you write that you were my brother?"

"I didn't."

Flynn swallowed hard. "Who did?"

The paramedic, this mook who'd been his savior, reached into his pocket as Flynn said, "Hey, now, no," and drew a tiny popgun .32.

The pistol was so tiny it nearly disappeared in his hand. Flynn held the .38 out at arm's length, pointed at the bad boy who'd gotten him out of the water, and said, "Don't."

"Don't let them bring me back."

"What? Who?"

"Any of them."

Flynn got it then as the EMT raised the pistol and shoved the barrel under his chin. The gloves he wore were so nice and thick he could hardly get his finger through the trigger guard. The guy didn't want to come back from the midnight road, didn't want anybody trying to save him. Flynn felt stupid holding a gun on a guy about to blast his own brains out but didn't know what else to do. A strong urge swept through him to get off a shot first. Make sure the bastard died by Flynn's hand and not his own.

He said, "Wait, hold it, don't—" His pleas sounded especially weak but the EMT paused a second because Flynn had told him to wait.

Actually listening to him. Standing there eager to hear whatever Flynn might say next.

Flynn came up empty for a second and said, "I don't even know your name."

"That doesn't matter."

Flynn supposed he was right. "How'd you find out about Emma Waltz?"

"You should've stayed dead."

"It's your fault I came back. Who knows your secret?"

"Everyone will know soon."

"How'd you learn to fire a rifle so well?"

"I never fired a gun in my life," the guy answered, and slowly began tugging on the trigger, like he might be able to feel the bullet burrow through him inch by inch, wanting to feel it all the way.

Smiling, two hot tears squirting across his cheeks, carving deep twin channels in the packed frozen crust covering him, he blew the top of his head off.

Flynn checked the EMT's pockets and found nothing. He was hoping for a cell phone but he thought that was probably what the guy had tossed into the water. So they couldn't find the Devil.

Flynn walked back toward the Goat, ready to search through it. He needed a name. He couldn't go around calling this guy the bad boy or God. He made his way to where the Dodge was parked and saw odd tracks in the snow. Footprints but a little off. Flynn couldn't make it out with the snow still coming down, erasing everything into a world of empty whiteness.

The GTO was gone. Someone else had been around.

That's why the tire tracks had gone up to the wall of the women's bathroom and then veered and wrapped back around. The driver had let someone out. Goddamn it, he should've realized. Somebody else had run to the far side of the bathroom and come around again while he'd been down on the beach.

"No," he said, because Mooney had been right.

There were two of them.

TWENTY-FIVE

They surrounded him under the shelter of the empty snack bar and prattled to one another, drinking coffee and taking photos and setting up the little protective lean-to the same way they had when Angela Soto had been murdered in the Stonybrook Hospital parking lot. They were nicer to him this time, maybe because he'd gone through his own rebirth of blood, and now he could be one of the boys.

Acting as if he'd shot the guy, they took away his .38 in an evidence bag and brought him a styrofoam cup of black coffee. They asked if he wanted cream or sugar. He said no. They walked in and out, sometimes laughing.

Raidin liked to cut a path all right, even when it folded up behind him in the swirling snow. He did it now, the other homicide dicks and forensic teams fading back a step or two as he stepped forward, still all in black, black breaking through all the white, looking as ill as he had the first time Flynn had seen him.

He was wearing a fedora. A fucking fedora, Jesus. Talk about a guy with a noir fetish.

He eyed first the bolt cutters laid up against the wall,

then the broken lock on the cement beneath the metal shutters of the hot-dog stand. Flynn was impressed. You'd think having a corpse out there in the freeze would be enough to overlook the little stuff, but no, Raidin took it all in, probably to make sure a new lock was bought for the owner of the stand, a letter of apology stamped by the commissioner.

Raidin had a lot to say but had to take a second to frame it correctly. "You're the one who caused all the pile-ups and backups on the Southern State. You could've killed somebody."

"Was anyone hurt?"

"No. So let's forget about that for now."

Flynn wanted to say, Hey, you brought it up, but he let it ride. "He threw something out into the water."

"Any idea what?"

"Black and small. Had some weight to it because it got some distance."

"How far out?"

"Forty feet?"

"It's gone forever."

"I know. I think maybe it was a cell phone."

"Start at the beginning."

Flynn did but for some reason left Emma Waltz out of the story. The urge to protect her hadn't lessened at all, and when he let his mind roll over he could still feel her in his arms, her compact warm solidity beneath him on the floor. He had to find her.

He cleared his throat and said how he'd opened his front door and was nearly blasted by someone at the far end of the parking lot. Three shots.

Raidin called someone over to go check Flynn's apartment and pull the slugs out of the floor.

Maybe they were close enough now, with another body between them, to ask questions and get real replies. To talk about wives and kids. Fear and heartache. For that grudging respect to possibly burgeon into something else. A friendship, a brotherhood. Raidin was maybe five years younger than Flynn but could be the older brother he needed, the father he'd been missing.

Flynn sipped the coffee. It was cold, and the shakes started to take over. The black nerve throbbed in time with them. After all of this Flynn suddenly felt chilly. He leaned back and sagged against the cement wall, feeling himself becoming at least half as hard and frozen as the stone.

He slid down to a sitting position, very aware of the coffee, not wanting to spill it. Raidin stamped forward and put his strong hands on the back of Flynn's neck and pressed his head down. Flynn was having trouble breathing but took the time to set the cup on the floor near him. Raidin said, "You'll be all right in a minute. Breathe deeply. Through your nose."

He did but it wasn't helping at all. Colorful lights pulsed and coiled at the edges of his vision. Someone brought a blanket and threw it over Flynn's shoulders. Raidin said, "When you can stand we'll go talk in one of the cruisers."

"No," Flynn said, the light-headedness beginning to ease. "It's okay now. Help me up."

Raidin got him by the elbows and lifted. Flynn was abruptly on his feet, staring into the man's eyes, the cop searching him, him searching the cop. Both of them probing deeper.

"Okay," Flynn said.

"Did you talk with him before he shot himself?"

"Yeah."

"What did he say?"

Flynn was still having trouble piecing it together. "He said I let his secret loose."

"What secret?"

"He liked to let people die. And someone else knew it. He said he met someone as sick as he was, sicker than he was. Maybe the one who took the Goat. He said the guy noticed his hands, saw it in his eyes."

"What about his eyes?"

"He said he let them go, just because he felt like it. Dozens of people over the years. He let them die."

"Son of a bitch."

Flynn lit a cigarette. "Except for Angela. He said he loved her enough to want to kill her."

"I suppose it made sense to him. And this is the guy who saved your life."

"Yeah, he said he didn't want to be brought back."

"No chance of that." Raidin thought about it all, his hard small pointed body like a knife held in a talented hand. "Who's he protecting?"

"I'm not sure that's the way it was."

"What do you mean?"

"He seemed to be angry. He called the other guy the Devil. Said the Devil talked to him with his own voice, his own words. Said he liked listening."

"Another fucking nut."

"Sure."

Tugging the fedora down, not bothering to wear it at a hip rakish angle, Raidin walked back to the others who were still taking photos. Flynn stuck his head out of the stand and saw the M.E.'s wagon parked next to the Charger.

They were getting ready to pack the little god away soon.

"His name was Petersen," Raidin told him. "Wayne Petersen."

"I asked him but he wouldn't tell me," Flynn said. "It's not over yet."

"Perhaps he was working with his day job partner. EMT's shift in pairs. We're checking on that now. I've covered a similar situation before. A male nurse who started poisoning his patients over at St. John's. He believed he was easing the pain of those who were suffering. Sometimes they pick up a god complex and can't wait to exert the power of death."

Flynn tried to see it. The guy shushing him, telling him to quiet down. Telling Flynn he was the luckiest son of a bitch he'd ever heard about. Saying how Flynn had angels watching over him they never taught the kids about in St. Vincent's.

"I want my gun back."

"We have to check it."

Again with the checking.

"You could sniff it and know it wasn't fired."

"We still need to check."

A uniformed cop stepped into the snack stand to draw Raidin aside and whisper in his ear, eyeing Flynn but not in an intimidating way. They still thought he'd probably capped the guy. Chased him down the Southern State heading the wrong way in order to punch his ticket out on the sand. It was a pretty good story, they liked it.

Flynn lit another cigarette and waited in the corner. The signs were making him hungry. Hot dogs. Hamburgers. Twenty flavors of ice cream. French fries. Nachos with fresh melted cheese. Pretzels. His father used to go in for the pretzels, the giant salty ones, eating about half of one before he started to tug off small wads to give to Flynn and his mother. His mother would chew heavily, absently, with a distant look in her eyes, waiting for the old man to start mixing it up with the lifeguards. On a good day it wouldn't happen until late afternoon, just before they were ready to leave anyway. It was like his father couldn't go back home without puffing his chest out just enough to give him a reason to feel tough.

They were breaking down the lean-to. The body was gone. Flynn could tell already that Raidin was getting bad news. If they'd tagged the partner, everybody would be smiling and flexing their muscles, running for their cruisers. The uniform cop slipped off.

"It wasn't the partner," Raidin said. "That guy's name is Bucky Ford. Have you ever heard of him?"

"No."

"He's working today. Less than an hour ago he saved an elderly man who'd slipped on ice in St. James and given himself a concussion. He has a new partner. Petersen was let go almost four weeks ago."

And he'd taken his zap paddles with him. "Why?"

"He started missing work, screwing up on the diagnoses at the emergency scenes, seemed distracted. They told him to take a vacation. He never came back from it."

"It started going downhill for him a few days after he saved my life." Flynn nodded, feeling the answer closing in on him, just not quickly enough. "Something happened to him. Something bent him." Perhaps Bragg had made contact, threatened him, forced him to become a part of this. If there was a Bragg, if the colonel wasn't dead in a swamp somewhere.

Or maybe Petersen had somehow gone so far out onto the midnight road trying to save Flynn that he'd gotten himself stuck on it.

"The rifle's ten years old and was registered to a sometime second-story thief and bank robber named Leo Coleman. Have you ever heard of him?"

"No."

"He's got a few priors, a couple of convictions, went down hard this last time and he's been in the can the last seven years."

"I don't know him."

"Probably sold it a long time ago to some idiot crony who didn't know enough not to buy a piece off someone who pulled jobs with it."

"Was Coleman ever hurt bad?"

"Why?"

"Maybe he fell off a roof once and Petersen took him to the hospital and stole the rifle along the way."

Frowning, Raidin said, "That doesn't make any sense."

"I know. I'm just trying to figure where he keeps crossing paths with all these people. It's got to be in the back of his ambulance. That might be how he knew Angela Soto. You said she OD'ed a couple of times. He must've been the one who caught the call. Saved her life and figured he owned it, could use it or end it whenever he liked."

"We're checking into it."

"Sure."

Raidin kept working it. "What secret of his do you know?"

"I have no idea."

"Yes, you do, you're just not aware of it."

"Same goddamn thing."

Another expansive moment settled around Flynn, the sense that the past and the present were colliding and sluicing toward a near future full of significance. Flynn didn't want to let the feeling go even though it left him vulnerable.

His life held a little more meaning in this minute than it had the minute before. The complexity of design tipped its hand and he could almost see the fates working behind the scenes, measuring out the length of his life, tying knots where he was meant to interact with others.

Raidin took him by the shoulder and said, "You're still in shock after that insane ride and all the rest of it. You need to see a psychiatrist, you know that?"

"I know that—"

"You're breathing too shallowly."

"Chest hurts a little—"

"Try to stay calm. I'm calling for a medic."

"I'm just—it's just that—"

"Try to relax. When was the last time you ate?"

"I don't know."

"You look like shit."

"You never answered me. Are you married? Do you have children?"

Raidin gave him a look that was a mixture of disappointment, anger and possibly even fear. Raidin walked back out into the blizzard, another faceless figure among other eddying figures to soon be swallowed by the snow and the endless cries of the ocean.

No medic ever showed but in five minutes Jessie Gray turned up. Other reporters were out there too, trying to stay warm in the parking lot, but Jessie slipped right in.

She came over and gave him a hard kiss, one filled with a misunderstood passion. Maybe as a show of thanks for constantly giving her something to do with her days. It kept her from watching the daytime shrink shows. She drew back and said, "Jesus Christ, you're cold. Your lips are blue." She lifted the blanket and drew it over his head, started to rub his hair with it. Ice crystals crackled and dropped to his shoulders. "You're freezing. My God, we need to get you out of here."

"I think I'll be okay."

"You'll get hypothermia." She took off her gloves and rubbed his face with her hands. It felt good. He smiled and knew he probably looked a little goofy.

"Thank you," he said.

"I do care about you, you know."

He lit another cigarette and let it hang. Everyone was strong but him. Here he was thinking of hot dogs and his dead father and sand castles, nearly passing out. He still had a way to go until this thing was through, and it was going to be tough. Something was twisting inside him, a piece of the puzzle sparking at the back of his brain. It was going to set fire soon. He had to be ready for it.

She looked into his eyes and said, "What's the matter?"

"I'm wondering where we fit into each other's personal journeys."

"It's okay if you don't like me."

"You're quick to say those kinds of things. Why are you so fast on that draw?"

"I told you already."

"Tell me again."

"I know I drive men crazy, the ones I'm interested in."

"Maybe you drive them crazy because you're not really interested in them at all."

It stopped her. She thought about it, and it was obvious she didn't want to. She had an interview to run, an article to write. She was rubbing the ice off him. She smiled and then sort of grimaced.

"What do you want from me?" she asked.

He thought about what a loaded question that could really be. The two of them in bed, the feel of her action and edge beside him. Her dark night demands, her willingness to impress. The way she often stared at him like a man of substance. Other times she gave him a glance that made it seem like she couldn't see his face anymore beneath the columns of ink. Her honesty, her in-your-face attitude. He liked it, he wanted it, and he was shamed by it. He hadn't even given her a chance. His mind had been set to disregard her from the beginning, even before she could ruin it herself. He cared too much about his gray hair. Christ, what a fuck-up. He thought of Emma Waltz and—

There it was.

He remembered where he'd seen the Goat before.

And he knew where the rifle had come from.

He stared over at Raidin, the man's fedora covered in white, the black raincoat snapping in the wind. He even took a step in that direction before the nerve burning inside him urged him to handle the next scene by himself.

What was one more mistake? It might already be too late.

Jessie Gray said his name and it didn't mean enough to stop him from wanting to roar out of there full throttle.

He turned to her, slowly, with some real affection. He understood she would eventually smooth out her burrs and quit frightening off the men she might care for and who might care for her. She was young. She had a reason. He was old and didn't. He thought, So here it is, where our personal journeys diverge again, for the last time. It's not so bad.

He told her the thing that mattered most to both of them now.

"Just write the end of the story," he said.

Flynn walked out into the snow, out into the parking lot and checked around, opening doors of the police cars until he saw the evidence bag with his .38 in it. He grabbed it and stuck it in his coat pocket, got into the Charger and got out of there.

The water had nearly gotten him again this time. He'd be back soon enough.

TWENTY-SIX

The note had been right. It really was all his fault.

The answer had been in front of him the entire time, but he had a head full of film noir. He set up his own red herrings. Too much Spencer Tracy in *Fury* and Dana Andrews in *Fallen Angel*. Bogie always on his mind.

He forgot clues. He couldn't do simple arithmetic. He thought of Danny too much and denied the world at hand. He let young women spook him and wasted energy on self-pity.

A row of three police cars came rallying toward Robert Moses, and Flynn swung past them on the bridge, needing to punch the gas pedal but waiting for his chance. His second chances had gone to waste. He took the Sagtikos up to the LIE and headed east, fighting the traffic and the storm every inch.

The sun had already begun to set, but the snow kept the sky and the streets bright with the burning white. It felt like he'd never be in complete darkness again. He'd shut his eyes and there would always be that glow seeping under his lids.

Pileups, wipeouts, and fender-benders peppered the

Expressway. People were pulled over trying to wait the blizzard out. Clearing their windshields and side windows and kicking snow out from around their tires so they wouldn't be totally buried. Groups of folks stood together on the shoulder and parked on the sides of entrance ramps trying to get their bearings. A couple of flares sputtered meaninglessly in the distance.

He pulled up in front of the house and knew he was too late. The windows were lit but empty of passing shadows.

He drew the .38 and tried the front door. It was locked. He went around back past all the children's toys, fighting down bile, trying to blank his mind of the ugly pictures that kept coming up.

He had to at least try to end this himself. It was purely selfish. If he didn't make the effort, he might never allow himself to live, to truly find love.

The back door was unlocked. He opened it in a crouch and slipped inside. A fan of snow followed him and broke against his back.

A groan whispered from the living room.

Sierra lay on the floor in a puddle of blood, battered worse than he'd ever seen anyone beaten. She'd been bludgeoned with a wooden baseball bat. It lay a couple feet away, almost completely red.

The only reason she was still alive was because of all the plastic work she'd had. Her wig was affixed to the far wall, stuck there by some drying fluid and tissue. It had probably been swept off her head at the first blow. Someone had come up behind her while she bent to pick up a scattering of toys. It looked like there was at least one plate in her skull. She wasn't going to get a chance for another.

The door here always opening and shutting, opening and shutting. Kids running in and out all day long. She wouldn't have even looked up when someone walked in behind her.

Flynn's breath stuck in his chest and he moved to her. She was trying to rise. She didn't yet realize that both her legs were broken. He checked the halls to see if anybody was around. No one.

He put his arms around her and tried to ease her back to the throw rug, but she was still all muscle and willful intent. He pulled a pillow from the couch and carefully pressed it to her head. She reached out and grabbed him by the shirt. He said, "It's me."

"Flynn?"

"Lie still, you're going to be okay."

"The children."

He didn't know what to say. It annoyed him to lie but he had no choice. He'd check in a minute. "They're okay."

"Don't let them . . . see me like this . . ."

"They won't."

He attempted to shrug free so he could get to the phone and call 911 but she wouldn't let him go. Okay, he thought, willing himself away from the moment, Okay, I'll get a fucking cell phone. It could come in handy at times like these. She shoved against him again, the agony making her flail.

One fist locked on his wrist. The bones there ground together and he hissed but didn't yank away.

"It's all right," he said. He needed to know how much she knew. "Who did this to you?"

"Didn't see him. From behind. Your friend . . . I guess."

"You're the only friend I have."

"Soon you'll have . . . no one."

"Shhh, help is coming."

"No one is coming." She was panting, her body twisting beneath his hands, but somehow it didn't affect her voice at all. He couldn't believe she was still talking. "But here we are together. This mean I'm the love interest?"

"Sure."

"Oh fuck, now I know it's bad." She smiled and blood pulsed over her bottom lip. "The hero always comes to the love interest's rescue. You're late."

"Sorry about that. I got a little hung up."

"I can't . . . I can't see anything."

"Relax."

"Tell me . . ."

"You're missing your left eye."

"Oh . . . God . . ."

"You're going to be all right."

"Don't . . . bullshit me."

"I'm not."

"Yes, you are."

He already knew the answer. He didn't have to ask the question. It was a waste of time and there was no time left. But the words refused to settle back and he was already saying them aloud, hating himself for not spending these seconds in prayer, speaking of love, eternity, salvation, the children, the children who might be dead in their

THE MIDNIGHT ROAD 269

rooms, not spending these seconds giving Sierra a little advice on what to expect on the midnight road.

"Your old clunker, what kind of car is it?"

"What?"

"You said Trevor and Nuddin would stay up at all hours, playing videos, on the computer, and out in the garage fixing up an old clunker. What kind?"

Her remaining eye, gazing into the distance, but puzzled, wondering why the hell he would ask such a thing now. He chewed his tongue, begging forgiveness.

She said, "One of my exes . . . it doesn't run."

He put his hand to the side of her wet face and rubbed, the way he had touched his mother in the hospital bed, where there was almost no flesh left to touch at all. "What kind?"

"An old . . . GTO."

The Goat. He'd seen Trevor and Nuddin working on it that day he'd stopped by, looking through the garage window. He'd only seen the hood, but it had made its impression. Everything sticking in his mind too far down to do any good until it was too late.

"What was your gun nut ex's name? The one who robbed banks. Was it Leo Coleman?"

"The fuck do you know . . . Leo? Why?"

"I'm sorry, Sierra, I'm so sorry."

And of course, that brought a smile to her lips. The plaintive whimper, the apology in the dark.

Her body shook and the broken bones clattered together. "Noir films always end badly."

"Yeah, but not for the woman. It's always the guy who winds up getting it in the neck."

"That's right, I forgot. I feel better now," she said, and with a sudden knowledge that filled her eye with absolute terror, she convulsed for twenty seconds and died. A small piece of Flynn's small heart broke off and tagged along with her.

TWENTY-SEVEN

A shadow thrown against a corpse.

Flynn spun and held the .38 out before him, trained on the boy Trevor, who stood there trembling. Flynn could see the kid was about to vomit and grabbed him by the collar and led him into the kitchen, where he threw up in the sink. The boy began to pass out and Flynn ran the water and woke him up with cold splashes. He holstered the .38 and carried the boy back into the living room and sat him on the couch close enough to the wall that the bloody wig almost touched the side of his face.

He went to the nearest room and threw the door open to find a black girl of about ten sleeping heavily, her eyes half-open. He tried to wake her. She groaned and licked her lips but didn't rouse from her stupor. He felt her neck and found her pulse to be strong and regular. He went from room to room, checking all the children. There were five of them. They were drugged but seemed to be fine. Kelly wasn't among them. Sierra had been a saint to handle so much, and he'd never once helped her out.

The boy sat there shivering in a warped calm. He

would never get over it, not even when he finally understood what he'd done and sought penance for it.

Flynn looked at the nearest bedroom door.

"What did he use on the kids?"

"Pills."

"What pills?"

"He wanted me to put them in the dinner tonight, before she got home. But there were so many. I only put in
about a third. I didn't—I didn't want—"

"You knew he was going to kill them all."

"No!"

"Where's the rest of the medication?"

"I flushed it."

"Do you have the bottles?"

"There were no bottles, he had them in baggies. Little
white pills."

Compliments of Petersen, the pudgy Tabasco-stinking
god who sometimes saved people and sometimes didn't,
just because he could.

Flynn grabbed the phone and dialed 911, barked the
address and said all that he knew about the state of the
children, told the excessively monotone but condescend-
ing voice on the other end that his friend was dead on the
floor.

The emergency operator buffeted him, devoid of
any empathy, "Sir? Sir. Are you sure, sir? Sir? Sir." Flynn
hung up.

"What happened, Trevor?"

"I don't know."

Flynn slapped the kid hard. "Tell me."

"I don't have anything to tell you!"

"Talk to me."

"Who the hell do you think you are? Oh my God. Goddamn it, goddamn it, Jesus."

So it was going to be like that. Flynn couldn't put up with it. He gripped the boy by the back of the neck and faced him toward Sierra, still on the floor, unheralded.

"Why did you do it?"

"I didn't do this!"

"Why were you helping Petersen? How do you even know him?"

"I don't!"

"Stop lying."

"I'm not!"

Abruptly, Flynn felt an incredible wash of pity for the boy, realizing Trevor really was only a stupid kid trying to make his way through an increasingly complex, intense, awful world. He took the boy in his arms and hugged him for a moment, doing a poor job of it. But requiring contact, hoping to give solace, to himself or the kid, or just by putting out a moment's goodwill in the midst of death. Then it was enough. Things were on track.

Flynn backed up and slapped Trevor, then backhanded him. Then did it again until the kid hit his knees and started sobbing.

"Talk. What's your secret, Trevor?"

His eyes swirling, Trevor tightened his legs as if he might make a run for it. Flynn went to the front door, opened it, let more of the ice in. He said, "You want to go out there? Go ahead. How far are you going to get?"

Trevor's bottom lip sagged and trembled. He was

trying desperately not to cry. He still couldn't fully comprehend the magnitude of what had gone on here, not even with Sierra laid out in front of them like this.

"What's your secret?" Flynn asked.

"I won't tell you."

"Your foster mother was my best friend, maybe my only friend."

"You don't look so sad to me," Trevor said.

"Judge your own heart, kid. You helped to murder her and two other people."

"It wasn't my fault!"

"I know that. You're just a teenager, Trevor. Teens need help in the best of times, much less trapped in a situation like you've been. So out with it!"

The kid sucked air hard, the edges of his mouth quivering violently. He hissed and spit bubbled, but he couldn't get the words out. He'd be blocked by various forms of trauma for decades to come, no different than Flynn. Not much anyway.

His face darkened and two fat tears squirted from his eyes and still the boy couldn't quite cry and couldn't say the thing that had led to Sierra's murder.

"Does it have something to do with your parents?" Flynn asked.

A long hesitation, his hands squeezing in fists, then loosening, then tightening. Finally he said, "My parents. Yes."

"What about them?"

"They—they—" Another pause. He was trying. Despite it all the boy was showing courage. Facing up to his greatest heartache and shame.

"What did they do?"

The words fell out of him like stones. "They never abused me. I hated them. I always hated them. My mother always nagging me with stories of her own life, of all the losers she knew. Her brothers, her father, her boyfriends, holding me up to them. All she knew were scumbags, why should I be different? Trying to make me feel guilty for things they did, for all their mistakes. My old man always staring at me. Both of them looking at me the same way. Coked out of their heads but always looking at me. Him wanting me to be better than him, better than I was, but never good enough, no matter what I did. Always staring, disappointed sometimes, and sometimes proud. He couldn't make up his mind. They made no sense. They were crazy. And all the time both of them doing coke, like that made everything okay, like that put them above all the losers they were always talking about. Selling enough so it didn't matter, you know? Always stoned but still going to work, still acting like they were fine middle-class examples, even when the drugs were out on the kitchen table and they were cutting them with baby powder. Screaming at me to cut the lawn, like that was important. Screaming at me to wax the cars. Always screaming. Telling me to do my homework while they put on the twist ties. I'd have to be crazy not to hate them. I had to save myself. It doesn't matter if nobody else understands, I know I did what I had to do. I got them in trouble. It was easy. I told a counselor at school. He sent me to the nurse's office to get an examination. You know what the clincher was? I cleaned my mother's brush and

took a few of her hairs and stuck them down my under-
wear. There it was. They were both busted for that. The
narcs and shit came afterward. I had to do it. Fuck cutting
the lawn."

The pressure of the dead increased. It wanted to cave
in his chest, crush him down into a square of pulp. He felt
the kids he'd failed tightening their hold, the unfulfilled
life of Grace Brooks gathering force. They weren't here
to condemn but to offer their own aid, to help him along
the course of his purpose.

"What were you going to do, kid?"

"I don't know."

"Yes, you do. You were going to clean up, weren't you?
You were going to try to hide her body?" Flynn could
barely open his mouth wide enough to speak. His jaws
kept tightening, he wanted to snarl. "Could you do that?
What, grab a chainsaw? Dump her on the side of Vet's
Highway? Bury her in the backyard?"

"No."

"Where is he, Trevor? Where is the rotten son of a
bitch?"

The footsteps in the snow. Flynn had known there was
something a little off about them.

The other shadow in the blizzard, the footsteps in the
snow, with the weight on the balls of his feet.

"Where is he? Where is Nuddin?"

The boy chewed his tongue until he got blood going.
Whenever he spoke all Flynn could see was more red.

"He knows my secret. He was going to tell. It didn't matter if anyone else listened."

"Nuddin doesn't talk."

"He's always talking! He never shuts up! He just talks... *quietly*. He knew my secret a few nights after we met. I told him. I needed to tell somebody. I thought he was retarded. I thought he was innocent. I thought he was my friend. But he's not. He's smart, or at least, something inside him is smart. A part of him. It can do amazing things. It's insane. It's evil."

Flynn could only think of the joyous smile, the humming, the hugging. "How did they keep in contact?"

"Petersen's name badge. He's in the phone book. On the Net. Nuddin knows computers too. Before I came here I had a little side business... nothing big, just ripping off cell phones and minute cards and selling them."

"You got him the phone."

"A friend of mine. I still have connections. I didn't know what he was doing at first. But his talk. He's got this way. It digs in. It doesn't let go. I don't think Petersen even knew who he was talking to at first. But they... brought it out of each other, this craziness, this sickness. Nuddin... he told me, he was always telling me, always whispering about it."

Flynn grabbed the boy by the throat and lifted. "Why didn't you tell anybody?"

"I couldn't!"

"You could've, damn you! You could've saved lives! You could've saved Sierra!"

"I couldn't!"

Flynn threw the kid down again. He wondered if he

had the strength to allow his greatest secret out into the world. If he had any secrets left.

"Petersen never fired the rifle, did he? He didn't kill Angela Soto."

"He knew her. He fucked her. He loved her. He had sex with her a lot of times and he saved her life when she overdosed once. He found her, tried to help her, but she couldn't be helped. He loved her, but he hated her because she wouldn't stop being a hooker. He was crazy about her. He was crazy. He brought her back after her heart stopped and from then on I guess he acted like he owned her life. He always wanted to kill her. But he couldn't do it, until he met Nuddin."

"Why in front of me?"

The kid's eyes were twirling in his head. "You know why. It was your fault. They wanted to hurt you. They wanted you to have blood in your face. They owned you too. He studied you. Researched you on the Net. Archives. He learned all about you. Read the papers, that girl reporter always writing about you. It didn't matter who brought you the message, so long as someone did. No matter who they killed they were blaming it on you, because you were the one who brought them together, see? You freed him from the cage. You set him loose on Petersen. You sent the sickness out. Nuddin doesn't like to be alone. He never wants to be alone. That's why he had me. That's why he had Petersen. He *needs* someone else with him. And Petersen needed someone to push him over the edge. You brought them together. It was all your fault, right?"

Jesus Christ, the logic of the retarded and the insane.

This kid refusing to take any responsibility. Petersen admitted that he'd already been letting people die, but that he'd never fired a gun. Enjoying the ride. And Nuddin ... what the hell was Nuddin?

"He found Leo Coleman's rifle in the garage," Flynn said, thinking about Sierra's ex, the bank robber, in a ten-gallon hat, throwing the rifle in Lake Ronkonkoma.

"An old Remington 30.06," Trevor told him. "All rusted and broken apart. Locked up in a trunk in the garage. That's the first thing he did when he got here, was go through the whole house, top to bottom, the entire garage, everywhere, every drawer. It was cute, when we caught him, you know, nobody could get mad. Just a retarded guy playing games. But he was just finding whatever he could use. He cleaned the pieces of the rifle and put them together. He's been trained. He could do it with his eyes closed. Nuddin's a natural. His father taught him, he said. The thing inside him, whatever part of him it is, it's good with guns. With cars. He knows an engine better than me. He can drive like a pro racer, but he hates being alone. When he came back today—"

"Sierra never noticed the car missing?"

"No, she's hardly ever here. She's always working. She's not going to think her clunker was gone. She's not going to notice another set of tire tracks in the snow. And Nuddin, he's good with people too. They'll do whatever he wants. He manipulates them. He looks at you and he knows. He gets inside you. We're the stupid ones."

Petersen making runs with Nuddin. Setting up kills because after all his time working to bring back the dead and restore the living he'd started to enjoy letting his evil loose. His own words in the Devil's mouth.

"Where is he now?"

"I don't know. But he's got Kelly."

"Jesus."

"He needs someone."

"Why not you?"

"He doesn't need me now. He knows you're coming for him."

Flynn nodded. They were traveling the circle, heading around the track, coming up behind the place where it had to end, where it had started.

He fingered the .38. "There's nowhere for you to run, Trevor. It's all going to come out into the light now. You realize that?"

"Yes. It's a relief. I never should have been afraid. Nothing's as bad as having it inside. Call the police. I'll wait for them."

Easy as that. Jesus. Flynn checked the children once more and found they were beginning to respond when he shook them. They were snapping out of it. He hoped none of them would fully awaken and see what had happened to Sierra.

He phoned Raidin and told him about the kid and Sierra and how it all tied in. He said nothing about Nuddin. He wasn't sure Raidin would believe him. He wasn't sure he believed it himself.

"Don't leave the scene," Raidin said.

"I have to."

"There are children there who need you to look after them."

"They're starting to come around. I can't do anything for them."

"Don't run. It'll make you a suspect."

"I'm already a suspect, just not a very good one. You know I didn't do any of this."

"Who did?"

"I'll find out. I'll finish this. It'll be over tonight. The kid will explain."

"You're going to crack up out there on the streets, the way you're juiced. Don't do it."

"I have to."

"If you flee, there will be a warrant out for you."

Flynn figured it was an empty threat. At this point they all were. What could stop him from going the last mile?

"I'll be out on the road," he said, and hung up.

He turned to the boy. Flynn said, "You don't have any more chances left, kid," then slugged the teen twice in the stomach and clipped him on the chin.

He caught Trevor as the boy flopped over unconscious and laid him on the couch three feet from his dead foster mother.

Flynn touched Sierra once more on the side of the face, dabbing the tips of his fingers in her sticky blood. It was an affirmation of life over death, of friendship and family over lonely steadfastness.

He started for the door when an idea struck him. It was so foolish and bizarre he thought it might actually work. If not, what was one more stupid act? He checked Sierra's bathroom and bedroom until he found what he needed. Then he got in the Charger and brought all his dead with him.

TWENTY-EIGHT

It took him almost two hours to get there because of the road conditions. The salters and sanders and plows tried to keep up, but even they were being entombed with snow. Flynn welded the front end of the Dodge to the brake lights of eighteen-wheelers and stuck with them, letting them forge the path ahead. It was as safe as it was going to get out here. The radio told him a state of emergency had been issued. It gave him hope that his fate was tied to something besides himself.

By the time he got off the Expressway, heading north, the night having fallen like a black blade slashing through a bucket of ice chips, he was the only car out there. Flynn liked the empty road. He skidded and barreled into the snow-choked shoulder, bounced off, looped into a veering donut and kept heading toward Port Jack. Nothing would stop him.

"You're going to die tonight," Zero said.

"No, I'm not."

"And she'll die with you."

"No fuckin' way."

The radio whispered about broken records: most consecutive days of blizzard, most snowfall, most consecutive days under twenty degrees. Greatest number of weather-related deaths. Car accidents. Frozen homeless. Sick elderly. The hospitals packed. The worst New York winter since they started collating weather data. The newscasters sounded surprised by the strain in their own voices. Jessie Gray had been right, people just hadn't been paying attention.

He could beat it. Inside the car he could do almost anything.

"He's going to kill you," Zero said.

"No, he's not."

"He's been waiting, because you're both just alike."

"You say the sweetest things, you know that?"

"You both live in your own worlds."

"Go choke on a chew toy, you little fucker."

It was almost over. He knew the storm would soon be finished. He and Kelly would drive back down the dark isolated Port Jack streets, and by the time they got back to the South Shore the temperature would've gone up enough to start water droplets falling from the icicles.

The dead dog asked, "You know who I really am, don't you?"

"You're my brain damage. Nobody can be dead for twenty-eight minutes and not suffer from it."

"You're crazy all right, but not from that."

"Is Sister Murteen really in hell?"

"She practically runs the place."

Zero moved even closer. "You have no love. There's no reason for you to stay. Marianne doesn't want you.

Jessie Gray only used you. Emma Waltz...well, you already know that's just ridiculous."

"Maybe."

"There's no one else. You have no one else."

What an awful thought.

That there was no one in the world who loved him. He vaguely wondered why he was putting himself through this, which hateful part of him was keeping the dog around. Why his doubts should take this form. Some men had to struggle with a faceless despair and here he was with a nasty French bulldog. He figured his father had it better, just be depressed in front of the TV.

He thought of Emma Waltz folding beneath the same pressures her entire adult life. He knew he had only one final shot at redemption. He had to save her somehow.

"I've got my reasons for staying."

"So do I."

"You'll be gone soon enough."

"So will you."

Flynn held back a sigh. The Charger's headlights flashed across the terrain and immediately the grim nerve worked through his chest again, twitching under his heart. He was here.

The GTO sat in the driveway, already almost buried under the snow. Nuddin wasn't only good with rifles, he was a damn fine driver too.

The Shepard house, black as the far end of the road.

The false mortar and fake ancient rock face, freezing metal and dark, empty windows like wide, blind eyes searching.

A good place for the endgame.

Flynn could only feel a growing sense of reality deepening around him, a resolve and call to purpose, an understanding of intent.

Love and fear entwined, that's what Mooney had said. If Petersen the Tabasco king had been the fear, then was Nuddin the love? What the hell did it mean?

Autistic, living in his own reality, but visiting ours on occasion. An idiot-savant murderer. A natural manipulator, a honed killer.

He's low-functioning autistic, so separated from the world that it hardly impacts on him.

It was good hearing Sierra's voice in his head again. She'd always helped him, had always loved him. He couldn't fully see that at the time, but it was obvious to him now. So was his own lack of appreciation and ingratitude. Even when she'd threatened to fire him she'd done it out of love for him. He was such a damn fool.

I wonder if he even felt any of the torture he was going through. He walks on the balls of his feet because there's more pressure exerted on the nerves. He likes to be hugged hard. He can stare into a mirror for hours, unable to fully realize he's looking at himself.

The Devil hates to be alone. He always needed someone to hear his voice of power, to listen to his whisper. It's how he worked. It was the completion of the circuit. It was someone else's evil that brought the savant to the surface.

Flynn got out of the car and made his way to the house, falling twice. The second time down he relaxed himself and went with the cold trying to consume him. He breathed in the snow and enjoyed the darkness trying to make him its own. He had no fear of the freeze. The light-headedness swarmed him. He hadn't eaten in days, hadn't slept at all. His exhaustion dulled him and dialed him down to nothing. He still wondered why his brother had saved his life that day, and if, after all these years, Flynn remained a good boy.

His eyes flashed open. He stood and got moving.

Trying the front door, he found it unlocked. He walked in feeling no pressure. He wasn't worried for himself. He didn't think he ever would be again.

The house was freezing. Someone had shut the heat off right after Shepard had been taken out of here, and no one had turned it back on.

He heard humming coming from somewhere deep in the house.

A girl softly murmuring a childish tune.

Flynn walked to the kitchen.

He found the door to the basement. It was back in place with the pins set back into the hinges.

He was playing it all wrong but something kept telling him this was the only way to play it. His brother's presence felt so strong around him now that he could imagine spinning around fast enough to catch sight of Danny.

His mind shifted into fantasies spreading to the two ends of fulfillment. In the first, he and Danny were partners, going shoulder to shoulder, brothers and friends, ready for glory, unbeatable. In the next, Flynn turned to see Danny behind him, the cigarette hanging out of the corner of his mouth, handsome and only marginally tortured of soul, selfish and suicidal, out to cause pain. Flynn punched him in the mouth and went down into the dark alone.

But some things couldn't be helped.

You decided on your course, and you saw it through.

Flynn went to hit the light but it was already on. A dim glow wafted across the bottom step.

He didn't draw his .38. It wasn't time yet.

It came back to him then, what Petersen had said right before he blew his own head off.

My evil was down deep where it was supposed to be, and he unlatched the cellar door.

Flynn descended the stairs.

Zero's plastic hamburger was still at the bottom of the stairwell where the dog had left it.

Nuddin sat with Kelly in the cage in the middle of the room with a butcher knife pressed to her throat.

The door was ajar, the key in the lock. She was shuddering from the cold.

Flynn looked at Nuddin's misshapen head and scars anew, realizing he had done all of that to himself, since he was a child. The thick, knotted welts and brandings that cross-thatched his body. The broken bones that tilted him one way, then another. Beating himself, crushing himself, destroying himself just to feel the contours of his own identity.

Nuddin started humming along with Kelly, and those gentle brown eyes an inch too far apart watched Flynn.

A pile of clothes had been set off to one side. Nuddin was covered in dried blood. After the first blow of the baseball bat, he'd stripped before continuing to beat Sierra to death. He made sure he covered himself with her, the streaming wet heat describing his own body. He'd cut himself too, and had been cutting himself since he'd been taken from this house. Old crusted wounds and new incisions curved and arced across his flesh.

His breathing came in short rasps, puffing clouds across the basement. He was actually sweating despite the chill.

For a moment Flynn couldn't imagine what it would be like to live in a body where you could feel almost nothing, not even the shape of your own skin. An instant later he realized, Oh yeah, he could, in fact, imagine it. In a fashion, he lived it. That's what this was all about.

Flynn just stared for another second. Sometimes you needed an extra breath to help you decide where it was you wanted to go next.

"Are you all right, Kelly?" he asked.

"Yes," she said.

"Don't be scared."

"I'm not."

"It's going to be okay."

"I know. He killed Sierra."

He wondered how much she had seen. "Has he been talking to you?"

"He doesn't talk. Usually."

"That's right, not usually. But he does, doesn't he?"

"Sometimes."

Nuddin smiled. It was utterly innocent and perhaps even loving, enough to break your heart.

The cage. Christina Shepard had said she was protecting him. All the scars—they were self-inflicted. Maybe she'd known about his penchant for connecting with evil. She'd known not to let him loose on the world.

Sierra had told Flynn about autistics, how they had trouble understanding the contours of their own bodies. Nuddin used the pain to give himself an identity. Flynn couldn't comprehend the willpower it would take to bash yourself in the head hard enough to dent your own skull. To twist your arms and break your own bones. How big a step was it before you were destroying other people?

He leaned down and stared through the bars.

"Hey, hello there," Nuddin whispered.

It was the same voice Flynn had heard on the phone that night. The one that had told him it was afflicted. Anguish and sorrow that murdered men in their sleep or kept them locked up for decades. Flynn had been so close. He remembered thinking the voice had no name, that the person had never been identified, lurking unseen and unknown and never understood.

So close, but he hadn't been able to see it.

"I'm your friend," Nuddin said. "Can you talk to me? Can you understand me?"

Saying the things that Flynn had first said to him. Using his own words. Flynn remembered how the first time he'd heard Nuddin's voice, through the heating vent, singing softly in the basement, his stomach tightened at the tune and his scalp had prickled. It was happening again.

Nuddin grinned, his gaze full of resolve. Nuddin, the thing inside Nuddin. He might not understand his purpose in life, but he recognized it and embraced it. That put him leagues ahead of most people in the world.

No one had cleaned up down here after that night. A

dried pool of gritty copper remained on the floor where Shepard had bled after being shot in the heart by his wife.

"I know your secret," Nuddin whispered.

He's got a voice that comes from hell. You can't resist.

It rang through Flynn and he felt his soul chime along with it. A voice that had no name, that had never been christened or identified. The hiss of your deepest lies and sins. The scream of your own human madness. The whisper of impending death. It was the sound of ice breaking beneath you.

Flynn was used to it by now.

"Big deal," he said.

Flynn unclipped the .38. Nuddin's eyes brightened and his smile twisted into a leer. He pressed the point of the knife harder into Kelly's neck and she let out a gasp but did nothing more.

Flynn thought she had the makings to be the strongest, most determined person he'd ever known. He hoped he would be around in ten years to see her graduate from high school, but he didn't think it was going to happen.

"Let Kelly go."

"No," Nuddin said. "No no no."

Flynn unloaded his pistol. He rattled the bullets in his fist for a moment before tossing them to one side of the basement, the empty gun to another.

"I'm not going to shoot you."

"Oh," Nuddin said. "Oh oh oh. That's bad."

"Why?"

"You're supposed to understand."

Here it was, a retarded guy with drool on his chin telling Flynn he was stupid. Flynn was punctured by the thought that Nuddin had been controlling and directing everything that had happened these past weeks. That he had, in fact, been in charge of Flynn's life because Flynn had allowed it. A multiedged personality—his dominant identity moronic, and the hidden killer beneath quiet and knowing and planning. It filled Flynn with awe.

"He doesn't hurt the family," Kelly said. "My mother told me. He doesn't hurt family. Never. But we have to keep him from everyone else."

The knife at her throat wavered an inch, then Nuddin retightened his grip and the blade straightened, aimed at her carotid. One yank and he'd tear her throat open.

All families have a dark secret.

Sometimes it's you.

He tried to imagine what it had been like for Bragg. A Southern gentleman with a family history of slavery, violence and murder. Coming from a clan that drowned babies at birth. Slowly going out of his own head as the cancer ate into his brain. What did Bragg see in the boy when he was born? Had he destroyed the records, or had there never been any? Had he taken on the burden of his own son in some form of penance, an act of defiance?

"I know your secret," Nuddin whispered.

"That doesn't matter to me."

But Nuddin seemed to think it should. His free hand started fluttering about, the awkwardly angled elbow striking the bars. That voice reaching out like a silken tongue moving into his ear. "You want to die."

"You're a real whiz with a rifle," Flynn said.

"Daddy taught me."

"Let Kelly go."

"No."

"You don't hurt family. Ever."

Nuddin grinned, lost in himself, perhaps even adrift from two selves. He shut his eyes, and a nervous tic twisted his face to the right until his nose pressed to Kelly's hair. "Almost never. I hurt Mama. From time to time."

Flynn recalled Sierra telling him how Bragg's wife had been cut to pieces from cancer surgery. Now he saw it. Nuddin taking away pieces of his mother over the years. Bragg trying to teach the boy all that he knew about guns and knives. Maybe trying to channel the thing inside the boy. Nuddin unable to fully understand anything except using the skills and weapons he'd been given. Flynn wondered how many missing folks had wound up in the Chatalaha River and nearby swamps thanks to Nuddin. Bragg too ashamed to admit the truth to anyone, the woman alone with her wounds and her son locked in a cage smashing his own head in. Maybe Nuddin was only as insane as his parents, as his sister.

"Let Kelly go," Flynn said, "and I'll come sit in there with you. I want to, okay? I think we should sit together for a while."

The whisper without sexual identity, not a male voice or a female one, and yet urgent and in pain, as if others' dark riddles and mysteries affected and tainted it. The whisper becoming a hiss. *"You want to die."*

"That's no secret. Even the fucking dog knows that."

"You want a child."

"Sure."

"You want to kill me."

"No."

"You want to kill us both."

"No."

"Me and Emma."

Nuddin's smile faltered and he cocked the oblong head. Perhaps it truly was Flynn's secret, the need to die and take Emma Waltz along with him. Perhaps his secret disgrace was knowing they'd both lived such miserable lives. It was a second-rate regret at best, no different than his father's.

Nuddin sensed there was no fear in Flynn at hearing his hidden heart spoken aloud. The knife drooped.

Kelly showed absolutely no fear at all. Flynn felt a great surge of love for her. He thought if only he'd found her five years earlier he might've saved his marriage. The love he couldn't provide his wife he might've been able to give to the kid.

"You want to take Emma with you into the water."

Flynn reached into his pocket and drew out the mirror he'd taken from Sierra's bathroom. It was covered with fine layers of powder and scuffed with mascara and lipstick. He held it up to Nuddin's face and watched his reaction.

Nuddin froze, seeing himself. No longer lost to himself. Meeting himself in the glass just a few inches away.

He reached out with his free hand to grab the mirror but Flynn wouldn't let it go. Nuddin tugged harder.

Soon he drew the knife away and used both hands to grip the mirror. Flynn gave it to him. Entranced, Nuddin peered deeper and began humming.

Nuddin went, La la la.

Flynn gestured for Kelly to come to him. She snaked

around Nuddin without touching him, easing against the bars.

"Go upstairs and out into my car. You can turn the key all the way to start the engine and get the heat going."

"What are you going to do?"

"Go, Kelly."

"You're going to kill him, aren't you?"

"No."

"You're going to because he killed Sierra."

He watched her rush up the stairs and another wash of affection went through him.

Flynn turned back and Nuddin was staring into his eyes.

They both went for the knife in the same instant. Flynn lunged into the cage and the two men grappled, slamming against the half-inch steel bars.

Nuddin's strength astonished Flynn. He had no idea where it was coming from, the power in this guy who was as light as balsa wood. The thing inside him was made of iron.

In a moment Nuddin had the knife. Flynn managed to grab his wrist but couldn't press him back at all. His other hand was trying to find purchase on Nuddin's sweaty chest. He came to the only slightly horrifying realization that he wasn't going to be able to win.

It made him cut loose with a sick giggle. You could die a lot of dopey ways but being stabbed in a cage while wrestling a naked autistic idiot-savant split personality was way the hell up there.

Flynn said, "No," between his teeth and Nuddin forced him back another inch, and another, until the back of his head was being wedged among the bars and the knife was still moving toward his throat.

There was no room to lash out with a kick. Nuddin's weight pressed against Flynn. The stink of blood made Flynn gag. He had time for maybe one final frenzied move but he had no idea what it should be.

His eyes spun and Nuddin smiled, still without an ounce of anger in him, his love no different now than when he was hugging Flynn in Sierra's home.

The thought enraged him. The mirror was on the cage floor and Flynn knew that somehow everything was wrapped up in that.

He brought the heel of his shoe down on it and the mirror cracked.

Flynn said, "Now look at yourself." Nuddin cocked his head, grinning, and angled his chin down to see.

Flynn swept the busted pieces forward with his toe. He was hoping to dig the shards into Nuddin's groin. Maybe that would be enough pain for the guy, but he didn't have enough leverage. The glass dug into Nuddin's thigh and he weakened his hold the slightest bit. Flynn ground his toe into the glass, shoving it farther into Nuddin's flesh.

It made Nuddin smile wider but he loosened his grip even more, enough for Flynn to make a final concerted effort. Instead of fighting, he flung himself out of the cage.

His shoulder caught against the lock and banged the door wide open against the bars. On his knees, Flynn reached, grabbed the steel door and tried to shut it.

It slammed on Nuddin's head. He hardly felt it. Flynn knew now that on the phone Nuddin hadn't been talking about an affliction of spirit. He hadn't been talking about the murders. When he'd said *I am afflicted* he meant with the malady of not being able to understand pain.

Flynn slammed the door again. The metal tore a gouge in Nuddin's forehead, smashed his nose and mashed his lips. He giggled and continued to come forward, the knife in front of him, slashing now. The blade caught Flynn across the arm of his coat, tearing through the fabric and digging into muscle. It hurt like hell and he held on to his hurt, knowing it was the thing that most differentiated him from Nuddin.

He threw himself against the door and got his hand on the key, hoping to simply lock Nuddin inside. But it wasn't going to go down that easy. It couldn't. The knife stabbed out and narrowly missed Flynn's eyes. Nuddin went, Oh oh oh. He shoved back and the cage door eased open farther and farther. Flynn shrugged himself against the bars and slammed the door once more.

A geyser of blood shot out in an arc that lashed Flynn's chest. Nuddin's face was smashed but he was still smiling.

"Stop it!" Flynn said and Nuddin came forward again, the knife slicing down. Bragg had taught him how to use edged weapons too. The blade slashed across Flynn's chest. It went deep enough that he felt the knife nick a rib. He screamed and fell hard on his back. No cool anymore, man, no way. Frantically he kicked out and shut the door on Nuddin's arm.

The cracking bone sounded like a gunshot as Nuddin tittered. He was enjoying being beaten to death, covered in hot blood.

Perhaps it meant he was showing some kind of love for

Sierra when he'd killed her the way he had. It was his ultimate expression of devotion.

Nuddin stabbed again and Flynn slammed the cage door.

It took five more times before Nuddin's eyes were gone and he'd stopped moving.

A brilliant smear of blood snaked across the back of his hand.

But the hand was steady.

The car chase, Petersen blasting himself, the murder of Sierra, and now having crossed the last line, having taken a life, and Flynn wasn't trembling. What did it say about him? About his death wish, about his inability to find another way besides becoming a killer. What about his secret? What about taking Emma into the water with him?

The pool of blood on the back of his hand didn't drop over the side of his wrist until he stood.

He picked up a shard of the mirror and stared at himself in it the way Nuddin had. Nuddin hadn't only been stronger than Flynn, he'd been smarter. He'd been right in his last note too.

They were brothers.

It took him ten minutes to maneuver up the stairs. He carefully took his coat off but couldn't keep from crying out, tore some dish towels into rags and staunched his wounds. It took a while to do even a half-assed job, but at least he wouldn't bleed to death. He washed his hands in the kitchen sink and a wave of nausea rolled over him. The stink of rotting food wafted from the refrigerator, and his stomach tumbled. He splashed water on his face and tried to pull it together.

He phoned Sierra's place and Raidin answered. Flynn had difficulty speaking. His voice sounded faraway from himself, the words unfamiliar.

Raidin said, "You're in shock. Where are you?"

"The Shepard house."

"The boy Trevor's been telling us everything that's been going on. It's fascinating and more than a little hard to believe."

"But you do believe it."

Raidin said nothing. That was good. It meant he did, but still wanted to investigate and reserve judgment. He was a solid cop through and through. Flynn found himself respecting Raidin even more, although he still had to even the score about that bullshit throat chop. And he wanted to say something about that fucking fedora.

"We've found some corroborating evidence. You shouldn't have left the children."

"How are they?"

"We've got a doctor looking them over, but they should be fine. We'll get somebody out there to you as soon as we can. Did you finish it?"

"Yes," Flynn said and that seemed to be enough for Raidin. But Flynn found himself explaining it, in detail, all that had happened. Trying to get it straight in his own head.

"We're pulled very thin," Raidin said. "It'll take us a while to get to you. The Port Jack department should be there soon though. Go with them. Don't give anybody any trouble."

"I've got Kelly. I'm not waiting. I'll be at my apartment. We can clear it all tomorrow."

"You'll never make it. You'll smash up on the streets."

"I'll make it."

He hung up and got out to the Dodge. Kelly sat there staring at him. He climbed in beside her, waiting for her to weep, but she wouldn't.

It was still snowing.

It wasn't over yet.

TWENTY-NINE

The slow rhythmic heartbeat of the wiper blades and the warm rush of air from the vents put Kelly to sleep on the way back. The resilience of kids astounded him. The resilience of some kids, anyway. Kelly had been through more than Flynn had been through as a child and seemed to handle it with dignity. She understood the realities of death and grief better than he had as a kid, perhaps even better than he did now. It made him shake his head in admiration.

He took her back to his apartment and Emma Waltz was still there.

He carried Kelly inside, asleep against his chest, and didn't want to let her go. Emma stared at the girl and then up at him, and Flynn asked, "Are you all right?"

"No," she told him. "I don't think so."

They were the first words he'd heard her say. He'd expected her voice to mean more to him, to carry the song of both their lives. Perhaps it did. The strained voice carried fortitude and intensity. It was husky and determined. He imagined it saying, Save me. He thought of it telling him, Make love to me.

The twin holes in the floor had been worked over by the cops, the bullets removed.

"Do you remember me?" he asked.

"Yes," she said. "Now, I do. I didn't when you showed up at the house. Afterward, I realized how much you looked like your brother."

"Except older."

"Yes. It's odd. Your being so much older than him now."

"When I was pulling out I saw you leave."

"I drove down to the end of the parking lot and waited there. I barely made it here with the storm, and I didn't want to try going all the way home again until it cleared. I didn't know what to do. I'm not a very comfortable driver and my car doesn't work that well in bad weather. The police came. I sat in my car and watched. I didn't know whether I should talk to them or not. When they left I came back inside. They left the door open."

"Why didn't you speak with them?"

"I don't know."

Nearly being shot but choosing to sit in the snow instead of running to the police.

He put Kelly on the couch and covered her with the only extra blanket he had. Emma Waltz sat at the far end, Kelly's feet brushing against her. They spoke quietly, the girl's presence somehow connecting them even more deeply.

Emma said, "You're bleeding. My God, what happened to you?"

His wounds had reopened. He shrugged out of his coat and shirt grunting in pain. He went to the bathroom and took a handful of painkillers. He got gauze, a bottle of hydrogen peroxide and a spool of tape but felt too tired to do anything with them. He sat in a kitchen chair stripped to the waist, covered with dried blood and scabbing cuts and gashes, his flesh looking so much like Nuddin's flesh now.

With the thought exhausting him further, Flynn uncapped the hydrogen peroxide and started to drift. Emma sat beside him and took the bottle from his hand. She swabbed his wounds and the abrupt burning pain brought him back with a strangled yelp.

She said, "I'm sorry."

He sucked air through his teeth. "It's okay. Thanks for helping."

"This one slash needs stitches to be closed properly."

"Maybe tomorrow."

"Did the man who shot at us do this?"

He nodded. "Yeah."

"What happened?"

"I killed him."

You'd think that might elicit a gasp or a shudder from her, but she continued tending to him, complacent and empty. She wasn't even curious, or if she was, it was tamped so far down that it didn't register.

There was no righteous follow-up. He'd just admitted to murder. Anything he said was going to be a non-sequitur, so he just followed his instinct.

"You told the police I'd hit you."

"Yes. It was Chad's idea."

"And you went along."

"Yes."

"Why?"

"Honestly, it's because he was there and you weren't."

Flynn nodded again. "Did you leave him after that? Did you kick him out?"

"No, I didn't."

They were the kind of questions you could ask someone else but never answer yourself. Why you stayed with someone, or why you left. He felt bold and capable only because he was more afraid than she was. She had struggled to find love and found angry men much weaker than herself. She gave more, she tried harder. She risked her blood and her bones. Flynn had never risked anything. He just beat the hell out of anybody who hurt a kid, keeping himself busy while his wife found Frickin' Alvin.

"Do you know what's been happening?" he asked.

"From the papers. I put it together afterward. Your name."

"Right."

"Why did you come to see me?"

"I had to."

She wet her lips. She tended him perfectly but without warmth. He could feel the chill between them.

"Why then?" she asked. "After so much time?"

"Same poor answer. I had to. That doesn't explain anything, but it's all I've got."

"I think it might be all I have too."

"Tell me what happened."

"Starting from when?"

He still had the note in his pocket. He drew it out. "From when you got this."

"What is it?"

"You had it with you when you came to my door." Then he realized he was telling her to start in the wrong place, but he couldn't see asking her to go back thirty years, to the day they'd first met. "No, tell me what occurred after I came to your place. Between you and Chad."

"He hit me. He thought I was having an affair. He refused to believe that I didn't know you and hadn't asked you there. He thought I'd paid you to beat him up. He thought you were going to steal his pot."

"One of those guys who gets paranoid when he smokes."

"No, not really. You're still oblivious to exactly what you did."

That stopped him. He frowned, knowing it was true. "Tell me."

"Walking into the house unannounced, a total stranger. The things you said."

"They were righteous."

"They were very frightening and embarrassing to me."

He told her, "I'm sorry."

"We filed the report and went home. Chad left later that evening. I hadn't seen him for two days when someone phoned me. I couldn't tell if it was a man or a woman. The person spoke in a whisper, with a great deal of"—Her fingers clenched the air trying to grab hold of the proper word—"zeal. It mentioned your name. It told me your address. It begged me to visit you, and in the morning I decided I would."

Flynn tried to see it. Imagining how Nuddin had researched him online, maybe gotten his hands on Flynn's file. Would Sierra have brought it home? Yes, in order to protect him. Doing her own investigation into Flynn and

Emma's background. Upset and angry but still looking out for Flynn, worrying over his paperwork. He'd asked her to check up on Emma and she had, and that had given Nuddin the edge.

"How'd you get the note?"

"When I got out of my car in your lot a young retarded man handed it to me. I thought it was one of those cards that say, 'I'm handicapped, please give what you can.' I gave him five dollars and he rushed away. I didn't know what the note said until just now. What does it mean?"

"It's nothing but a bad joke."

In her sleep, Kelly wailed once. She quietly called for her mother and father, sat up and immediately fell back on the couch, sobbing into the cushions without awareness. She whimpered for Zero and Nuddin. She said Flynn's name and he took a strange pride in it.

He sat with her and held her and rubbed her back while Emma Waltz watched him. The girl's warmth against him moved him toward hope. He knew she'd be able to get past her pain now. It wasn't quite as bad as he and Sierra had predicted, but this was merely the first wave. It would catch up to Kelly again and again over the next several months and years, but eventually she would make a precarious peace with all that had transpired. He pressed his lips to her brow the way a father might.

He fell asleep on the couch holding her like that and woke hours later in the deep morning with Emma Waltz still watching him, still with her coat on.

He thought, Here it is. Here's our chance to save each other.

"Why are you here?" he asked.

She tried to say something but didn't make it. The planes and angles of her face dropped and diverged. She shook her head so that the layers of hair rose and fell and swam, and finally she shrugged. Minor human motions with the unspeakable accents of life behind them. She bent and stroked Kelly's forehead. He knew she felt the same longing he did and he could find no words of explanation. He thought it might be like this forever, lost in a mire of silent experience.

"I could probably love you, you know," he said. It was sincere and heartfelt, but sounded weird even to himself.

Embarrassed, he went to his bedroom and lay there, his wounds tight and painful but securing him to the texture of life.

An hour later, as the windows brightened with dawn, she crept into bed with him and lay down with her clothes on, even her coat and shoes. She turned on her side and he reached around and held her, waiting for her to cry. She didn't. She hadn't for thirty years. He knew what it had done to him, and thought for her it must be much worse. The years with men like Chad, who bent her arms back until she went to her knees. Driven to endure pain and terror with ignorant, caustic men, young and old. That's why she was here. She didn't just want him to smack open her cut lip and give her another shiner.

He was much more special than that. She wanted him to go the extra mile down the midnight road for her. She was here to die and he was supposed to kill her.

THIRTY

In the morning, Kelly Shepard said, "I want to see my dad."

Flynn threw back a handful of painkillers and took her to the hospital. Emma Waltz riding shotgun, Kelly in the back staring ahead expressionless except for a muted concern. He hadn't even asked Emma along, she'd simply gotten into the Charger as if it had always been expected. She slid in without hesitation, despite what had happened the last time she'd been in it.

The snow had tapered off but still hadn't quit. It wouldn't until he figured out his next move. The plows had been busy all night long and had done a better job than Flynn had expected. Things wouldn't be quite as rough today.

When they got to the hospital, Emma waited in the little alcove where Flynn had first met Jessie Gray. He held Kelly's hand and led her to her father's room. Shepard looked the same except he'd lost a few more pounds.

Kelly moved to the bedside very slowly, took her father's hand and hugged it to her. She began to cry and Flynn mentally commanded Shepard to wake the hell up, do everybody a fucking favor.

But the man slept on. A nurse walked in and asked if Flynn was family. He said, "Yes, I'm his cousin Ferdinand."

The nurse wandered off. Kelly's face was slathered in tears but she almost afforded him the gift of a smile.

They got back out to the Dodge and Kelly asked, "Where am I going now?"

"To where I work. Child Protective Services. They'll find you another family to go with for a while, but first I want you to talk with somebody."

"Can't I stay with you?"

"No," Flynn said. "I wish you could, but I've got some problems I have to work out first."

"I don't know if I want to talk to anybody right now."

"Well, that's okay. Maybe you could just listen to him for a while?"

"All right."

He drove out to the CPS headquarters. More than half the staff was out because of the blizzard, and the rest hadn't heard about Sierra yet. Raidin must've had a hell of a time forcing Jessie Gray to sit on the story, but he'd managed to swing it. There was too much that had to be worked through, evidence to sift. No word would leak out until Raidin tracked down Flynn and got everything proven, bagged, written up, stamped, and filed.

Kelly walked down the hall between Flynn and Emma, holding their hands. It could've been the portrait of a normal family. The promise of possibility reemerged.

When they got to Mooney's door he told them, "Wait here for a minute."

He knocked and stuck his head in. Mooney looked up

from a folder and sniffed. Flynn entered and shut the door behind him.

He said, "You've got your work cut out for you today, Dale, so clear your desk and focus. Sierra was murdered last night. You'll hear about it later this afternoon. It was ugly. You remember Kelly Shepard. She needs to talk to someone. She may have witnessed Sierra being killed. She's certainly been through a hell of a lot. She also needs to be placed with a new foster family."

It was a lot to process. Mooney's left eye twitched and he swallowed thickly. He started to ask about Sierra and thought better of it. All in all he handled it pretty well. He said, "She's here now?"

"Yes."

"Give me a moment."

"Sure. And thanks, Dale."

Flynn stepped out, dropped to one knee before Kelly, and said, "Listen, maybe you remember this guy's name is Dale Mooney. You two are just going to chat some more. If there's something you don't want to discuss, you tell him and that'll be the end of it. But I want you to try."

"Okay."

"He's a pretty up-front person and he'll do his best to help you."

Her eyes grew wet but she didn't cry. "Are you going to stay?"

"No. But I'll make sure everything works out right this time, okay?"

"Okay."

"Trust me."

"I do. Is my father ever going to wake up?"

"I don't know," Flynn said.

Mooney opened the door and smiled. "Kelly? It's so nice to see you again. Will you please come inside?"

Emma Waltz, attractive in her hard way, couldn't meet his eyes. Flynn moved to her, those bruises a bit less noticeable than they had been last night. He kissed her and she didn't respond. He saw she had expected him to be someone else, to say and do other things. The actions of her other men, the actions of his own brother. She was confused by the way he was handling himself. She wavered and said, "I have to leave."

"Going home to Chad?"

"Yes," she said.

"Is that what you want to do?"

"Yes."

"Do you love him?"

"Yes."

"You're a liar, Emma Waltz. What would Patty think of that?"

It got through, hearing her sister's name. It brought heat into her eyes and her lips firmed. Flynn liked the look. He'd be willing to be hated so long as it fired her up. He kissed her again and she pressed her hands against his chest to shove him away. Good, he liked that too.

Their impasse would soon turn lethal for one or both of them. Flynn had to break it any way he could or give Emma what she wanted.

He turned away and said, "Before I drop you back at your car, I want you to take a ride with me."

She licked her lips, hoping now might be her chance to get snuffed. "All right."

He knew the place but not the means of atonement.

PRIVATE BEACH. NO ENTRY EXCEPT FOR RESIDENTS.

They were back where it had all started and ended for them. They couldn't get away from the sign. It followed them through life. Flynn's face shifted into a hideous expression of joy and doubt. The great mysteries continued to spin outward and roped him in tighter and tighter.

The old man started coughing in his ear again. His mother sighed. Your family never let go of you, no matter how long they'd been gone.

"Why are you doing this?" Emma asked.

"Why are you here with me?" he said.

"I don't know. I feel like it was always supposed to be this way."

"It's not. We're not going to die."

"I don't care if we do."

"You're going to, Emma, you're going to start caring."

"I don't think I can."

"We'll see."

Survivor guilt. Danny hadn't realized what he was doing when he booted Flynn and Emma from the car. He hadn't been saving them or setting them free, he'd just been letting the towing cable out. For thirty years the

winch had been pulling them closer and closer to the water. Now they were either going in together or cutting
loose together.

He gunned it toward the beach, the same way Danny
had. It was time to give up the car or give up his life. He
saw the stupidity of it all with an intense clarity, but there
wasn't anything he could do alone. He eased down farther on the pedal and the Charger bounced wildly over ice
down the snow-covered road. In the distance he watched
the tide starting to rise, as if trying to reach the car.

It wasn't only about life, but about cool. Action. Charm.
Hipness. Breath.

From the backseat Danny seemed to be urging him not
to do it. That made Flynn smile, knowing his brother
didn't want him dead. Saying to him, Take it to the edge
of the water, on a straight run. Give it your all, but don't
go in, you hear me, you don't need to go in.

From back there Zero said, "Of course you do. That's
what this is all about. You're dead. You've always been
dead. Didn't I already tell you?" It was the first time the
dog had ever spoken to him in front of another person.
Of course it would be Emma, who was also dead. She
didn't react to Flynn's brain damage, but he thought she
must've heard.

Flynn glanced over at her and said, "Are you scared?"
"No."
"Do you care? Do you even want to live?"
"No."

What could you do with that? How did you work
around it? He should know. They started down this road

together. Flynn put his hand on her knee the way Danny used to always grip his girlfriends. Lightly, friendly. It had something to do with sex but more about partnership, about traveling together.

He fought for words and put the hammer down. The world whipped past them even faster while they sat there, stuck in and out of time. He started to speak and quit, tried again and came out with a noise he'd never made before in his life.

He cleared his throat, a little surprised at how calm he felt. "You're not the only one who jumped the rails so early on, Emma. Nobody gets out of childhood undamaged."

She said nothing.

"You were a kid, you can't blame yourself for what happened. You can't even blame them. Danny and Patricia were only kids too. They were stupid but that's no reason to hate them. We all have pain to deal with. Everybody's got a story to tell. A dead daddy, a greasy-fingered uncle. A mean mommy. A failed algebra test. We all hurt. You don't have to feel pain more deeply than the rest of us, Emma. You don't have to allow yourself to be hurt anymore. You deserve better. Patricia would want better for you."

She said nothing.

He gripped the wheel tighter. "Fine."

He jammed down on the gas. The car bucked and jounced as they went over the curb toward the snow-covered sand. They hit a dune and went airborne.

She reached out against the dashboard and dug her

nails in. Her grimace tightened until she appeared skeletal, already dead. She turned away, pressed her face against her shoulder, sinking farther into the seat and growing smaller and smaller until he could hardly see her. Until she wasn't even there anymore.

"All right, fuck it," Flynn said. "Let's do what they couldn't. Let's hit the water."

"You know who I am, don't you?" Zero asked.

"Yes."

"I'm the angel of death."

The constant wind at the shore blew the snow into sloping drifts that uncovered saw grass and sand. The beach where his brother had made love to Patricia Waltz and other girls opened wide. The rooftops of the neighboring mansions offered black scratches against the white sky.

Zero's voice, his own voice, said, "You've always been mine, whenever I wanted you."

"Not anymore, mutt."

"Forever," Zero said, "you're mine forever, because that's what you want. You're mine until you hit the bottom of hell. Until we—"

A huge fist reached forward from the backseat and grabbed the French bulldog by the collar of its little plastic coat, roughly shaking it once. Zero's eyes bugged farther, his lips peeled back into a hateful, knowing snarl. The angel of death was pulled away, only to reappear an instant later at Flynn's left shoulder, pressed hard against the inside of the driver's window. The dog yelped and looked at Flynn, sort of grinning, indignant and frothing.

The knuckles of the hand holding the dog rapped twice on the glass, vying for Flynn's attention.

He finally understood and rolled the window down. The hand shoved the dead dog out and Flynn rolled the window back up, free of the tormenting voice of his self-hatred. He glanced at the rearview but Danny wasn't there anymore. His brother had appeared just long enough to show Flynn he was still loved and protected.

He put his hand to Emma's chin and slowly turned her face and forced her to look out the windshield as they closed in on the furious ocean.

"Last chance, Emma. I think I can save you if you'll let me. And more than that. I need you. I need you to give me a reason to get beyond the next minute. It's a lot to be responsible for, these feelings, these words, especially coming from a stranger. But we're not really strangers, are we?"

The Charger roared through the storm fencing and flew out over the snow. Sand, ice and smashed bits of wood exploded up across the hood.

Flynn yanked the wheel hard, the Charger bouncing down the beach and fishtailing like mad.

You had to have a reason. He glanced at the side of Emma's face, thinking she could be beautiful, if only—

The right-front tire plunged and the Charger rocked wildly forward but kept going, jolting and bouncing harder and harder as the tires lost all traction and the car began to spin in a wide looping circle. He wondered if the shocks would hold. They whirled out of control. He gunned the gas and they reeled, the circle widening as they were tossed about. She fell up against him and he wrapped his free arm around her, holding her close because if you had to die, it was better to die with somebody else. He pressed his lips to her cheek and tasted salt. She was crying.

"Stop us," she whimpered. "Please."

It might be too late.

He slammed the brakes and tore at the wheel but he couldn't break the circuit as they kept going around and around, the engine screaming and the tires flying insanely across the ice. He thought, Too late, we can't make it. Look at this shit. The car lurched, the shocks screeching. They ripped into the water and the force of the sea stopped them like a wall of cement. Flynn and Emma both slammed forward. She cracked her face against the dash and he banged his nose hard against the steering wheel. Noir was gone, it was time for color. Blood burst across the inside of the cracked windshield. It was a sickening sight but a real one, a fleshly one. Metal shrieked and crumpled. The two front tires burst and the radiator exploded. She sat quivering in the seat, her fists pressed to her cheeks, her nose broken and pouring blood, her fiery eyes staring into the blue. The sorrow inside loosened and flowed. Emma said her sister's name once, a quiet farewell from a lifetime away as the waves broke across the hood. She fell against him and the tears she'd been holding back for three decades came gently at first and then with greater power. Their blood ran together. He lit a cigarette before his pack got wet and stared out over the waves. Water poured in through the vents. It was going to be impossible getting the doors open. They'd have to get out through the windows and swim in the fierce tide. It was going to be tough. But they still had another minute for that. He held her tightly, waiting for his own tears to come, and thought, *I'm alive.*

ABOUT THE AUTHOR

TOM PICCIRILLI lives in Colorado where, besides writing, he spends an inordinate amount of time watching trash cult films and reading Gold Medal classic noir and hardboiled novels. He's a fan of Asian cinema, especially horror movies, pinky violence, and samurai flicks. He also likes walking his dogs around the neighborhood. Are you starting to get the hint that he doesn't have a particularly active social life? Well to heck with you, buddy, yours isn't much better. Give him any static and he'll smack you in the mush, dig? Tom also enjoys making new friends. He's the author of fifteen novels including *The Dead Letters, Headstone City, November Mourns,* and *A Choir of Ill Children.* He's a four-time winner of the Bram Stoker Award and a final nominee for the World Fantasy Award. To learn more, check out his official website, Epitaphs, at www.tompiccirilli.com.

Don't miss
Tom Piccirilli's
exciting new novel

THE
COLD SPOT

Coming from Bantam Books
in summer 2008

*Read on for an exclusive peek, and
pick up your copy at your favorite bookseller.*

THE COLD SPOT
On sale summer 2008

Chase was laughing with the others during the poker game when his grandfather threw down his cards, said, "Lady Luck's still pissed I left her for dead in Vegas," took a deep pull on his beer, and with no expression at all shot Walcroft in the head.

Only Chase was startled. He leaped back in his seat knocking over some loose cash and an ashtray, the world tilting left while he went right. Jonah had palmed his .22 in his left hand and had it pressed to Walcroft's temple, a thin trail of smoke spiraling in the air and the smell of burning hair and skin wafting across the table into Chase's face.

You'd think it would be disgusting, acrid, but it was actually sort of fragrant. There was almost no blood. One small pop had filled the hotel room, quieter than striking a nail with a hammer. It didn't even frighten the pigeons off the sill.

Walcroft blinked twice, licked his lips, tried to rise and fell over backward as the slug rattled around inside his skull scrambling his brains. The whites of his eyes quickly turned a bright, glistening red as he lay there clawing at the rug, twitching.

The others were already in motion. Chase saw it had been set up in advance, well-planned, but nobody had let him in on it. They didn't entirely trust him. Jonah opened the closet door, and Grayson and Rook lifted Walcroft's body and carried it across the room. Walcroft was trying to talk, a strange sound coming from far back in his throat. He was blinking, trying to focus his gaze, his hands still trembling.

Chase thought, He's staring at me.

They tossed Walcroft in the corner of the empty closet, slammed the door, and immediately began cleaning the place.

No one looked at Chase which meant everybody was looking at him. Nobody said anything as they wiped down the room. So that was how it was going to be.

The room continued leaning and Chase had to angle his chin so things would straighten out. He shuddered once but covered it pretty well by bending and picking up the ashtray. They wouldn't want the butts tossed in the trash, they contained DNA. Maybe. Who the fuck knew. They were evidence anyway, some keen cop might nail Rook because he always tore the filter off his Camels. It was a clue.

Chase carefully split the cotton nubs apart, stepped to the bathroom, and threw them in the toilet. He washed out the ashtray. Maybe it was the right thing to do, maybe not. It could be downright stupid. It felt insane. What really mattered was they had to see he was trying, that he was very much a part of the crew.

He dove for the cold spot deep inside himself and seemed to miss it. He couldn't look at his face in the mirror. His heart slammed at his ribs, trying to squeeze through. Beginning to pant, he noticed he wasn't breathing through his nose. He started again. He made sure he left no prints on the toilet handle or around the sink. He tried to hurl himself into the cold spot again and this time felt himself begin to freeze and harden.

When he got out of the bathroom the closet door was open a crack. Walcroft was still squirming and had kicked it back open. One shoe had come off and a folded hundred-dollar bill had fallen out. Rook said, "Son of a bitch," grabbed a pillow off one of the beds, and drew his .38. Walcroft kept making the sound.

Chase knew then he would hear it for years to come, in the harbor of his worst nightmares, and that when his own loneliest moment in the world came to pass he'd be doing the same thing, making that same noise. Rook stepped into the closet, stuffed the pillow down on Walcroft's face to stifle the shot, and pulled the trigger. There was a loud cough and a short burst of flame. This time the pigeons flew off. With his teeth clenched, Rook tamped out the pillowcase, which was on fire. He nabbed the c-note and shut the door again. That was finally the end of it.

Chase was fifteen and he'd been pulling scores with his grandfather for almost five years. First as a kid running two- and three-man grifts, a few short cons, kitten burglaries—as Walcroft had called them—and then working his way up to taking part in an occasional heist. He knew Jonah always packed guns during jobs, but so far he'd never seen him fire one, much less kill a man.

Now this, one of his own friends, a part of his own string.

The score had gone down smooth as newborn ass. They hit a bookie joint run out the back of a fish market owned by the North Jersey mob. Jonah had explained how years ago nobody would've dared mess with any of the syndicates, but the days of the mob families' real power were long over. They squabbled among themselves more than they battled the FBI. Sons put their fathers under. Wives turned informant on their Mafia boss husbands. Everybody flipped eventually.

So the four of them went after the book. It was sometimes a little tough putting the string together because a lot of pros wouldn't work with someone named Jonah, despite his first-rate rep. It was one of the reasons why Chase started as a driver so early on, just so they wouldn't need to find the extra guy.

Chase sat behind the wheel of a stolen '72 Chevy Nova that he'd tuned on his own. He'd also done the body work and repainted it himself. A Turbo 350 transmission, 454 bored engine, solid lift camshaft, and a Flowmaster 3 exhaust so the car practically hummed like a struck chord. The horsepower seeped into his chest.

Part of being a wheelman was putting everything you had into a car and then letting it go again. After the heist they'd be able to get rid of it to a local chop shop for an extra ten grand, which he'd keep himself. For what Jonah called his college fund. It was a joke to all the crews they ran with, how young he was. It took a while but eventually they came to respect him. For his scouting and driving skills, his nerves, and the way he kept his mouth shut.

Rook and Grayson came out of the fish market with a sack of cash each. Jonah followed carrying another two. Five seconds later Walcroft came prancing out the door holding a giant yellowfin tuna, smiling widely so that all you saw were his bright eyes and perfect teeth under the ski mask. It got Chase laughing.

They'd expected forty grand, maybe a little more since the fish market was the hub for six different books who all turned in their receipts on Friday noon, in time to get to the bank before the midday rush. Not a major score, but an easy one to keep them afloat until the next big thing came along.

They climbed into the Nova, Walcroft hugging the fish to him for another second and saying, "I shall miss you, my friend, but now, back to the smelly depths of Joisey with you," before tossing it in the parking lot. Chase let out a chuckle and eased down on the throttle, moving smoothly out of there.

They had a hotel room on the lower west side of Manhattan. Chase had the way perfectly mapped, the streetlights timed, and hit the street heading east just as some of the mob boys came running outside. One of the fat ginzos tripped over the fish and took a header. Both Chase and Walcroft started laughing harder.

The goombas rushed for their Acuras and Tauruses. Nobody had too nice a car in case the IRS was watching. They followed the Nova for about a mile until Chase made a left turn from the right lane and bolted through a stale yellow light.

This was a family town. The mob mooks had grand-children going to the school on the corner, their family priests were in the crosswalk heading to the local rectory. The Mafia gave it up without hardly a fight, too worried about running over a nun or crossing guard. It almost made Chase a little maudlin, thinking these guys had a home they cared for more than they did their own cash. He hadn't stayed in the same town for more than three months since he was ten years old.

He'd been ahead almost a hundred and fifty bucks in the game. Walcroft about the same. Now Chase realized the others had let them win to distract them. He wondered if he'd been a little sharper and seen Jonah palming the gun, and had dared to warn Walcroft, would his grandfather have shot him in the head too.

Rook and Grayson finished wiping the room. There hadn't been much to do, they'd been playing cards for less than an hour. They took their split of the score and said nothing to Chase, which meant they were saying a lot.

He listened to their footsteps recede down the hall and then sat back in his chair. Icy sweat burst across his forehead and prickled his scalp. He stared at the closet and whispered, *"Pleading for murderers to step forward."*

Chase had liked Walcroft. The man had taught Chase a little about computerized engines and how to circumvent the LoJack and other GPS tracking systems. Unlike all of Jonah's other cronies who'd bothered to teach Chase anything, Walcroft was young, only about twenty-five, and knew about the modern systems. The other pros and wheelmen were Jonah's age. They'd been at it for decades and only wanted to steal cars that came off the line pre-1970 because they were simpler to boost and reminded them of their youth.

A surge of nausea hit Chase like a fist. He wanted a bit of something but all the liquor bottles were gone. He spread his hands across the table and held himself in place until his stomach stopped rolling.

"Wipe that table down again," Jonah said. There was no heat in his steel-gray eyes, no ice.

A confidence man knew how to read human nature. He could see down through the gulf of complex emotion and know what people were feeling, which way they were likely to jump. Chase had gotten pretty good at it over the last few years on the grift.

At least he'd thought so. Now he looked at Jonah and tried to read him. He couldn't. There were no signs. Nothing but the hardness of stone.

Jonah stood five-nine, about two-twenty of rigid muscle, powerfully built. Fifty-five years old, compact, everything coiled, always giving off intense vibes. Mostly white hair buzzed down into a crewcut, just a flicker of silver on top. Huge forearms with some faded prison tats almost entirely covered by matted black hair.

There was a quiet but overpowering sense of danger to him, like he'd always speak softly and be perfectly calm even while he was kicking your teeth out. You knew if you ever took a run at him you'd have to kill him before he'd quit the fight. If he lost and you left him alive, he'd catch up with you at the end of a empty desert highway, barefoot on melting asphalt if he had to. You'd never stop looking over your shoulder. He'd mastered the ability of letting you know all this in the first three seconds after you met him. Nobody ever fucked with him.

Now that lethal cool was filling the room. Chase had always thought it was for the other thugs and never for him, but here it was, turned all the way up, Jonah just watching.

So now Chase knew.

One wrong move and he'd be quivering in the closet. He met his grandfather's eyes and held firm, as cold as he could be.

"I liked him," Chase said. "Tell me it wasn't because of the fish. You didn't snuff him because he was dancing around with the goddamn fish."

"He was wired," Jonah said.

"What? For who?"

"Who knows?"

Chase shook his head but didn't shift his gaze. "No. No way."

"It's true."

"I didn't see a wire."

"Even so."

There was nowhere else to go with it now but to check.

Chase stood and started to make his way to the closet. Jonah blocked him and said, "We need to leave."

"We were going to stay here for three days."

"We've got another job waiting to be cased. We have to be in Baltimore by midnight."

"I want to see it."

"We don't have time for this. We need to go. Now."

Unable to do anything but repeat himself, like a brat demanding presents. "I want to see it."

"Rook took the tape and microphone."

"I didn't see him do that either."

"You were too busy trying not to throw up."

Said in the same flat tone as everything else Jonah ever said, but somehow there was still a hint of insult in it.

"Walcroft's chest will be shaved."

"It wasn't on his chest. It was down his pants."

"Then his goddamn pubes will be shaved."

Jonah crowded him now, refusing to get out of his way.

Had this been coming for a while? Chase wouldn't have thought so twenty minutes ago but abruptly he felt a cold fury asserting itself within him. As if this was the natural course for them to follow, the only one, and always had been. The two of them standing here together face-to-face with a dead man in the closet.

The air thickened with potential violence. Chase

glanced down at Jonah's hand to see if he was still palming the .22. Jonah had his hand cupped to the side of his leg. Jesus Christ, he was. It had really come down to this.

Time to let it go, but Chase couldn't seem to do so. It was stupid, he could sense Jonah's thin patience about to snap, but maybe that's what he wanted. He wondered if his need to push the point had anything to do with his parents, with the way his father had ended up.

"Why would Walcroft suddenly start wearing a wire?" Chase asked.

"You say that like it's an actual question."

Maybe it wasn't. Everybody eventually flipped. Chase moved another step forward so that their chests nearly touched. He realized there was no way he could beat Jonah, but at least the man would have to work a little harder for it than a quick tap to the temple. All these years, all the talk about blood and family, of fatherhood and childhood, the discussions about unfulfilled vengeance, going after his mother's killer, and they'd come down to this. Two kids in a sandbox.

"Why did you really ace him?"

"We need to leave."

"You didn't even blink," Chase said. "You've done it before."

"You asking for any special reason?"

"I'm not asking. I can see it now. You've done it before."

"Only when I had to."

"You didn't even let me in on it."

"Would you have wanted to be?"

Probably not but what was he going to say? "What if I'd hesitated? Those two would have killed me too."

"There was no chance of you hesitating. I taught you better than that. You're a pro."

It was a comment meant to appeal to Chase's vanity. There was no substance or emotion behind it. Jonah didn't quite understand how regular people felt about things, and when he tried to play to any kind of sentiment he always wound up way off base.

"I'm through," Chase said.

"You're not through."

"I'm going my own way."

"Turning your back on blood?"

"No," Chase told him. "You ever need me for something other than a score, let me know. I'll be there."

That almost made Jonah smile, except he didn't know how to do that either. "Going to start doing scores on your own? More second-story kitten burglaries, shimmying up the drain pipe? Knock over liquor stores and gas stations? Home invasions? You'll get picked up on your first run."

"A minute ago I was a pro."

Jonah stared at him, eyes empty of everything. You looked into them for too long and it would drive you straight out of your skull. "You're a string man now. You're part of a chain. You're a driver. You going to start working for other crews?"

"I don't know. Maybe I'll retire."

"And deliver newspapers?"

Gripping Chase's arm, Jonah dug his fingers in deep. It hurt like hell. In the past two years Chase had grown to six feet and gained thirty pounds of muscle, but he knew the cold spot inside him wasn't as deep or icy as the one inside his grandfather. He didn't think it ever would be. He wondered for perhaps the ten thousandth time how his fatally weak father could have come from this man. Chase fought to remain expressionless.

His mind squirmed and buzzed with all his failed tasks and unaccomplished dreams. He hadn't yet killed the man who'd murdered his mother. He'd never made a major score. He hadn't even gotten laid yet.

"I don't have any answers," Chase admitted. "I just know we're through after this." He tried to shrug free but couldn't break his grandfather's hold. "He wasn't even dead yet."

"Close enough."

When you've got nowhere to go you go back to the beginning. "I didn't see a wire. I don't believe it."

"You've got an overabundance of faith."

"Not anymore. Let me go."

"Okay, then try it on your own," Jonah said, releasing him. "But wipe the table again before you do. You know how to get in touch with me if you need to."